# A Gift to the Heart

## A Twist Upon a Regency Tale
### Book 12

## By Jude Knight

## ARE YOU SIGNED UP FOR DRAGONBLADE'S BLOG?

You'll get the latest news and information on exclusive giveaways, exclusive excerpts, coming releases, sales, free books, cover reveals and more.

Check out our complete list of authors, too!

No spam, no junk. That's a promise!

### Sign Up Here

www.dragonbladepublishing.com

*Dearest Reader;*

*Thank you for your support of a small press. At Dragonblade Publishing, we strive to bring you the highest quality Historical Romance from some of the best authors in the business. Without your support, there is no 'us', so we sincerely hope you adore these stories and find some new favorite authors along the way.*

*Happy Reading!*

*CEO, Dragonblade Publishing*

When Cilla Wintergreen supports her sister's plans to punish the man who ruined their friend, she helps in a miscarriage of justice, for they catch the wrong man. But no harm is done, except to her imagination. She cannot forget the sight of their victim, half naked, his torso shining in the candle light. Just as well she is unlikely to meet him again. Until she does.

When Drake Sanderson is mistaken for his licentious older brother Colin, he readily forgives the women who captured him. After all, they release him when they realize he isn't Colin. But the event changes his life, for one of those women captures his heart, and he won't give up until she agrees to be his wife or marries another.

When Livy Wintergreen tries to take revenge on a cruel seducer, and catches the wrong man, she puts in train a series of events she could not have imagined. For she had long thought she was too old, too contentious, and too independent to find a man to love her.

When Bane Sanderson rescues his brother from female revelers out for retribution, he did not expect their queen to consume his heart and mind, until courting her seems the only sensible course of action. If she is not put off by his scars, his irregular birth will disgust her. But he must try.

# Chapter One

## CILLA

*31st December 1816*

AT THE TIME, Lucilla Wintergreen thought the New Year's Eve rumpus to be perfectly justified. Justice in action, in fact. Unwise, perhaps, but only because she did not want even a hint of it reaching her father. For if Papa knew what she and the other young women at the party had done, he would shut her sister Olivia in her room forever, and he would never let Cilla out of his sight again.

Papa had not wanted her and Livy to go, but Aunt Ginny had talked him round, assuring him that it was an all-female party. "Even Jasper won't be there," she had said. "He is going to stay with friends. It will be all my own daughters, goddaughters, their sisters, and their mothers. I want my nieces with me. Other girls of Cilla's age will be there. Younger girls, too. It is disgraceful, by the way, that Cilla has not yet made her come out. The girl is nineteen, after all."

"You shall leave me to know what is best for my daughter," Father had said.

They had a fabulous time at the party. Cilla already knew and liked her cousins. Pearl was nineteen, the same age as her. Beryl and Ruby, the twins, were a year younger. The other guests included at least a dozen other single young women, as well as matrons of all ages and a smattering of older widows and spinsters. Cilla had soon made several new friends.

As for Livy, away from Papa and in an all-female environment, she blossomed. It helped that, two days into the party, her slice of the Christmas pudding contained a silver crown, making her the Lady of Misrule for the whole two weeks of the party.

Livy threw herself into the role, showing the sly humor she normally shared only with Cilla. It fueled a seemingly endless succession of merry tricks and hilarious games, and inspired others to offer suggestions of their own.

Everyone was enjoying themselves. Everyone, that is, except Aurora Thornton, a school friend of the Marple sisters from the village of Amblecote, who did her best to join in but was clearly unhappy. Cilla tried to draw her out of her shell, but to no avail.

"It is odd," one of the cousins said. "Rory is not normally like this."

"She was happy when the party started," said another cousin. "Very happy. I thought she had a suitor, but if she did, he has disappointed her."

Poor girl. Cilla had never had a suitor. From the stories she was hearing this week, perhaps that was a good thing.

In the end, what caused Aurora to sob her heart out on Cilla's shoulder was a game, for one of the girls claimed she could read the cards and tell fortunes, and the fortune she told for Aurora was of a tall fair-headed man who would be faithful and true.

"But he wasn't," Aurora wailed. "Colin was not faithful, and he wasn't true. He made all kinds of promises, and they were all lies, for he is ma- ma- ma- ma- married!" The final word was broken by sobs, and even though the young ladies—the mothers and aunts were closeted with a bottle of port and had left the damsels to their own devices—even though the young ladies gathered closely around, it was some time before the story was told.

She had had a secret suitor, who became her lover. He was a

neighbor of the Marples, and so Aurora had arrived full of hope, certain she would be able to arrange to see him, to find out why he had not visited for several weeks.

And on Christmas Day, when the house party attended church at Marpleton, she *did* see him—in his pew with a woman and two children. A few questions to those who lived locally soon confirmed they were his family—his wife and their offspring. He also had a couple of brothers living with him, but they were not part of Aurora's story so could be ignored.

He owned a business making and selling medicinals, Cilla discovered, and bought bottles and jars from the glass-makers of Amblecote, which explained what he was doing in that village, but not why he dared to seduce the daughter of the local vicar.

"Well," said Livy, when she understood all, "you are not with child, and nobody knows except us. And we are all your friends, Aurora, and will keep your secret. The question is, what do we do to Colin Sanderson to embarrass him in public the way he has embarrassed you in private?"

Cilla had never been prouder of Livy. Though some of the maidens had been horrified to have a ruined woman among them, Livy had reminded them that Aurora was a sheltered innocent and Sanderson a mature man who should have known better.

And a girl from Oxfordshire said that Aurora was like the ladies who were helped by the Countess of Sutton, who was the daughter-in-law of the Duke of Winshire. "She and some other ladies support a village for women who are in trouble because of men, Aurora. If you need help, you could go to them. Even the Duchess of Winshire is in favor of the village."

Those who were inclined to be critical were impressed that such high society ladies were on the side of women whose reputations had been dragged in the dust because of the misbehavior of men.

Livy was still focused on Sanderson. "He set out to ruin her," she said, fiercely. "Who is to say that any of us would have fared better, believing his lies and his promises as Aurora did?"

And one by one, they nodded their heads, and assured Aurora of their silence and support.

Even the most censorious promised to keep the secret, and all of them had suggestions about how to make Sanderson pay. The plan they came up with for New Year's Eve was masterly, Cilla thought.

New Year's Eve, in Marplestead, was the Festival of the Lady of Misrule, where the women took over the town and the men stayed indoors out of their way. It was the perfect time to make a fool out of a lying deceiver.

They had to enlist the boot boy who was sweet on Cilla's eldest cousin to lure the Sanderson mountebank to the tavern in the village, but everything else, they could handle themselves.

It would be the highlight of the party.

# BANE

WOLFBANE SANDERSON LIVED in Marplestead, not at Bancroft House near Marpleton with his two half-brothers—Mandrake, Bane's dearest friend and the nearest to him in age, and Hemlock, the eldest, who had insisted on the name Colin since he was seventeen.

On the death of their father, Colin had inherited his father's estate, including Sanderson Medicinals. Larkspur, their only sister, and the child of Father's third wife, was married and gone by then, and Colin had evicted Bane, who was the son of Father's mistress, as soon as the funeral was over and the will had been read. He tolerated Drake, son of the second wife. In fact, he ignored his younger half-brother as much as he could. Drake in turn tolerated him, because living as cheaply as possible suited the plans that Drake and Bane had made for their eventual escape.

"Can I come and stay with you?" he asked Bane a few days

before Christmas. "Frances has taken the children to visit her parents, and Colin has invited some of his lordly friends to stay while she is away. You know what sort of a party that is going to be," said Mandrake, wrinkling his nose.

Bane wondered idly which came first—the decision by Frances, Colin's wife, to take the children to her parents, or the invitation from Colin to be with the dissolute aristocrats he called friends.

"You are welcome to stay with me, Drake," he said. "Plenty of room in the barn loft."

If Colin guessed where Drake had gone while he and his guests drank themselves stupid and misbehaved with the prostitutes he had imported from the nearest town, he didn't care.

The party had become the talk of the three villages in the vicinity by New Year's Eve. Not only were the villagers fascinated by the goings on at Bancroft House, but the local viscount, Lord Marple, was also part of it. Though he was at least a decade younger than Colin, he already had a reputation for dissolute carousing, as did his dear friend Curston.

Perhaps it was in the blood, for Lady Marple, the young viscount's mother, had developed a certain amount of notoriety herself since her husband died. Indeed, local gossip had it that Curston and Marple had first met because their parents were lovers.

That said, she was a widow and discreet, so her suspected sins could be forgiven, especially since the house party at her place was an all-lady affair apparently designed to allow her daughters to make friends before they made their debut at the coming Season.

The villagers had their gossip updated every day when the servants from the two major houses collected mail, purchased milk, or otherwise met up with the neighbors, and the news circulated swiftly from that point.

Everyone agreed that Lady Marple was behaving just as she

should, and Colin was riding for a fall.

On the day before New Year, Drake was in Bane's office at the blacksmith's forge. He had made a hot toddy while he waited for Bane to finish totaling a column in the accounts for the local baker. Bane's share stood at his elbow. The baker had poor handwriting and the tendency to transpose numbers, so Bane didn't need to muddle his brain with alcohol.

"Colin would hate to know that you do the books for all the tradesmen and shopkeepers in Marplestead and most in the other two local villages," Drake commented.

"No one is going to tell him," Bane pointed out. *Ah. That was a seven, not a one. The man always forgot to cross them.* "The blacksmith owns his forge, but most in Marpleton and a few of the others pay rent to Colin."

"Silly duffer," Drake said. "He cut off his nose to spite his face when he threw you out. Lucky for him he has Frannie, who has taken over the books for Sanderson's Medicinals. He'd do well, if he'd listen to her advice."

"Not likely, and he was certainly not going to listen to mine." Father's will had reminded Colin that Bane, the base-born son, had been educated to manage the accounts for the business. Since Colin had deeply resented his father spending money on Bane's education, his reaction was to toss Bane out of both job and home. "I've been comfortable enough in my rooms above the blacksmith's barn," Bane added.

"Not for much longer." Drake had finished half his toddy and was waxing loquacious. Bane knew perfectly well that they planned to be in London by Spring, shaking the dust off their feet as they left their boyhood haunts.

A knock on the door stopped Drake from embarking on a soliloquy about how much more convenient a London location would be for keeping track of their investments and finding new ones.

"Come in," said Bane.

It was a boy from Marplestead Manor—an orphan the house

employed to clean boots, carry firewood, run messages, and other tasks beneath the other servants. "Sir," he said to Drake, "Are you the Mr. Sanderson who lives in Marpleton?"

"I am," Drake agreed.

"Then this note is for you, sir," the boy said.

He handed it over. Drake opened the seal and read it, then handed it to Bane. It was written in a feminine hand. If that was not clue enough the sender was a woman, the ink was purple and the paper a soft blue that had been liberally doused with a floral perfume. Bane grimaced. He didn't even need to hold it to his nose to inhale the scent. It had been not so much sprinkled as drenched.

"It's not a good night for a man to be out in Marplestead," Bane said, but he might as well have saved his breath.

"I don't plan to be out for long," said Drake, "but the lady invites me to a private celebration. What sort of a gentleman would I be if I ignored her?"

"A wise one?"

But Drake only laughed.

"Who is it?" Bane asked. If it proved to be one of the maids at the tavern, he would worry less. But the hand seemed too fine for a tavern maid, and Drake wasn't aware of any with a name starting with "A"—the flourishing initial that was the letter's only signature.

Bane shrugged. "I cannot bring a likely candidate to mind," he admitted, "but I daresay I shall know her when I see her."

Bane wasn't easy in his mind, but Drake was a grown man. Bane had no right to prevent him, nor any way to do it, either.

"I'll walk with you," he said, instead. "I'm going that way."

It wasn't true. The blacksmith's barn was in the opposite direction. Nonetheless, Bane accompanied his brother to the tavern. "I'm here," Drake announced, when they arrived. "I don't need my minder any more, Bane."

Bane couldn't resist one more warning. "Be careful, Drake, Tonight is a night for the ladies to take their revenge." By tradition, New Year's Eve in Marplestead belonged to the ladies, and anything that happened on that night was ignored by the entire neighborhood the following day. A drunken husband might wake up in a pig wallow. An unfaithful one in the stocks. The ladies were inventive, determined, and disguised, so no one knew who had done what.

Drake cut him off with an impatient gesture. "I won't do anything my fair correspondent doesn't wish, Bane. I never have. The ladies have no reason to go after me. Will you be safe going home?"

"I'll be fine," Bane insisted. "It isn't far."

Bane figured the revelers would leave him alone. Rumors about the face he kept hidden had grown over the past fifteen years, since his father had brought him to Bancroft House wounded and near death.

Bane still wore the hood that Drake's mother had demanded, so she need not look upon the scarred wreck of his right cheek, but in truth, the mark of the knife attack that had nearly taken his life had faded since he arrived at his father's house, ten years' of age, grievously wounded, and not expected to live. His face might not be pretty, but Bane had seen worse.

The hood also threw his mismatched eyes into shadow—and it had been those that had led to his scarring. Wearing it was a habit. And on a night like tonight, something of a protection.

Sure enough, he made it home safely, though he did see a group of a dozen or so women—masked and costumed. They glanced at him and dismissed him. Was one of them the person who had written to Bane? He paused just inside the gate to watch them pass the tavern and keep walking, so probably not.

"The wife is out," said the blacksmith, when Bane poked his head into the kitchen to see if supper was ready. "It's Misrule Night. Don't know what they're up to, and I'm not going to ask, but it has them all a twitter. Supper is on the table."

Bread, cheese, and a big slab of plum cake. Good enough. Bane poured himself an ale and sat down, as did the blacksmith.

They ate in silence—when the lady of the house was home, she chattered enough for all three of them, but the blacksmith was a man of few words, and Bane had been eating alone for most of his life.

Besides, his mind was not on the food or the company, but on his brother. Something about the whole situation didn't sit right. Drake was popular with the ladies, but—as far as Bane knew—this was the first time he'd ever received an anonymous invitation. Not, in itself, suspicious, but Bane didn't like the timing. He couldn't stop thinking about the fact that, on Misrule Night, women used their temporary freedom to seek revenge.

Revenge for what, though? Drake was, as Bane had cause to know, the kindest, most giving of men, with a positive talent for staying on pleasant terms with his *amours* both during and after their liaisons.

He had almost finished his ale when a hullabaloo started from outside—the rata-tat-tat of drums, the shriek of whistles, and clanging sounds that put him in mind of kitchens.

"Better check," said the blacksmith, and got up to open the door, just in time for the parade to pass in front of the smithy and then the cottage alongside it.

The noise makers came first. The clanging, Bane noted, was made by various types of spoons against pot lids. The women all wore costumes and masks, like the group he'd seen earlier. Even their own mothers would not have known them.

More women, similarly garbed, followed the noise makers. They were oddly positioned, in long lines, and it took Bane a minute to realize they were pulling on ropes—at least half a dozen ropes, each with eight or nine women haulers. Others danced among them with lamps, lighting the whole scene.

As he craned his neck to see what they were dragging, he noticed that doors and windows were being opened up and down the village street. The men of the village were silent witnesses to whatever was happening.

"It is a shaming," said the blacksmith. He sounded awed.

"There hasn't been one in Marplestead for seven years! I wonder who it is?"

A shaming. Bane had never seen one, but he had heard about the last one. The man had been a serial fornicator, seducing one girl after the other with meaningless promises. After being led through the whole village and around the major farms and manors all one Misrule Night, he had left town and had never returned.

The object at the end of the ropes was plodding into view. It was a donkey, stolidly ignoring the ropes, the noise, and the murmuring of the onlookers. That, Bane saw at a glance.

What took his attention was not the steed but the rider. He was male. Since he wore nothing but knee breeches and a head-concealing mask in the form of a goat's head, his gender was beyond a doubt. The broad shoulders and the muscular torso, arms, and thighs also bore witness.

He sat backward on the ass, bound to the saddle with rope, swaying slightly as if he was drunk.

With a jolt of shock, Bane realized he knew that torso, those arms! He narrowed his eyes as the rider drew level, and was aided by one of the dancers, who lifted her lamp so it shone on the rider's elbow.

"It is Drake," Bane said.

"Really?" asked the blacksmith. "What has Drake done to deserve a shaming?"

"Nothing," Bane said, grimly, and took a step forward, but the blacksmith grabbed his arm.

"If you go out there, you'll be joining him."

"I can't leave him there," Bane protested, but the blacksmith was right. He'd not get Drake free without using his brain instead of just reacting. "I need my horse," he said. "And a good knife. I'll grab him when they take him off the donkey to throw him into the pond."

"They'll overpower you," the blacksmith warned. "There are what? Fifty of them? One of you."

"I can't fight them. Not women," Bane admitted. "But I must try. If I get dunked alongside Drake, so be it."

The blacksmith pursed his lips. "Cut the goat mask off," he advised. "Let them see they've got the wrong man."

That might work. Bane left for the barn, where he also stabled his horse.

He wanted to merely bridle the horse and be off after his brother, but his common sense told him that he might need the stability of saddle and stirrups. It took several minutes, even with the blacksmith's help, but at last he was in the saddle and galloping after the Misrule party.

They had reached the pond and were dragging Drake from the saddle, none too gently. Fortunately for Drake, only a few of the women—ten at most—were involved in the dismounting. The rest were not even watching. Rather, they waited on the edge of the pond for the next event in the night's entertainment. Bane grinned. He would give them something to watch.

He set the horse at a gallop, straight at the cluster around Drake, pulling up only at the last minute. They had, as he'd hoped, leapt out of the way, and Bane reached down and grabbed the rope that bound Drake's arms to his body. "Mount behind me," he shouted, and heaved as Drake jumped and scrambled until he was seated behind Bane.

The horse danced and skittered. Nightshade was skittish at the best of times, and he was taking exception to the torches, the masked ladies, the noise, the load, and the whole situation. That was a help, for the women who might have objected to losing their prisoner were keeping their distance.

"This is my brother Mandrake Sanderson," Bane shouted. "He has done nothing worthy of a shaming." He was pretending with his hands to be attempting to control the horse, but in truth, his calves and heels were encouraging its jittery behavior.

A woman with the crown and staff of the Lady of Misrule stepped forward—an Amazon with dark curly hair. He could not see much of her face behind her half-mask, but what he could see distracted him for a moment. She was stunning.

"Mandrake?" she asked. "Not Colin?"

Bane hoped it was her readiness to listen to reason that soothed his anger, and not his awareness of her as an attractive female. Or perhaps it was just that Colin probably deserved whatever the women cared to dish out. They had made a mistake, and Bane had rescued Drake before they could half-drown him. Or all the way drown him, which old timers said had sometimes happened.

"Not Colin," he replied. "I'll show you." Bane twisted in the saddle so he could use his knife to cut the ropes, an act Nightshade made more difficult than it needed to be. "Drake, take the head off," he said.

"I don't feel too good," said Drake, in a voice that quavered all over the register, but he fumbled with the mask and lifted it free. His eyes looked odd. They must have given him something.

As Nightshade calmed, the women gathered closer.

"It *is* Drake," said one of the women. Bane couldn't be sure, but he thought he recognized the voice of the blacksmith's wife.

"Mr. Colin Sanderson is older," explained another to the Lady of Misrule.

"We made a mistake," said a third. "The rider is Mr. Bane Sanderson. He is the other brother."

Bane, conscious of the absurdity of good manners in this moment, nonetheless bowed as well as he could from horseback. Drake bowed with him, murmuring sleepily against Bane's back, "How'd'y'do."

"What was he given?" he demanded. "Drake, I mean. To make him compliant."

"Only laudanum, and not much," said the Lady of Misrule. "He will be perfectly well after a sleep. I do not suppose your brother Colin plans to come into the village tonight?"

Bane had to laugh at the cheek of the woman. "My sincere regrets, my lady, but I doubt it," he said. "You could try another perfumed note."

The woman considered it for a moment, but shook her head. "I suppose by now word of the shaming will have reached him," she said. She took a deep breath and let it out. "I shall have to consult with the other ladies. Please tell your brother Drake that we apologize for our mistake."

Bane, in lieu of raising the hat he'd left behind in his haste, settled for touching the side of his forehead. "I shall pass that on, my lady."

He turned the horse, being careful not to dislodge his sleepy brother, and rode back to the blacksmith's barn. He'd be staying awake tonight, so he could keep watch over Drake until the drug was out of his system.

But as the blacksmith helped him to get Drake into the barn, Bane's thoughts were not of his brother but of the Lady of Misrule. She wasn't a local lass. In fact, by her accent, she was educated and refined. She must be one of the guests at the all-female house party up at Marplehurst Hall.

Far, far above his touch, then.

And she was magnificent.

# Chapter Two

## LIVY

LIVY HAD COME down to earth with a crash. Everything had been going so well. Sanderson had come in response to the letter. He had drunk the wine she had given him and passed out. Her collaborators had helped to strip him and put on the goat's head. Exactly as they had planned.

And, oh, the uplifting sensation of striking back at all the men who thought they could have whatever they pleased while denying the same freedom to women!

Pacing beside the ass, surrounded by her temporary subjects, she had felt powerful, free, and above all, accepted. And then *he* had arrived. The man in the hood. Riding through the gathered women to haul their prisoner up onto his horse, and then delivering the devastating words that laid bare her mistake.

It didn't help that something about his voice, his posture, his sheer *presence* made her tingle, and not in an unpleasant way. A ridiculous and shaming reaction to a complete stranger she had just offended.

Why had she insisted on having none of the locals in the room before Sanderson had been blinded by the goat head? She had meant to protect them from retaliation, and instead, she had led them into a debacle.

Though they didn't seem downhearted. They were carrying on with the plans they'd had for the evening before the Maplehurst Hall party had joined them. Blankets had been spread out on the ground. Some of the matrons were carrying around baskets of food.

Several of the villagers were passing out jugs of wine. A group was singing. Livy had heard the tune before, but the scandalous lyrics were new to her.

"Come along, Miss Wintergreen," said a girl from the village that Livy had met earlier in the evening. "Come and have fun."

Livy allowed herself to be led to where her sister and other people from the house party were sitting, all mixed in with the villagers and other neighbors. "I am so sorry," she said to them. "My mistake has ruined the evening."

"Not your mistake," someone protested. "You had no way of knowing that the silly boy would take the letter to the wrong brother."

The whole neighborhood—but not the house party—had known that Colin Sanderson was holding a scandalous gathering at his house for Livy's cousin Jasper Marple and his friends, all of whom were apparently cut from the same cloth. Mrs. Sanderson had gone to spend Christmas with her mother and had given every maid under forty leave to do likewise. Mr. Sanderson had responded by bringing in a carriage load of scandalous women from the nearest town.

"It sounds as if Colin Sanderson well and truly deserved a shaming," Cilla observed. "What a pity we got the wrong brother. We didn't even know there *was* more than one brother."

"If I had asked someone who knows him to look..." Livy said.

"They are kind of alike," another of the villagers offered. "Mr. Drake and Mr. Colin. Though I doubt Mr. Colin Sanderson looks so good with his shirt off! Mr. Drake works on the farms and such."

That remark set all the women into talking about the two

younger Sanderson brothers, and Livy heard more than she wanted to know about how kind Mr. Drake was, and how Mr. Bane could be depended on to lend a helping hand to anyone in need.

Livy learned there were four Sandersons—their father had had three sons and a daughter, all with different mothers. Each was named for one of the plants whose medicinal properties were the foundation of the family fortune, though the eldest insisted on being called Colin rather than Hemlock.

Apparently, the eldest brother did not get on with the other two. Mr. Bane was the odd one out, dark where the others were fair, and the villagers conceded that one could not altogether blame Mr. Sanderson for not wanting his father's by-blow to live under his roof—"even if he has been raised as a gentleman, and even if his father wanted him to stay."

They agreed, though, that Mr. Sanderson was unkind to his legitimate half-brother as well. "Maybe because Mr. Bane and Mr. Drake are as thick as thieves. Always have been, ever since Mr. Sanderson—the old Mr. Sanderson, who was their father— brought Mr. Bane home."

Livy learned the odd fact that Mr. Bane always wore a hood to conceal his face, and the various neighborhood speculations about his reasons. A base-born son with a ruined face. A pity he was the first man Livy had ever met that produced that disquieting tingle.

*Papa would be horrified if you announced a* tendre *for a merchant's scarred bastard son.* It was the first cheering thought Livy had had since Bane Sanderson crashed her party. If it wasn't certain to backfire on her when her father went rampaging to Mr. Sanderson to order him to withdraw his suit, she might try it.

# BANE

IN THE MORNING, Drake was a bit sluggish but otherwise unharmed. "Nothing but a few bruises, Bane. I am fine. Sorry they didn't get Colin as they intended, though. I wonder what they had against him? Knowing Colin, he probably seduced someone he shouldn't. Ah, well. Misrule Night will come around again in Marplestead in just under a year. We can hope they get the right Sanderson next time."

He was fully recovered by the time the revelers at Bancroft Hall went home, and Drake prepared to do likewise.

"If Colin has heard what happened, you might be going home to trouble," Bane warned. "He won't want to risk you telling Frannie that the revelers thought you were him." Everyone knew that the victims of Misrule Night had done something scandalous, even if no one ever said what it was. Word had spread through the neighborhood that the shaming had been intended for Colin Sanderson, and if no one knew the specific reason for it, everyone agreed that they were not surprised.

Drake waved off the warning. "Leaving aside that I would never tell Colin's wife anything to distress her, poor woman, we are nearly ready to go out on our own. If Colin throws me out, shall we just move our leaving date up a bit?"

"Done," said Bane. "Just keep your distance, Drake. Don't let him goad you into a fight."

He fretted right through the morning, until Drake turned up at the blacksmith's on the riding horse he had purchased last year, leading his older horse, which was carrying laden saddle bags.

"I was packing when he turned up, told me I was a disgrace, and threw me out," said Drake. "I was so tempted to tell him they mistook me for him." He flashed an evil grin. "But it will be better if it comes as a surprise."

"Much better," Bane agreed. Colin would be meeting quite a few cold shoulders in the neighborhood next time he ventured from home. And perhaps at home, as well, for several of the matrons had apparently declared their intention to have a word with his wife. Poor Frannie. As if she did not know what Colin was like!

"I've a few commissions to finish up here. Can you hire a gig and pick me up in half an hour? We'll take the last trunk to Wart."

Wart was Viscount Wharton, who was their next-door neighbor. He was the same age as Bane and Drake, and an old companion on many a boyhood adventure. They'd seen him after Father's funeral, and had asked him if he'd store some trunks for them, and in the following months, transferred to his place the items they wanted to keep but didn't want to take with them.

They both had a few last things to add to the store, from Bane's barn and Drake's bedroom. They would take only what they could carry. Without their horses, for Wart had promised to care for them, too.

He must have seen them from a window, for he was out on the steps when the gig drew up in the carriage way, and had footmen carrying the trunks inside before Drake and Bane could reach for them.

"The grooms will look after your horses," he said. "Come in for a drink. Stay the night, if you wish."

"We'll take that drink," Bane said, speaking for them both.

"But we won't stay, Wart." Drake finished the thought. "We've been cast out into the world and are off to seek our fortunes."

Wart grinned as he led them to his library. 'Off to seek our fortunes' had been one of their favorite games when they were boys. "It'll be London then?" he asked.

Bane exchanged a look with Drake. They had decided on London, but it was not because of their childhood game. Was it?

Drake shrugged. "London is the biggest city in England; perhaps in the world. Parliament is there. Merchants from all over the world are there, and those with investments to sell. Where better?"

*Where, indeed.* Five years ago, when their sister Larkspur had married, Father had given Drake and Bane what Drake liked to call their dowries. Five thousand pounds each made ten thousand. They'd put five thousand into government bonds—the Funds, as they were called—and sought investment opportunities for the rest, continuing to live at home while their money went out into the world to grow. When Bane was thrown out after Father's death, he worked for board and keep, rather than touch any part of their joint capital.

They had both taken to heart a saying of Father's—"The rich don't work for money. Their money works for them."

"And the Marriage Mart," said Wart, helpfully, as he poured them each a drink. "The quickest way to make a fortune is to marry one."

Wart should know. After he inherited the viscountcy, he had taken the impoverished title to London and had bartered it for an heiress. One he liked, furthermore. In fact, if Bane was reading the signs right, Lord and Lady Wharton might have married on mere liking, but in Bane's opinion, they were well on the way to becoming a love match.

"Alfred," said the lady herself from the doorway of the library. "You did not tell me we were to have visitors."

The gentlemen, who had been lounging in the comfortable chairs by the fire, stood as soon as they realized she was there. "We called unexpectedly, Lady Wharton," he explained. "Bane and I are leaving, and came to say goodbye to your husband."

"Sanderson has thrown them out and they are off to seek their fortunes," Wart explained.

Bane winced at the frank explanation, but no doubt the Sanderson servants would have spread the news all over the countryside before nightfall.

Lady Wharton, faced with a merchant's bastard who was also her husband's best friend, proved her mettle, and instead of objecting to Bane's presence, said, "You must stay with us until you have managed to settle your affairs, Mr. Sanderson, Mr.

Wolfbane Sanderson."

"I asked 'em," Wart said. "But they're keen to get to the fortune bit. They won't stay."

The lady went up further in Bane's estimation when she did not show her relief. "I shall wish you every success then, gentlemen."

Drake did the pretty, bowing gracefully. "Thank you, Lady Wharton. It was very kind of you to ask us to stay, and we appreciate your good wishes."

She curtseyed in response. "You are my husband's dearest friends. Of course, I wish you well."

Very nicely said. Bane bowed, too. "We shall say goodbye then, my lady."

"Farewell, rather," said Wart. "Lady Wharton and I are for London, too. Lady Wharton believes I should take my seat in the house. And you should check out the social scene. I'm sure I can get you some invitations. Perhaps you shall be as fortunate as I am." His smile at his lady could only be described as fatuous, and hers back was every bit as inane. It was definitely becoming a love match.

"The last thing I need," said Drake, as they drove down the carriageway, "is a wife. Not that any woman I might meet at a *ton* affair is going to be interested in the third son of a merchant."

"That goes double for me," Bane pointed out. "Not only am I the second son of a merchant, but my mother was the man's mistress." Or had been. By the time she died, her erratic behavior had ended the relationship, though—to give Father due credit— he never failed to send money for his son's upkeep, even if Ma did spend it on laudanum and other substances.

"Anyway," said Drake, "We're not looking for wives, are we?"

"Good lord, no," Bane agreed. And why Lady Misrule's lovely form should suddenly appear in his imagination, he refused to consider.

# Chapter Three

## DRAKE

*March 1817, North Midlands*

W HEN BUSINESS CALLED them to Sheffield, Drake and Bane allowed an extra day for the journey. Better to have a day at leisure in the area than to be late for their meeting. Drake already had an idea of how they might spend the day, but he didn't say anything until they were waiting for fresh horses at the last staging post before their destination.

To Drake's surprise, it was Bane that raised the idea. "We should visit Lark," he said. "While we are in the area."

*Yes, exactly.* Though Drake hadn't expected Bane to think of it.

Bane had never been close to their half-sister, Larkspur, and nor had Drake since Bane came into his life. Lark was five years younger than the two half-brothers, and her mother had refused to allow her to associate with Bane. Since Bane and Drake were usually together, that meant she had little to do with either brother.

Their father had arranged a marriage for Lark six years ago, into the Hampton family, whose fortune was based on china and coal. Since the marriage, the Hamptons had branched out into managing canal cargoes, with Phillip, Lark's husband, as the manager of the new division.

"She might not want to see us," Drake warned. Or she might want to see Drake, her legitimate half-brother, and not Bane, her mother's scapegoat for all their father's sins.

Bane shrugged. "What is the worst that can happen? She might show us both the door. She might be pleased to see you but not me. It is worth the trial, Drake. I've been thinking about her for a while. Father married her off as soon as she was out of mourning for her mother, and as far as I am aware, he ignored her from that day on. And Colin hasn't visited her, that I know of."

"Or written to her," Drake agreed. "Or, at least, I've never seen her address on a letter, coming or going, and neither Colin nor Frannie has ever mentioned hearing from her or writing to her."

"Then she is on her own, without family," Bane said. "Which is not a problem if her husband is a good man, and if his family has accepted her. But what if they haven't? I want her to know she can call on me in need. Even if she doesn't know me or even want to."

He was right. Drake had been thinking only that he'd like to see his sister. Before Bane arrived, he had been very close to Lark—before Drake was forced to choose between protecting the unexpected brother who was still recovering from a gruesome injury or being allowed to visit the sweet child in the nursery. He had always treasured stolen moments when he had been able to collaborate with the nursery staff—and later the governess—to sneak her a treat, or take her on a quick outing, such as to the woods to pick daffodils or to the stables to visit a new litter of kittens.

"She can depend on both of us," Drake said. "Let's go and tell her."

Chesterfield was only a few miles farther on, and it was just past noon. They rode the distance in less than an hour and left their horses at the most prominent of the local inns, guessing that it would also be a sorting house for the Royal Mail. As it was, they soon found, and when they asked after their sister's address, they were directed to the innkeeper, who was also postmaster.

"Can you direct us to the residence of Mr. and Mrs. Phillip Hampton?" Bane asked.

The innkeeper gave them an address. "Would you wish to book a room for the night, sirs?" he asked.

"We are not certain whether we will be staying," Drake told him, "but we would like to leave our baggage for a couple of hours."

They gave the man a couple of coins and walked to the outskirts of Chesterfield, where the Hampton house, Three Oaks, was as easy to find as the innkeeper had predicted.

The family was wealthy enough to afford a man to answer the door, which was the task of a maid at the Sanderson house. "Drake and Bane Sanderson to see Mrs. Hampton," Bane announced them to the man, who looked as if he was trying to decide whether to bring the visitors inside to wait or to leave them standing on the doorstep.

"We are Mrs. Hampton's brothers," Drake said.

Apparently, Lark was at home, for the man opted to show them into a little room just inside the door—one of those bland rooms with uncomfortable benches that houses often had for unexpected, and possibly unwanted, guests. "I shall see if Mrs. Hampton is receiving," he said, resolving the question of whether or not to bow by nodding his head before he hurried away.

He had not been gone for long when Lark burst into the room. For a moment, Drake thought she was going to hurl herself into his arms, but she stopped just inside the door. "It is you!" she declared. "Drake and Bane! Whatever are you doing in Chesterfield? But never mind that. You shall tell me in a minute. Come through to the parlor." She beckoned them to follow her, paused in the hallway to order refreshments served, and led them into a parlor that, while still being elegantly appointed, showed every sign of being in regular use by the family.

Lark seated herself in the smaller of two chairs with matching blue and white paisley upholstery and waved them to two other chairs that picked up the blue and white in a floral design that was reminiscent of Indian fabrics Drake had seen.

Indeed, now that he had noticed it, the blue and white theme was repeated in the tiles of the fireplace, the vases of flowers that adorned the room, and a selection of china plates, jugs, and bowls on a sideboard.

"Now," Lark said. "What brings you to my door? Not that I am not pleased to see you! But it has been five years! Is it because Colin threw you out? Do you need a place to stay? You are welcome of course. I am certain Phillip will agree with me. He cannot understand our family, though I have tried to explain to him that my mother had us living in three armed camps, with Father the only common link between us. But here you are! I certainly did not expect this when I woke up this morning."

"We are pleased to see you, too," said Drake, when Lark paused for breath. "You have apparently heard that we no longer live in Marpleton?"

"I often exchange letters with Polly Freemantle, the vicar's daughter, who married the squire," Lark explained. "She told me about Bane going to live in Marplestead after Father died, and about the shaming that caught Drake instead of Colin, and that Colin used it as an excuse to turn you out, too, Drake. But that was two months ago. *Do* you need a place to stay?"

"We have moved to London," Bane told her. To rooms in a respectable but inexpensive lodging house, where they could live as cheaply as possible while growing steadily wealthier.

"We were about to do so anyway," said Drake, getting his word in quickly before Lark took flight again. He'd forgotten that about her—how excitement made her chatter. Nervousness, too. The name Lark suited her, in fact, better than Larkspur, for she was a bird in joyous flight rather than a plant that remained rooted to the ground. And he loved her for it.

"Our investments needed closer attention, and London is the

best place for us at the moment."

"We are on our way to Sheffield," Bane explained. "We think of you often, Drake and I. We couldn't come so close without visiting, but we had no idea whether we would be welcome."

Lark burst into tears.

Drake exchanged a worried look with Bane. A crying woman was not something they had much experience with. Bane produced a handkerchief and went to kneel at Lark's feet. He patted her on the shoulder, and cast another glance at Drake, shrugging his own shoulders to show how far out of his depth he felt. At least he was doing something!

"Don't cry, Lark," Drake said, hearing how feeble he sounded even as he said it.

"I am just so happy," Lark sobbed. "You think of me. I thought I had no family in the world except for Phillip and the children."

Bane patted her shoulder again, and Drake dared to approach and pat her other shoulder. Fortunately, after a moment or two, she mopped up her tears with Bane's handkerchief. And just in time, for the manservant and a maid arrived with tea makings and a tray of refreshments. Both of them glared at Drake and Bane, and Lark had to reassure them that her brothers had made her very happy.

"I am glad to hear that," Drake said. "You had us worried. But it is a relief to Bane and myself to know that our sister's servants are protective."

"Mrs. Hampton don't need nobody upsetting her," the maid said. "Especially not at the moment."

"I cry easily when I am breeding," Lark explained. "You know that, Flora. I cried for five minutes last week when Frederick counted to ten, and yesterday the sunset was so beautiful that Phillip had to loan me his handkerchief for mine was hopelessly wet. I do apologize, Drake and Bane. I did not mean to worry you. Run along, Flora, Finch. I shall pour for my brothers."

Drake guessed that one of the servants must have sent for

Lark's husband, for she was surprised when he arrived home no more than thirty minutes later. By then, the brothers had explained their errand in Sheffield, and were making themselves known to Lark's two children, brought down from the nursery by their nursemaid.

"Phillip," Lark said, when Hampton strode into the room. "You are home early. Is something wrong?"

Hampton narrowed his eyes at Drake and Bane, who were on the floor building a tower with Frederick. Tabitha, who was two, took that moment to knock the tower down, and Frederick would have objected, loudly, except that Bane cheered and clapped. "Excellent, Tabitha. Frederick, say hello to your Papa, and then let us build the tower higher."

Crisis averted, and Hampton emerged from a hug with both his children with a broad welcoming grin. "I did not know we were expecting your brothers, my dear. Are they staying?"

"Will you?" asked Lark. "I can put you up if you do not mind sharing a bedroom. Will you at least stay for dinner? And then it will be too late to go on to Sheffield, so you should stay."

Drake said that they'd left their bags at the inn, but Hampton said that would not be a problem. "I shall send a servant with a note to collect your things. It would please my wife above all things if you stay."

Given the gulf that time and Lark's mother had dug between them, the evening went off very well. Lark was keen to ask about friends of hers from their home neighborhood, and to hear about what Drake and Bane were doing.

They explained about their "dowries".

"We put half of what Father gave us into the funds, and the interest is enough to cover our living expenses," Drake explained. Rent, food, candles and heating, clothing—they lived frugally, but well enough.

As well as their money in the Funds, they had—at least on paper—another fourteen thousand pounds, the other half of Father's original gift having grown nearly three-fold. "Most of the rest of the money is out in various investments," Bane said. "We own shares in several ships' cargoes. We also hold stocks in a canal company, a venture seeking to grow tea in Ceylon, a woolen mill, and several other enterprises."

Drake added, "In the past eighteen months, we have been using a broker to trade on a Stock Exchange." He had been given two thousand pounds with which to trade stocks, and had grown it to more than six thousand, plus his commission.

"I imagine you have working capital, as well," said Phillip, Lark's husband, and the brothers both nodded. It would almost halve if they decided to support the device they had come north to Sheffield to see.

"We are heading for Sheffield to look at a new investment. An innovative, new hydraulic press particularly optimized for silversmithing." The inventor's prototype had already attracted several orders, and the inventor had patented the design. He was looking for investors to provide the money to allow him to build the machines.

Lark's husband, Phillip, was intrigued, and asked many questions. The brothers discovered he was a genial fellow with wide ranging interests beyond the canal system and the cargoes on which his family were making a second fortune to go with their first—they organized boats for people with cargo and cargo for people with boats, helping to make sure that neither side was kept waiting and that everyone made a profit, including Phillip's family.

Lark had another brief bout of tears as they parted for bed. "I have always admired you both, and I am thrilled to meet you again. Do stay in my life, brothers mine. I want my children to know that I have family, too. Until I met Phillip's family, I did not realize how peculiar our family is. And I love Phillip's family, but I did not understand until you came today how lonely I have been for my own."

When Bane and Drake left for Sheffield in the morning, they were farewelled by Lark, Phillip, and the children. The children demanded hugs, and then Lark lined up for hers, and Phillip vigorously shook their hands, saying, "This has meant so much to my wife." They promised to keep in touch, and to visit again. "Perhaps for Christmas," Lark suggested.

They were easily on time for their afternoon meeting in Sheffield. It turned out to be not only with Silas Pentworth, but with his wife, Anne. Pentworth demonstrated the prototype, a half-size model, and it worked as well, if not better, than they expected. Drake and Ben both had questions—about the design, the function, possible issues with scaling up, and costs to potential customers of refitting their factories.

Mrs. Pentworth answered as many of the questions as her husband, Pentworth deferring to her on all issues of design as well as some of the others. Bane put his finger on the notion that had just occurred to Drake. "This is your design, Mrs. Pentworth, is it not?"

The couple exchanged glances and Pentworth replied, "We worked on it together," he said. His nostrils flared and he looked defiant when he added, "Anne had the original idea and designed the parts."

"Silas made the parts, and put them together. He refined the design," said Mrs. Pentworth, sounding defensive.

"I congratulate you both," Bane said, and Drake nodded. He wondered if the couple had encountered investors who did not want to work with a woman. Those investors were fools, in Drake's opinion. His own father's fortune was based on recipes developed by Colin's mother, and Frannie was far more involved in the management of the business than Colin.

Drake could name any number of other merchants, artisans, and traders whose enterprises depended on a talented female member of the family. Even in the upper classes, women often took a role in business. The whole neighborhood knew that Lady Marple continued to manage her son's estates, even though he was of age.

The brothers had several more questions, but the upshot was

not in doubt. Drake turned over and over in his fingers one of the small forks that the prototype had turned out, all the same, all perfect except for a little finishing and polishing. Changing the shape would be as simple as changing the die inside the machine.

"Two thousand pounds in return for a fifty percent share, twenty-five percent for each of us," Bane said.

"A forty percent share," Pentworth responded, with a glance at his wife. "Twenty percent each."

That was the percentage the brothers had hoped for.

"Done." Bane held out his hand for Pentworth to shake and Drake offered his to Mrs. Pentworth. Then Bane shook Mrs. Pentworth's hand and Drake, Pentworth's. They had a deal. Given the potential for industries outside of cutlery making, Drake and Bane expected to make back their investment in three or four years, and after that, any earnings would be pure profit.

Money working for them, just as Father had recommended.

# Chapter Four

## LIVY

*March 1817, Liverpool*

"LIVY, DARLING," SAID Cilla, "must you argue with Papa over dinner? You know it upsets his digestion, and then he is grumpy for days."

Livy winced slightly, for what Cilla said was true, but truly, Pa was impossible. "I only said I didn't see any point in a London season," she argued. "You'd think he'd be pleased not to have the expense!"

This was all Aunt Ginny's fault. Even after the true story of the Misrule Mishap had become common knowledge among the female half of Marplestead and its surrounding countryside, Aunt Ginny was delighted with her nieces, or at least with Cilla, and wanted them to come to London with her when she presented her daughters, all three at once, in the coming season.

Livy knew she was being unfair. Pa had always gone along with his wife's desire to see her daughters join their cousins and have their turn among the upper classes in London. But Livy's seasons had been a disaster and Cilla had been ill last year, when it should have been her turn.

This year, Pa still said that Cilla was delicate. Papa had *always* insisted that Cilla was delicate. Mama had been delicate, and Cilla looked just like her, but—apart from the severe ague last year—had always kept excellent health.

Livy said that Mama's delicacy was caused by Papa's habit of bellowing, which might be true, but did not go down well with Papa. Delicate or not, Livy's sister had a will of iron, and she was determined to join her cousins. The outcome was a foregone conclusion. Cilla was going, and so Pa insisted that Livy must go, too.

Furthermore, even Pa was coming. He had had a miserable Christmas, and refused to be left on his own again. He decided to take a house in London, leave a skeleton staff to look after their home just outside of Liverpool, and uproot everyone else for the three months from the first of April until the 30th of June.

Livy still did not want to go. Cilla should, Livy agreed. Cilla was pretty, personable, polite, and pleasant. A plethora of "p" words, and all highly desirable in a wife. She was also young—not as young as her youngest cousin, but still not yet twenty. To add to her appeal, she was an heiress. With Aunt Ginny as her chaperone, Cilla would have the one final criteria to make her irresistible to a well-born but poverty-stricken gentleman—an eligible connection.

As for herself, Livy had already had two-and-a-bit miserable seasons. She was more handsome than pretty, and none of the other "p" words applied. She was six years older than her sister. Yes, she was also an heiress, and Aunt Ginny was as much her connection as Cilla's. But all the other counts against her meant she was not marriage material.

Furthermore, she was happy in that state. Apart from one youthful mistake, she had never met a man to whom she wished to shackle herself.

The irritating internal voice that refused to accept the lies she told herself threw up a mental image. *Nonsense.* After all, she had not really met Mr. Bane Sanderson, had she? Undoubtedly, he would be a disappointment if she knew him better.

"Let me stay home and look after the house and the estate,"

she begged her father.

He refused, but she kept arguing. "Take Cilla, Pa. She would like to find a husband, and I'm sure she will easily attract the gentlemen. But leave me at home."

In deference to Pa's digestion, she stopped besieging him over dinner, but she sought him out several times a day with new arguments for taking Cilla and leaving her, until Pa finally blew up.

"Enough, Olivia. No more arguments. No more complaints. You are coming to London. You are joining in the season. Furthermore, you will make yourself agreeable to the gentlemen. For I tell you this, girl. I shall not see Cilla married before you. If you do not marry, then neither does Cilla. And it shall be your fault."

It was the one thing that could silence Livy—the thought that Cilla might miss out on anything her heart desired. "But surely, Cilla, if you meet someone you care about, Pa will change his mind," Livy said.

Cilla's, "Ye-e-es," was not convincing, and rightly so, for once Pa dug his toes in, the whole earth would be easier to budge. But Cilla was not downcast. Not at all. "Look on the bright side, Livy. Now I can enjoy myself without any fear of being stuck in a marriage that suits Papa or Aunt Ginny, and does not suit me at all. If I cannot marry before you, and you do not want to marry, then we shall have all the fun of London and none of the trials."

It was not so much that Livy did not *want* to marry as that she was sure she could not. Even if the incident in her first season had never happened, she had the habit of speaking her mind, and no plans to change. A man who was not interested in her views and opinions was not one she wanted to spend her life with. Unfortunately, in the three years she had gone to London, none of the eligible men she had met appreciated outspoken women.

Except in her first season, and that was a lie. Livy had every reason, as a result of that season, to sympathize with Aurora. She, of all people, was in a position to understand that a girl was only ruined if people knew. And only Livy and a certain man, long gone to face a judgement higher than hers, knew what had spoiled Livy's first season so thoroughly.

Shortly after the incident that didn't ruin her, her mother's illness had cut her season short. What with nursing Mama and then mourning her, it had been two years ago before she again went to London.

It had not been like the first time, with Mama. She was much older, much warier, and much less tolerant of male arrogance and stupidity. Also, she had missed Cilla, and was determined to blot her copy book with her paid chaperone so she would be sent home. Sure enough, six interminable weeks into the season, the chaperone had thrown up her hands and written to Papa.

Livy had been spared the rest of the season, though she'd had weeks of grumbling from Papa. But last year, Pa insisted on trying again. "I promised your mother that you would have your chance," he insisted. That time, Livy was even more miserable, even more of a fish out of water, and—she could concede it, if only to herself—even more grumpy and difficult. And last year, Pa had insisted on her seeing the season out.

At least this time she would have her sister and cousins with her, but she did not suppose that would protect her from the consequences of her well-earned reputation as a difficult woman.

She had worked hard to become one. The wits and the gossips made fun of her. Suitors wouldn't touch her with a barge pole, even if she did have a large dowry and was the eldest daughter of a fabulously rich man.

They would flock to Cilla, of that Livy had no doubt. But in the end, Cilla wanted to go to London, and Pa refused to leave Livy behind, so go to London Livy must.

"You might meet the Countess of Sutton," Cilla pointed out. Unlikely, Livy thought. She doubted if Aunt Ginny moved in such exalted circles. And if she did meet the esteemed lady, what would she say? *"Please, my lady, I want to help ruined girls like you do, but I have no access to money beyond a few coins, and in Liverpool, people tell me either that fallen women have bought their fate on themselves, or that the work is not for unmarried women."* In fact, one cleric had frowned at her from under bristling eyebrows and said, "One must question the morals of an unmarried woman with an interest in such miserable creatures."

Horrid man.

No doubt, Countess Sutton would also turn her away. However, they were leaving for London at the end of this week, and Livy could think of no way to stop it.

# CILLA

PAPA HAD RIDDEN most of the way from home to the inn where they would stop for the night. He said he could not be confined in a coach with Livy while she was sulking. Cilla knew better on both counts. Papa got sick in carriages and would ride on his horse even in the rain to avoid such embarrassment.

And Livy was not sulking but anxious. When Livy was worried, upset, or frightened, her response was to snap and snarl. For Cilla's sake, she had been trying to keep her mouth shut on all the angry comments she wanted to make. The result was what her father called a sullen silence.

Truly, though neither Livy nor Papa would appreciate the comparison, the pair were more alike than they cared to think. Papa could not see that Livy's sniping was a defensive measure, used when she felt threatened or out of sorts, and Livy refused to believe that Papa's complaints and remonstrations arose from bewilderment over and concern about his elder daughter.

At least with Papa not in the carriage, Livy was able to relax. Since neither of them suffered from Papa's complaint, they took it in turns to read out loud. They speculated about who might be in Town that they had met at Aunt Ginny's house party. They discussed fashions, for the first order of business, Aunt Ginny had written, was to see to their wardrobes.

Even Barker, their shared maid, joined the conversation instead of insisting on the distance she assured them was only proper. Barker was a devoted reader of Ackerman's and other fashion periodicals, and had strong opinions about how to turn them out to do her credit.

It was a long day, though, and Cilla felt stiff and achy when she climbed down from the carriage at the inn. God bless Papa, who had arrived first and ordered a hot bath to be set up in their room as soon as they arrived. They had a cup of tea in their private parlor while footmen with buckets hurried to and from the bedchamber under Barker's supervision.

Dinner would be served in the private parlor, too, Papa told them. They would have time for a leisurely soak before dressing for the meal. Livy rolled her eyes. Cilla knew what she meant. It did seem silly to dress for dinner when it was only the three of them, and when they had been traveling all day.

But such was the way things were done in the upper classes. Papa was ever mindful of the manners of those he wished his daughters to emulate. There was no point in objecting, and fortunately, Papa didn't see Livy's eyeroll.

Livy had the first bath. Cilla had realized that the gown she wished to wear the next day—the one in which she would be arriving in London—was packed in the trunk that was still on the second carriage. Barker said she could fetch it, but Cilla wanted to stretch her legs, so she claimed that she wasn't sure what she wanted. They both headed downstairs after locking the door to the suite the girls were sharing.

Cilla was slightly in the lead as they turned the corner of the stairs. As she did so, a gentleman appeared, going up the steps as they went down. And later she thought it was possible she had been hurrying. Or perhaps the gentleman was, for they collided, Cilla slipped and would have fallen, and he clutched her to him until she found her feet again.

She looked up into green eyes to give her apologies and her

thanks, and the words died on her lips. It was the man they had mistakenly attempted to dunk on Misrule Night. Drake Sanderson. His name was etched in her mind, in the place where embarrassing memories were kept.

"I do apologize, Miss," he said. "I hope you are unhurt."

He had a warm voice that set something in her shivering, and not in an unpleasant way.

"I am unhurt," she agreed. "You caught me. Thank you."

Barker cleared her throat, and Mr. Sanderson started and removed his hands from Cilla's waist. "I beg your pardon," he said. "Again." He had taken a step backward and down, so that her head was now a little above his. Fair, curly hair and those startlingly green eyes. A handsome face with a firm jaw, strongly marked brows, and a three-cornered smile.

The memory of him stripped to his breeches stopped her breath for a moment as she stared at him and he gazed back.

Her maid coughed, and then said, "Miss, we need to get back to your sister."

Mr. Sanderson blinked as if waking from a dream, and Cilla felt exactly the same—as if they had met in a place out of time and wordlessly shared something to treasure.

"May I have the privilege of knowing the name of the lady with whom I collided?" Mr. Sanderson asked. "I am Drake Sanderson, and I am on my way back to London, where I live."

Cilla waved Barker's incipient protest into silence. "I am also traveling to London, with my sister and my father," she admitted. "My aunt, Lady Marple, is bringing me out this year. I am Lucilla Wintergreen." After all, how could he find her if he did not know who she was or where she was likely to be? And Lucilla very much hoped that he would find her.

This feeling she had being near him meant something, but exactly *what* remained to be seen.

"We must go, Miss Cilla," Barker insisted, glaring at Mr. Sanderson.

"Save me a dance at your debut ball," Mr. Sanderson begged.

"I'll be there."

"I will," said Cilla, and allowed Barker to hurry her away, satisfied that Mr. Sanderson was not unaffected by…whatever it was.

# DRAKE

DRAKE WATCHED THE young lady go. He recognized the name, of course. Miss Wintergreen had been Lady Misrule last New Year's Eve. Not this Miss Wintergreen, though. The one he remembered meeting—the one who had slipped a drug into his drink—was altogether larger than this dainty lady, with her blue, blue eyes and dark ringlets. As far as Drake could remember, Lady Misrule's hair was not as dark nor were her eyes as blue.

Had Miss Cilla been there? Did she know about her sister's mischief?

He was almost certain he could talk Lady Marple into giving him and Bane invitations to Miss Cilla's debut ball. The Marples and the Sandersons had long lived in the same neighborhood, and he'd known her and her daughters since he was knee high to a grasshopper. She was a pleasant lady, though somewhat high in the instep.

Talking Bane into going with him might be a different matter, but that he was also determined to do. He needed his brother to watch his back in alien territory.

He continued upstairs to the room they had taken for the night after their carriage back to London broke down. Bane was lounging in a chair by the window, once again studying the diagrams of the engine that was now carrying a fair chunk of their hopes and dreams.

"The carriage wheel is an easy fix, the wheelwright says," Drake reported. "He'll have it ready for us to carry on in the morning."

"That's good. I've ordered dinner for us both. It should be here any minute. The innkeeper must have links with the coast—the brandy is excellent." Bane pointed toward the bottle.

As Drake poured himself a drink, he said, "I bumped into a Miss Wintergreen on the stairs. She is on her way to London for the season."

Bane straightened. "Lady Misrule?"

"Her sister. Miss Lucilla. *Cilla*, her maid called her. I gather her sister is with her. Lady Marple is holding a ball for Miss Cilla. And, I must suppose, the Marple sisters, since they are also making their debut."

"Lady Misrule is going to London," Bane said. His choice of words and the flat delivery indicated a level of interest that surprised Drake. Perhaps Bane would be easy to persuade into the ball, after all. Drake wished he could see his brother's face, but Bane was still wearing his hood, conscious that a servant would soon be here with dinner.

Sure enough, there was a knock on the door which proved to be a maid with a heavy tray.

Drake said nothing further until she'd left, the door was locked, and Bane had removed his hood. They had served themselves and begun eating before he commented, "I told Miss Lucilla that I'd like to dance with her at her debut ball."

"What is the chance of that?" Bane said, dismissively.

"Quite good, actually. I think if we make a call on Lady Marple we might be able to come away with an invitation each."

Bane's hands stilled over his food, then he finished loading his fork and took the mouthful. He looked up from his plate then, saying nothing until he had swallowed. Drake refused to be spooked into filling the silence. He took a mouthful of his own. Bane would speak when he had thought through what he wanted to say.

And he did. "Is she pretty?"

"Miss Cilla? Lovely. Eyes like stars and curves to die for." Watching Bane carefully, he added, "Nothing like her sister."

"Miss Wintergreen is lovely," Bane snapped back, with an edge of indignation on the lady's behalf. Interesting.

"Indeed," Drake agreed, peaceably. He had noted her looks in an academic kind of a way before she drugged him, but he had not been attracted to her. "Lovely in a warrior queen kind of a way," he explained.

She had intimidated him, to tell the truth. "Miss Cilla is *petite*, almost a head shorter than me, and I am not a tall man, as you know. What else can I tell you? Her hair is dark, her eyes blue, and her complexion like porcelain. Except for something about the shape of the face, one would not believe them related."

"Miss Wintergreen is a very good height, brown hair suits her, and her eyes are an intriguing shade of silver." Bane sounded as if he had given the matter some thought. Very interesting.

"A good height for a giant like you," Drake retorted without heat. Bane had always been big for his age, and had shot past Colin in height when he was only twelve and Colin was fifteen. It was, in Colin's opinion, another of Bane's sins.

"So, you want to go to this ball?" Bane asked.

"Yes." Even if he wanted to prevaricate, it wouldn't work with this closest of brothers.

"Then you should go." Bane paused. Drake tried to think of a convincing argument, but Bane continued, "I'll come too, if you like. If Lady Marple doesn't refuse me."

Extremely interesting! The Amazon might not be to Drake's taste, but apparently, she suited Bane. Drake wished him every success!

# Chapter Five

## BANE

WHILE IN MARPLESTEAD, Miss Wintergreen had made her opinion of marriage so clear that word had spread across the parish. On the other hand, Bane had met quite a number of sprigs of nobility—in his home neighborhood and since he and Drake moved to London—who probably had helped her form that opinion.

Marriage! Was he really thinking of such a thing after an acquaintance that comprised the exchange of half a dozen words over the drugged body of his brother?

Probably not. After all, while he might suspect there was more to her than she showed the public, that didn't necessarily mean he had a chance with her. Even if she was a shipping owner's daughter venturing into the perilous seas of the upper-class marriage market, that didn't mean she was so without options she would overlook his scars and his birth.

Or that, on further acquaintance, he would even like her.

Say, rather, he was considering the possibility of *thinking* about marriage. He should take another look at the lady to see if his attraction warranted any further action. With this in mind, he went to the stables and gave a groom a coin, and the promise of another, to send him a message when the Wintergreen carriage was ready.

That allowed him to be in the hall that led to the stable yard when the Wintergreen ladies came down the stairs, escorted by an older gentleman who had a look of the smaller and younger of the two ladies. Miss Lucilla, that would be. Pretty enough, but not as compelling as the older, more statuesque, lady, who had paused on the stairs and was gazing at him.

Yes, she warranted further action.

Bane, with a deep breath, put his hood back and stood his ground. She might as well know what he looked like before he chanced his arm. The right-hand side of his face was unsightly. The scar from the knife slash ran right up from his chin through his eye to his forehead—the eye was brown on that side, and smaller than the green eye on his unblemished side. His mouth drooped on the damaged side, too, giving him a lop-sided smile. She was not the type to faint at the sight of him, but he braced himself for signs of distaste. Or worse.

"Come along, Olivia," the father said, his tone impatient.

"Mr. Wintergreen," said Bane, seizing the moment, "allow me to introduce myself, sir. I had the pleasure of encountering your daughters when they were staying with their aunt, Lady Marple, at her country estate." He bowed. "Bane Sanderson, sir."

"Bane?" said Mr. Wintergreen, frowning. "What kind of a name is that?"

Miss Lucilla hissed, "Papa!"

Bane inclined his head. "A cross my father's sons must bear, sir. He named us after some of the herbs that made his fortune. Hemlock is the eldest, and then Drake and myself—Mandrake and Wolfbane. Our sister's name is Larkspur."

A spark of interest diluted that irritation. "Sanderson's Medicinals," Mr. Wintergreen concluded.

"Yes, sir. My father's company, and now my elder brother's."

"Three sons, eh? I was not so fortunate. I suppose you are sniffing after my Cilla. I warn you, she wants to marry for love.

She does not have to marry at all, if she does not wish to. And she'll have her choice of young lords, mark you."

With his eyes on Miss Olivia Wintergreen's grey ones, Bane replied, "I beg your pardon for contradicting you, sir, but it is your older daughter who has attracted my attention. I believe my brother Drake intends to call on your younger daughter, however."

Miss Lucilla's eyes widened, but she smiled. Miss Wintergreen looked startled and then annoyed. She opened her mouth, but whatever she was about to say, a nudge from her sister silenced her.

Mr. Wintergreen snorted. "Olivia?" His astonishment was no compliment to his daughter, who glared at him. Mr. Wintergreen ignored her, and when he spoke, his irritation had gone as if it never existed. "Well, I never. I suppose we may expect to see you in London then, young man. Come along, girls. We must not keep the horses waiting."

"Good day, Mr. Sanderson," said Miss Lucilla as she passed him.

Miss Wintergreen stopped. "What do you mean by that nonsense?" she demanded.

"Exactly what I said," Bane replied. "You have caught my notice. I should like to know more."

Her snort was very similar to her father's. "I trust you are not claiming to have fallen in love with me over your brother's..." she trailed off, but her father and sister had passed through the door and no one else was within listening distance.

"Not in love," he responded. "Not yet, in any case. But I am attracted, admiring, and interested."

"You must be soft in the head," she scolded, and then walked past him towards the door without saying farewell.

"I shall see you in London, Miss Wintergreen," he called after her.

At the door she stopped, turned to look at him, and raised an elegant eyebrow. "So you say," she replied, and left.

It was a start. And one of the counts against him had not deterred her—she had not flinched at his scars, nor shown any reluctance to look him in the face.

She really was a magnificent woman.

# LIVY

IT DID NOT take Pa long to share his story about the Sanderson brothers with Aunt Ginny. Papa had taken a house in the same street as the Marple London residence, and Aunt Ginny walked across the street the following morning.

Livy and Cilla, who were sitting on the terrace enjoying a cup of tea in the spring sunshine, could hear Papa leading her into the parlor just one open window away from them.

"Before I send for my daughters, Virginia, I have something to say. We met two young men at one of our stops on the way to London. They apparently encountered Lucilla and Olivia in Marplestead, and they wish to pursue their interest."

Cilla made to get up, presumably to either remove herself or to let Pa know he had an audience. Livy frowned at her and gestured for her to sit again and be quiet.

"Really, Horace?" said Aunt Ginny. "How charming. Who are they?"

"Mandrake and Wolfbane Sanderson. Their father was Sanderson Medicinals. Apparently their older brother is at the helm now."

Aunt Ginny commented, "Young Drake and his half-brother, Bane. Merchants, at best. Cilla can do better, Horace. Livy, too. She is a fine-looking woman, and some men prefer women who are a little older."

"Sanderson Medicinals," Pa repeated. "There's money there, Virginia."

"The eldest brother got it all, unfortunately. Not that the

younger sons are destitute. Rumor has it that, after his daughter married, Old Mr. Sanderson gave them both a sum of money and told them to make their own way. They are both good boys, and they certainly haven't been wasting their money in riotous living. I daresay they are living on the interest."

"It bears looking into," Pa said. "Cilla's young to be thinking of marriage, and need not feel pressured to make any choices, but I'd like to see Livy settled, and that is a fact. If Bane Sanderson has money, he might do for Livy."

"He is not a real Sanderson," Aunt Ginny said, and Livy could hear the sneer in the word "real". "He is George Sanderson's son, right enough, but no one knows who his mother was. George Sanderson brought him home and made Ethel—Ethel was his third wife, his daughter Larkspur's mother—made her give him houseroom. The boy was very sick, and not expected to live, and by the time it was clear he would recover, Drake had taken to him. He would not hear of Bane being sent away."

"A by-blow, eh? He looks quite different from the other lad," Pa commented.

"Yes. The other two brothers have the look of their father, but Bane must take after his mother's family, for he is altogether larger, and his coloring is quite different. In any case, Drake and Bane have been inseparable ever since, and it is quite true that George Sanderson never made a difference between the boys. Ethel hated Bane, though, and the eldest brother didn't like him, either."

"He appears well spoken enough," Pa commented.

"He is well-educated, it is true," Aunt Ginny acknowledged. "I see no harm in him. He has the manners of a gentleman, is a hard worker, and is of sober habits. But as a husband for my niece? Setting aside the ugly scars and the mismatched eyes, he is illegitimate, Horace. One cannot get past it."

"He plans to call, he and his brother. Will you deny him the house?"

Livy almost objected. How unfair, to hold his father's sins

against the poor man! She opened her mouth but Cilla put a hand on hers and touched her mouth with her forefinger, turning the tables neatly. Livy subsided. Cilla was correct. They would look very much in the wrong if she spoke up now, after listening to the conversation so far.

Aunt Ginny, who had been silent for several seconds, spoke decisively. "No, I think not. I have a soft spot for both lads, and whatever they are doing in London, it might harm their chances to be turned away. No one needs to know about Bane's tarnished birth, Horace. And if he shows an interest in Livy, then perhaps other men will do likewise. It would be a different story if he was enamored of Cilla. She has a soft heart, and might be inclined to encourage him."

"I see what you mean," Pa commented. "Livy is determined not to marry, so he may court her and do no harm. And perhaps some good, as you say. Men want what other men want, and he seems to be the type others will emulate in spite of his faults."

"I will have a word with Livy," Aunt Ginny said. "It would be best if she understands that Bane Sanderson is not eligible. On the whole, I am not displeased about this. Not displeased at all. I must send the brothers an invitation to the debut ball."

"If you think it best, Virginia," Pa said. "You know much more about these things than I."

"Mind you, it will do no good for them to call in the next week," Aunt Ginny mused. "Oh, Horace, the girls and I are going to have so much fun! Now, I have written out the budget you asked for, and I have made an appointment with my modiste for this afternoon. My daughters have a fitting for the gowns we have ordered, and it will be a good opportunity to make a start on a wardrobe for Cilla and Livy."

"One more thing, Virginia," said Pa. "I will stand the ready for the season, but I shall not have any rumors about you and Viscount Curston."

"Horace!" Aunt Ginny's voice was accusing. "Someone has been filling your ears with lies! I am a perfectly proper widow."

"That may be, by the standards of the upper sort. But I don't want my daughters thinking that kind of behavior is acceptable."

"I have done nothing of which I ought to be ashamed," Aunt Ginny insisted. "A lady is entitled to some fun after her husband dies, Horace. That does not apply to this year, however. I am bringing my daughters out this year, and your nieces, too. What is acceptable for a widow is not acceptable for a mother of marriageable daughters. I shall be a pattern of rectitude, I assure you."

Pa made a harumphing sound, then said, "Let me look at these figures, then, Virginia."

Cilla stood and gestured to the garden door, which was further along the terrace. Livy nodded. It was for the best. She did not regret listening, though. What they had said about Mr. Bane Sanderson was intriguing. Her heart went out to the small boy who had been brought, ill and possibly dying, to a house where his father's legal wife ruled, and where he was hated.

How fortunate that he'd had his brother's love. Was that why old Mr. Sanderson had allowed him to stay? Where would he have gone if Mr. Drake had not stood up for him? And where did he come from? His mother's home? Was she still alive, the mistress? Had she not wanted her son?

Livy's mind was teeming with questions.

So, apparently was Cilla's, but not about Bane Sanderson. When it was time to leave for the modiste appointment, Cilla peppered Aunt Ginny and the cousins with questions about fabrics, styles, colors, until Livy was certain that her brain was going to dissolve and leak out of her ears.

She expected it to be worse at the modiste's, but Aunt Ginny held her back for a moment before they went in the door. "Livy, my dear, here is a list of what you absolutely must have. I want no argument from you, my dear, about quantities. But for fabrics, styles and colors, I will trust you and Madame Beauvillier to work things out. You are twenty-five, my dear, and do not need to stick to the fashions suitable for your sister and cousins."

Livy could hardly believe her ears. "I can decide for myself?"

"I will have final approval," Aunt Ginny said. "At least until you have more experience in walking the fine line between what is appropriate for an unmarried lady and for a matron of the same age. But I trust your common sense, my dear. You will not dress in a way that reflects badly on your sister and cousins. If in doubt, ask Madame Beauvillier, or refer the question to me. But yes. You can decide for yourself."

*This might be fun after all.* But probably not. She would still have to suffer through hours of being measured, of looking at fashion magazines, of trying to seem as if she understood or cared about the difference between two shades of powder blue.

Aunt Ginny introduced her to the modiste, and took herself and the girls off to another room with Madame Beauvillier's assistant.

"Well, Miss Wintergreen, Lady Marple did not tell me about your extraordinary eyes," Madame said. "I think I must revise my thoughts about the colors to suggest. What say you to silver?"

*Extraordinary eyes?* Livy only just prevented herself from sneaking a peek in the mirror. She followed Madame into yet a third room with an internal sigh. Extraordinary or not, her eyes were about to be overwhelmed until they dropped out with boredom.

But it was not that way at all.

Madame Beauvillier at no point treated her as if she was nothing more than a doll to be dressed and undressed. She had already made a number of choices, based on Aunt Ginny's description of Livy, "But if you have other preferences, Miss Wintergreen, name them," she said.

"I can only tell you what does not suit me, Madame," Livy explained. "For I have been wearing it. Everything selected for me by my last year's sponsor and the sponsor from the year before was too frilly for me, and too pale."

"The walking dress you are wearing is becoming," Madame commented. "Though a stronger shade would better suit your coloring. I take it you selected it yourself?"

"I chose the color." Livy smiled down at her peach-tinted skirts. She had wanted a poppy-like shade, but Barker had been horrified, and even Cilla had hesitated, so she had changed her mind.

But she was pleased with the outfit. Cilla said she looked wonderful, Aunt Ginny had given a nod of approval, and even Papa had said, "Pleased to see you taking care of your appearance, Olivia."

"My sister sketched a cut that she thought would suit me, and I liked it, so we had it made up by a local dressmaker. What color would you recommend?"

"Perhaps this?" The modiste held up a swatch that was the shade of poppy Livy had wanted to choose, or near to it. "*Ponceau*, it is called. I would not suggest using it in the evening— it might be thought fast. But for day wear, it is quite acceptable, particularly teamed with trims or other garments in a more subdued shade. Or we could make a jacket in ponceau with a skirt in, let us say, a gray brocade with narrow ponceau stripes. Yes, that could work very well."

She looked intently at Livy, mostly focusing on her face but also scanning the rest of her frame. "You have a queenly form, Miss Wintergreen. A small lady like your sister can dress in frills, though I do not recommend it, and with fair skin, dark hair, and eyes of such an intense blue, the pastels that wash you out will be a perfect setting for her kind of beauty. Your beauty is of a different type. Your gray eyes are most unusual, and your hair…"

She paused to consider her words. Livy answered for her. "Is brown, as is my skin, if I am not careful to wear a hat at all times."

"Your hair is a light brown, with hints of gold and copper, and your complexion is excellent. Some shades will make your skin look sallow and your hair look dull, but if we choose the right colors, you will glow, that I can promise you."

*Glow.* Livy had never considered that she might be able to glow.

"My clothing will be your setting," said Madame Beauvillier. "Let me show you what I mean. Colors first. Come and stand in front of the mirror."

There followed a magical half hour, as the modiste laid lengths of cloth over Livy's shoulder and explained how the shade was complementing Livy's skin, hair, and eyes—or the reverse. And Livy, who had always chosen colors purely by whether she liked them, could see what Madame Beauvillier was trying to show her.

They had a pile of suitable tones and a larger pile of rejects before they moved on to the next stage.

"Let us consider silhouettes," said Madame. "You are tall and curvy, Miss Wintergreen. We must dress you to make the most of these assets."

"Assets?" Livy's laugh had nothing of humor in it. "The fashion is for slender and diminutive, Madame Beauvillier. Not for giants with large..." she indicated her breasts and hips with a gesture.

Madame snorted. "Fashion! Fashion is a way to sell gowns and other items. This year waists are up. Next year they are down. Today Pomona green is all the rage. Tomorrow, coquelicot pink. Ribbons are in. No, lace. No, flounces. No, ribbons again. Today's fashions, slavishly followed, look stunning on fashion dolls and ladies who look like them—thin like a stick with no shape."

"Nonetheless..." Livy ventured. She did not want people to laugh at her, as they did at Mr. Addison, an elderly gentleman who still wore the powdered wig and embroidered coats of his youth.

"We shall not, of course, ignore fashion altogether. You need not fear that. We shall reinterpret it to do you credit. Here." Madame picked up a sketchpad and pencil. "I shall show you what I mean."

Once again, she talked as she worked, explaining the impact of long vertical lines, how some fabrics draped better when cut on the bias, how undergarments that were correctly fitted were the cornerstone of both comfort and good looks.

Walking gowns, riding habits, evening gowns, morning dresses, coats of various lengths, all came flowing off her pencil, page after page of them.

"Unfussy, but superbly well cut," she instructed. "Your current costume is almost correct, though I would not have chosen that shade of red, and I suggest we remove the bow, and replace the broad trim with a narrower one. Thus." Another sketch, this time quite clearly Livy herself.

"And a turban cap or toque rather than a bonnet," she said, finishing the head with a few strokes.

"You have made me pretty." It came out as an accusation, though Livy was intrigued rather than irritated.

"Not pretty, exactly," Madame said, thoughtfully. "Beautiful, rather. Pretty is largely a matter of fashion, and the fashion is currently for dark-haired dolls like your sister. You have something better than dark hair, which will fade to white in time. You have good bones. You will be beautiful into old age."

That was nonsense. Wasn't it? Madame wanted to sell her dresses, of course. "I shall happily settle for being presentable, Madame Beauvillier," she said.

"You do not believe me." Madame put down her pencil and smiled. "It does not matter. I shall dress you, and others will see your beauty. Perhaps, then, you will believe."

Without warning, she clapped her hands together. Livy only just kept herself from flinching. A servant bustled into the room so quickly that she must have been hovering outside the door.

"Serve tea, Mary. Tell Doris I shall need her in… shall we say forty-five minutes? Miss Wintergreen, we shall take tea while you choose designs and fabrics for your initial order. Then one of my ladies will take your measurements."

That wasn't quite the end of it. Aunt Ginny joined them to see what had been decided, and declared herself pleased. "We have made a very good start today," she declared, as she gathered up the other four girls and swept them all towards the door. "Come along, darlings. We have earned a visit to Gunter's!"

"I am delighted with Aunt Ginny's modiste," Cilla whispered to Livy. I cannot wait to show you my new gowns. Are you happy with yours?"

"She is going to dress me in colors I like, and leave off all the fussy trims," Livy said, unsure how else to explain Madame's astounding approach. Beautiful? Livy? No, Madame Beauvillier was exaggerating. But Livy was hopeful that she would not have to blush for her gowns.

"I think I shall look acceptable in her garments," she answered.

# Chapter Six

THE BROTHERS HAD called on Mr. Wintergreen the day after they arrived in London, only to be told that he was not at home, and neither were the Wintergreen sisters. They next called on Lady Marple, but they were unsuccessful there, too. Her ladyship had gone out, and was not—in any case—receiving today.

For the next three days, the message was the same.

That wasn't all they did, of course. After two weeks out of London, they had catching up to do—meetings to attend, letters to answer, reports to read. Their solicitor had drawn up a contract following their written instructions, and one of their earliest meetings was to sign it so it could be sent to the Pentworths in Sheffield. Then there was a meeting with their bank, who didn't have a co-operative agreement with a Sheffield bank, which meant another meeting with another bank who *did* have such an agreement and could act as an intermediary.

As soon as Pentworth had signed and returned the contract, their bank would transfer the required sum to the partner bank, who would notify the Sheffield bank, so the inventor could draw down the money. It had been a busy few days.

"Sometimes, I think I'd like to be one of the idle rich," said Drake.

"You'd be bored witless in less than a week," Bane assured him.

On the fourth day, an invitation was delivered to them at their lodgings. "Drake," Bane said, "this is from Lady Marple. We have been invited to her ball, which is three Thursdays from now."

Drake held out his hand and inspected the card. "Excellent!" he said.

Bane was reading the note that came with the card. It was a brief message to tell them they would find the ladies at home if they called on Thursday after three in the afternoon. Two more days. He showed it to Drake. "Is she encouraging us, do you think?"

"We'll find out when we visit, I expect." Bane was very familiar with how the landed gentry and aristocracy froze out those they considered beneath them.

Drake had something else on his mind. "If we are going to attend balls, we will need made-to-measure evening clothes," he said. He had a good point. They didn't want to stand out for the wrong reasons, and tailor-made clothes would help them to fit in. On the other hand, Bane had heard that a Bond Street tailor charged like a wounded bull. "What do you suggest?"

Drake grimaced. "I don't suggest we go to a fashionable tailor and then fail to pay him, like an aristocrat. Or waste our capital on clothing. But there's a man I've heard of in Spitalfields—a German tailor called Swartz. He's very good, apparently."

"We can take a look," Bane agreed.

They could afford it. They had more than enough to dress like dukes if they chose. But they both agreed. Capital was for investing, not dissipating. To pay Bond Street rates to outfit them with fashionable clothing—at ten guineas for a single evening jacket each and perhaps a guinea and half for each shirt—would mean either cutting back on eating or digging into their capital.

"In a way, fine clothes are also an investment," Drake pointed out. "We'll be mixing with people we might want as investors in our own ventures, and meeting possible brides."

"By which you mean the Wintergreen sisters," Bane offered. "I agree to fine clothes, but not to Bond Street prices."

It was true, though. If they wished to pursue an acquaintance with the sisters, they needed to be part of the social scene. Bane didn't much like the idea of facing the ton, but even less did he like the idea of other people courting Miss Wintergreen, and possibly winning her, while he stayed away. "I'm in favor of buying whatever we need at the best price we can manage," he said. "Though if we are going out into Society, I'm wearing my hood."

He told Mr. Swartz the same thing when they visited him to decide whether to employ his services. The man's eyes widened, but all he said was, "Perhaps a black silk one, sir. For evening." That and his prices, which were half those of Bond Street, made up Bane's mind, and Drake agreed.

Indeed, the order they placed was larger than they had originally intended. They would be able to turn themselves out creditably during the day, as well as for evening events.

"After all," Drake said, as they left, "what is the point of being wealthy if we never spend anything?"

"If you are thinking of marrying, you might need to be able to convince the girl's father that you can support a wife," Bane pointed out.

"What about you?" Drake asked. "Do you look at Miss Olivia Wintergreen and hear wedding bells?"

Bane wouldn't go quite that far. "I hear the possibility of wedding bells, I suppose." From his side of the equation. He doubted that the lady would consider him.

Drake nodded. "Exactly. We need to spend time with them and see if this attraction survives and maybe grows into something more."

"I expect their father would prefer a title for them," Bane warned. "I'm sure he'd prefer a husband who wasn't born a scandal."

"The scandal was Father's, Bane," Drake pointed out, as he always did. But Society didn't think that way.

No point in arguing with Drake. They'd covered this ground before. "We have an hour before the meeting with our broker," he said. "Three Crowns for a bite?"

The cook at the Three Crowns inn had a light hand with pastry and a deft touch with spices. Besides, the innkeeper was as good a brewer as his wife was a cook, and kept a good cellar besides.

They were soon seated at a table in the corner, enjoying a meat pie with mashed potato and mushy peas, and a mug of the host's best brown ale. "Isn't that our broker?" Drake asked, pointing with his chin, to a man who was just walking in the door.

He, too, had arrived early, perhaps for another meeting, for he was in earnest conversation with another gentleman. A fashionable gentleman, at that. The cut, style, and quality of the man's clothing suggested wealth and social position, an impression that brought forcibly home to Bane how right Drake had been to insist on visiting the tailor.

The broker didn't notice them in their shadowy corner, and the innkeeper found the pair a table in a sunny window, obviously a premium spot reserved for men of the quality of the broker's companion.

Bane continued to watch while the two of them sat and talked, the broker scribbling notes in the same notebook he'd used when taking instructions from Drake and Bane. A business meeting, then. One of the inn's servants brought the two men a meal, and they continued their discussion as they ate.

Bane and Drake had finished their own meal and their table had been cleared by the time the pair they were watching were done. The gentleman stood and the broker hastened to do likewise, holding out his hand to grasp the one extended toward him.

"Come on," said Drake, pushing out of his chair. He strode

across the room toward the other two, Bane following behind, wondering what his brother was up to.

The broker's eyes widened and he smiled, then said to the other man, "My lord, these are the brothers I told you about. Mr. Sanderson and Mr. Sanderson, well met, sirs. Lord Andrew Winderfield, may I present Mr. Wolfbane Sanderson and Mr. Mandrake Sanderson?"

Lord Andrew—which meant he was the younger son of a duke or a marquess, if Bane remembered rightly. He presented his hand to each of them in turn. His grip was firm and his smile friendly. "Mr. Atkins tells me you might be prepared to act as a reference, gentlemen. The investment club to which I belong is thinking of commissioning his services as a broker."

"We have been pleased with his performance, Lord Andrew," Bane confirmed. "We have only recently moved to London, but he has been acting on our behalf for three years, and to excellent effect."

The aristocrat nodded. "A good recommendation, indeed. Perhaps you would be kind enough to speak to the other members of my little group? We meet here tomorrow at around this time. Please, join us for another of Mrs. Waters' delectable pies. She bakes them fresh every day."

"Thank you. We shall," said Drake, before Bane could make a polite excuse. And perhaps his brother was correct. It couldn't hurt to give their broker a helping hand, and—if they were about to venture into society—it was not a bad idea to do a favor for a group of nobles.

## CILLA

DRESSED IN THE palest of pinks, Cilla checked her reflection in the mirror then moved out of the way so that Livy could have a turn. Today was Cilla's first experience of London-style afternoon calls.

In a way, she supposed, it was Livy's, too, for her sister had never looked lovelier.

Livy was staring into the mirror as if she could not believe her eyes. For today, she had chosen a day dress in mazarine blue silk. The fabric had been woven with self-color stripes, shiny and dull, shiny and dull. Apart from a minute ruffle at the hem, cuffs, high waist and neckline, it was unadorned. The shade made her hair look darker and her eyes more silver than Cilla had ever seen them, and the superb cut flattered her figure.

"You look lovely, Livy," Cilla said, sincerely.

Livy's smile suggested that she almost believed it. "So do you, Cilla darling. Shall we go down?"

They had come over to Aunt Ginny's house after breakfast, for a dance lesson and then another shopping trip, this time for dancing slippers and other footwear. Rather than go home to change, they had arranged for Barker to bring an afternoon change of clothing over to the Marples'.

So, to attend Aunt Ginny's afternoon calls, all they needed to do was walk downstairs.

They met their cousins on the stairs, Pearl looking lovely in white, Beryl in pale green, and Ruby in the softest of blues.

"Oooh," said Beryl. "I do wish I was old enough to wear real colors. I would kill to be able to wear that gown, Livy. You look wonderful in it."

Aunt Ginny came out of her bedchamber, dressed in a gown of a rich red in which she did not look nearly old enough to be a widow with four adult children. Cilla found herself calculating her aunt's age. Jasper, her eldest, was twenty-two, and Aunt Ginny had been eighteen when he was born, which meant Aunt Ginny was more than twice as old as Cilla.

Cilla hoped she looked as good when she was forty.

"You all look charming, young ladies," said Aunt Ginny. "Now, where is Jasper? We must be sitting in the parlor before the guests start to arrive."

"His lordship has already gone down, my lady," said the

footman who was stationed at the top of the stairs.

Aunt Ginny waved her daughters ahead of them, took Livy's arm, and gestured to Cilla to walk with them. "Now, girls, I sent a note to the Sanderson brothers, telling them today was our day for visitors. I wanted to warn you that they are not eligible, my dears. But they are attractive young men with beautiful manners, and it never hurts the eligible men to think other men find you attractive."

"Not eligible?" Livy demanded. "In what way? Because they are not gentry, you mean? *We* are not gentry."

"Yes, Olivia," Aunt Ginny agreed, "but you could be. Women can marry up. Look at me. With my husband's title and my father's—now my brother's—wealth, I am accepted in the highest levels of Society. Men, however, are born into their status. Unfair. But that is how Society is. We can find you both far better husbands than the younger sons of a merchant."

Cilla wasn't at all certain she wanted to marry up. In her admittedly limited experience, young men who earned their own way were far more interesting—and less arrogant—than those idle young gentlemen whose status depended entirely on their birth-lines. She didn't feel she could argue with Aunt Ginny, however. The lady was, after all, putting herself out to give Livy and Cilla a season.

Livy had no such qualms. "I am not certain I ever want to marry," she said, "but if I do, I will choose a man for his qualities, not for his family."

"We have no time to talk about that now," Aunt Ginny told her. "There is the doorbell. Quickly, girls, take your places. Look busy. Jasper, do you have your book? Read to us, but stop immediately when guests arrive. We do not expect large numbers today, but I fancy we shall have a few gentlemen stopping by, and my friend Mrs. Sandrow and her daughters."

Aunt Ginny had instructed them to have some sort of hand-work so they could occupy themselves between visitors. "Nothing is sadder, girls," she had said, "than arriving at a home to find oneself the only visitor, and all the family sitting in their best staring hopefully at the door."

From the look on her face, Livy was about to suggest any number of sadder things. Cilla shook her head, and Livy grimaced, but kept her peace. Cilla took her quilling project out of the basket she had left by her chair before going upstairs to dress.

Livy took out her mesh sticks and cord—she was netting something. Possibly a reticule. Each of the cousins also had a project—Pearl was knitting and Ruby and Beryl were both embroidering slippers.

They were just in time. Jasper had not read a word from his book before the door to the parlor opened, and the butler announced Mr. Andrews.

Cilla had met Mr. Andrews. He was one of Jasper's friends, and even more immature and irresponsible than Jasper. Given the martyred look he cast around the room, he was here under duress—either Jasper or, more probably, Aunt Ginny had twisted his arm so that her daughters and nieces would not be entirely bereft of callers on their first day "at home".

Ignoring the fact that Mr. Andrews had been present at several meals over the past week, Aunt Ginny introduced him to everyone except Jasper. Cilla and the cousins smiled at the poor man, which—from the looks of him—made him even more uncomfortable. Livy glared, and he cast a panicked glance toward the door.

Before he could escape, Mrs. Sandrow arrived. Her two daughters were great friends of the cousins, and the introductions were perfunctory at best, as the newcomers sat and dived straight into gossip about who was in town, who had sent out invitations, and who had not yet arrived.

Under cover of the conversation, Jasper rescued Mr. Andrews and carried him off to the window seat, where the pair of them fell into a discussion of a horse Mr. Andrews wanted to buy, though Jasper decried it as more flash than substance, and a bag of bones in a horse skin.

Since Cilla had nothing to contribute to either conversation, she focused on quilling a series of petals for the flowers that would be a feature of her design. Livy, she noted after a quick glance, was listening to the horse conversation, the netting project set up over her knees but her hands still.

"Mr. Drake Sanderson and Mr. Bane Sanderson," announced the butler.

Was it Cilla's imagination, or did all the females in the room straighten? Mr. Bane had a hood on—silk, Cilla thought, from the way it draped, pulled forward so his face was in deep shadow. Other than that, both men were smartly dressed in coats that fitted snugly, neatly tied cravats, and smart pantaloons. They looked as fashionable as Jasper and his friend, and much more manly. Next to the Sanderson brothers, Cilla's cousin and Mr. Andrews still had the slightly weedy look of growing boys.

"Drake and Bane," said Aunt Ginny. "Welcome. Mrs. Sandrow, Miss Sandrow, and Miss Mary Sandrow, may I make known to you Mr. Mandrake Sanderson and Mr. Wolfbane Sanderson. Their family home borders on our country estate. Gentlemen, you know my daughters and Jasper, of course. And I believe you have met my nieces. May I make known to you Mr. Andrews? Mr. Andrews, Mr. Sanderson and Mr. Sanderson. Come and sit next to me, Bane, dear, and tell me what you have been doing since you left Marplestead. Drake, you, too, dear. Sit next to Bane. That's it. What may I make you to drink? Tea? Chocolate?"

"A glass of brandy?" Jasper offered.

"Tea, thank you," said Bane. "Milk. No sugar."

"Chocolate, if you please," Drake requested.

Cilla heard Mr. Andrews's whisper and Jasper's reply. "Who are they?" asked Mr. Andrews.

"Neighbors." Jasper sounded dismissive. "A merchant family. Brother sells patent medicines. Not our sort. Mama thinks we should be nice to them because," he put on a higher pitched voice that Cilla guessed was supposed to be his Mama, "'They can't help their origins, and they are nice boys'. Their brother is not too bad, but he inherited everything. This pair have no money, and what is a shopkeeper with no money?"

Her cousin and his friend were not as quiet as they clearly thought they were, and Drake cast them a sharp glance, then shifted his gaze to Cilla. His grin and his laughing eyes coaxed her to be amused at their condescending remarks.

Cilla wasn't amused. She was angry. She would be having words with Jasper once they were in private.

Livy didn't wait. "*I am their sort,*" she said to Jasper. Thank goodness she kept her voice low, too. "From a merchant family. Your mother's family, as it happens, so does that make you my sort, too?"

Jasper flushed. "It's not like that," he said. "You don't understand. Children take their bloodlines from their father. You're a girl. If anyone is fool enough to marry a scold like you, you'll ascend—or descend—to his level. Choose wisely." He sneered. "As if a shrew like you will have a choice."

Drake excused himself from the group with Aunt Ginny, and approached the corner where Cilla and Livy were glaring at Justin. "That's enough, Marple," he said. "You shame your mother when you speak so rudely to a young lady of her family."

His jaw set, Jasper was about to let fly with another insult, but he must have seen past Drake to where his mother was staring at them, her expression concerned. He stood. "Mama, Andy and I are going to see a man about a horse," he said. "Come on, Andy."

Drake pulled the seat Jasper had been using up beside Cilla and sat down. "He is a silly cub," he said to Cilla. "Don't let him upset you."

"I do not know him well," Cilla said. "He has never visited us when Aunt Ginny does. Lady Marple, I mean. And when we are visiting Maplehurst Hall, Jasper is always least in sight. Aunt Ginny says he can have no interest in such young ladies as his sisters and his cousins."

"He was always a bit arrogant," Drake commented, "but becoming a viscount before he was sixteen can't have helped."

"Do you think he is right?" Cilla asked him. "Will people judge us because our father is in trade?"

"Some people will," Drake replied. "Some people, not all. Hypothetical situation. You have a choice between marrying a bankrupt earl who doesn't like you but needs your dowry, and me—son of Sanderson of Sanderson Medicinals, and a trader in my own right."

He raised one eyebrow and one corner of his mouth kicked up in a grin. "On the one hand, you are doomed to live your life alone, while your husband spends your dowry on gambling, women, and drink. You are invited to every fashionable event, where your husband flaunts his mistress in your face."

Cilla grimaced.

"Make the other choice," Drake said, "and you live a comfortable life with a husband and children who adore you, and many friends. You are not invited everywhere, but you are invited to events hosted by those you like and who like you in return."

Livy must have been listening, for she added, "Or marry neither of them, but instead find a rich handsome titled man who falls in love with you, and you both live happily ever after. Or consider the risk of putting your wealth, your happiness, and your very life in the hands of a man who might prove to be a tyrant, and remain single."

Her voice had risen as she proclaimed the last sentiment, and Mrs. Sandrow heard. She raised a lorgnette to her eyes and commented, "I am surprised to hear such sentiments from a girl you are sponsoring, Lady Marple. I say it out of concern."

She put down her cup and stood. "The felicities of marriage and motherhood are reward enough for any proper-thinking lady, Miss Wintergreen. I trust you will discover the truth of that before it is too late for you. Come along, girls. We have other calls to make this afternoon."

Her two daughters rose obediently to their feet.

"Delightful to see you, Mrs. Sandrow, as always," said Aunt Ginny.

"And you, Lady Marple. Tell your cook to put more sugar in the biscuits, dear. I say it out of concern."

She sailed toward the door, her two daughters bobbing in her wake, and stopped to allow the entrance of a gentleman and his adult son. Cilla had met them, too, at dinner. Viscount Curston, who was a good friend of Aunt Ginny's, and his son, who was one of Jasper's boon companions.

Soon the older of the two visitors was ensconced next to Aunt Ginny, Mr. Bane Sanderson having been evicted for the purpose. His son had been handed over to the cousins. Cilla wasn't paying much attention, because she was still considering Drake's comparatives.

Bane had taken the spare chair next to Livy, and they were bickering about whether or not a husband was necessarily a tyrant. They seemed to be enjoying themselves, so Cilla felt no need to intervene and keep the peace. Instead, she asked Drake the question that was bothering her.

"Was that a proposal?"

"If it had been," he hedged, "would you have been inclined to say *yes?*"

It scared Cilla to realize how tempted she was to call his bluff—if it was a bluff. "Not on so short an acquaintance, Mr. Sanderson," she replied.

"Then by all means let us become better acquainted." Mr. Sanderson said, calmly. He leaned closer towards her. "And next time I propose, I shall leave you in no doubt about my intentions."

# Chapter Seven

## LIVY

Mr. Bane Sanderson was a provoking creature. "Not all husbands are tyrants," he'd said when he'd folded his large frame into the chair beside her.

Obviously true. The bakery they patronized in Liverpool was owned by a happy couple. The husband ran to the shop that sold the baked goods his wife made. Each depended on the other and each respected the skills of the other. "Perhaps it is just gentlemen who make bad husbands, then," Livy replied.

"And you know a vast number of couples in the gentry and aristocracy?" Bane asked. He sounded serious and sincere, but the twinkle in his eyes confirmed it was a sarcastic question.

"Enough," she replied. Barely any, to tell the truth. But she had read the newspapers and listened to scandalous gossip. "My aunt says that one must expect husbands to stray, and that gentlemen are expected to be idle. Apparently, Jasper agrees with her."

"I agree your cousin would make a bad husband." Bane smirked. "Unless he grows up a bit, which is unlikely if his mother encourages him."

Bane was not saying anything Livy hadn't thought, but she

was annoyed at the criticism. "He became viscount when he was only sixteen," she explained. "It must have been difficult for him." That, at least, was what Aunt Ginny said.

"More difficult still for his mother," he retorted. "Unless *her* husband was a tyrant? I daresay being a widow is preferable, in that case. You should add that to your options. Marry someone rich with one foot in the grave and look forward to being a wealthy widow."

"Risky," she responded. "With a young woman as his bride, he might rally. And she might have to wait another five years or longer to enjoy the fruits of her sacrifice."

"True," he acknowledged. "Though at least that would give her time to provide Lord Senescence with some children for her to enjoy once she is living in blessed widowhood."

"What if he is cruel, as well as a tyrant?" Livy wondered. "Those five years would be interminable."

"It might have been fifteen years. But let us be optimistic and imagine our imaginary bride knew a little bit about herb craft, and managed to introduce hemlock into the warm milk he drank before bed every night, even on the nights he came to perform his marital duty, despite her complaining it made his breath smell like the rancid effusions of an old goat."

Livy chuckled. "Why, Mr. Sanderson. Are you advocating murder as a remedy to a bad marriage?"

"A rather permanent one, and far easier than divorce," Bane declared. "With an old man, and his wife a virtuous lady known for her mild temperament and generous heart, no one is likely to disbelieve her account of things."

"True enough," Livy acknowledged. "You have convinced me, sir. I shall add the option of a wealthy old man and early widowhood."

"Now, if it was you and me, the matter would be different," Bane said. "I being a young man in robust health, and you being known as a lady of fixed opinions who does not suffer fools at all, let alone gladly. If you marry me and then poison me, Miss

Wintergreen, do not expect to get away with it."

"Since I do not intend to marry at all," Livy retorted, "you are safe, Mr. Sanderson."

"Perhaps I do not wish to be safe, Miss Wintergreen."

Aunt Ginny suddenly seemed to recall their existence. "Livy, Cilla. Come and speak with Lord Curston and Mr. Curston, my dears.

"We must be going, before we outstay our welcome," Bane murmured to his brother Drake.

"If Bane and I asked your aunt for permission to take the pair of you walking in Hyde Park tomorrow, would you be willing?" Drake asked Cilla.

"Yes," she said. "Livy?"

The urge to say an enthusiastic "yes" was so disturbing that Livy nearly said "no," but the outing was what Cilla wanted, so Livy curbed her reaction. "If you wish it," she said, instead.

Drake bowed courteously to Aunt Ginny, put his proposed excursion to her, and asked her approval, all while Bane looked on.

Aunt Ginny frowned as she thought. "Very well," she said, at last. "I can see no objection, provided you escort all five of my charges, and that you remain as a group throughout the entire outing."

The brothers bowed their thanks, arranged a time, and left. The room seemed duller and smaller without Bane in it. How ridiculous of her to feel that way!

The company was certainly not as stimulating. Mr. Curston paid her a few compliments which sounded as if he had found them in a book, since no one in their right mind would have applied them to Livy. *Shy flower from the countryside, indeed! Was the man blind?*

But no, for his eyes were working perfectly well when he leered at her chest. Indeed, she didn't think he looked above her neckline once while he spoke to her.

After the Curstons left, they entertained a succession of other visitors, but not one had anything to say that was of interest to Livy. It was all fashion, people Livy didn't know, and horses. Livy couldn't contribute, so she sat and finished her reticule and thought about Bane Sanderson.

What was it about the annoying man? He was, beyond a doubt, an imposing person, with his height, his broad shoulders, his slightly aloof air. He tended to leave his brother to do the talking, but when he spoke, he made sense. Or clever nonsense, as he had during their verbal jousting that afternoon.

Why did he wear that hood? Was it just to increase the sense of mystery? Or to cover the scar she had seen that morning at the inn? It was just a scar, though. Nothing for him to be ashamed of. According to the women she'd met on Misrule Night, he had arrived at the Sanderson home in Marpleton with a wounded and infected cheek, close to death. Even once he was past the crisis, he had not been expected to keep the sight in his eye. Once he was well enough to move about the house, his father's wife had insisted on him wearing a hood to hide his face. Perhaps it had become a habit.

Cilla nudged her, and Livy became aware that all the guests had left, and Aunt Ginny was talking. "I am cautiously pleased, my dears," she was saying. "You will note it was mainly my friends and their children this time. Word will get out, and we may expect to find others leaving their cards in the coming weeks. We shall, of course, be making calls ourselves now that we have wardrobes fit for the purpose."

She poured herself a fresh cup of tea and took a sip.

"You behaved very well, though Olivia, I will thank you to ignore Jasper when he is being provocative. I do not know precisely what he said—" she put up a hand to forestall Livy, who had been about to tell her—"and I do not wish to know. A lady does not lose her temper in public."

She gave a decisive nod, as if she vigorously agreed with herself.

"Cilla and Livy, I noticed that you showed unusual favor to

the Sanderson brothers, speaking with them for several minutes. It will not do, girls. I grant you, they are attractive and personable young men, but not well-born. Not at all."

Livy managed to stop the angry words that sprang to her lips, but before she thought of a politer way to make her point, Cilla forestalled her.

"The Sanderson brothers came to speak with us, Aunt Ginny, which none of the other young men did. It would have been rude of us to snub them."

Exactly! Well said, Cilla.

"The other young men do not know you, Lucilla. Their reticence is merely because they have not yet learned your family history and the size of your dowry. Once they know you are worth pursuing, they shall definitely seek you out."

*How cold! How... self-seeking.*

"I hesitated to agree to your excursion tomorrow afternoon, because it cannot be good for the pair of you, situated as you are, to be seen accepting the courtship of two young men such as Bane and Drake Sanderson. And yet, if I had turned them down in front of our other visitors, I would be making a public show of their unworthiness to woo my nieces."

"But you *do* believe them to be unworthy," Livy said.

"Not in themselves, Olivia. I judge them to be fine young men. But an alliance with them will not enhance the family's reputation, and may—I am sorry, my dears, but it is the truth—may damage the chances of your cousins making an eligible match."

"I am sure Society will forgive you when you disown us, Aunt Ginny." *Oops.* Livy had not intended to say that out loud.

"That is another thing, Olivia," said Aunt Ginny. "What might be considered wit in a man is unbecoming in a young lady. When I disown you, indeed. Did I disown your father? No, I did not. And even Lord Marple accepted I was right to maintain the connection, and to accept Horace's gifts when the harvest did not go as one would wish. But that is quite beside the point. You, yourself, told me that you do not have a partiality for either of the Sandersons. I trust you are not about to change your answer, so the occasion for being disowned does not arise."

"Livy was only funning you, Aunt Ginny," Cilla said. "You know how she is."

"Livy would do better to treat this as the serious business it is. Girls, your whole future may well be decided in the next few months. I expect all five of you to give careful thought to each eligible young man who presents himself."

She shifted slightly to straighten, and began counting characteristics on her fingers, as she gave them what they had privately agreed to call, *The Husband Lecture*. "Is he well-born? Is he kind and respectful? Does he have a healthy income? Does he have a title, or is he in line for one?"

By now, all five of them could repeat it word for word. "You are choosing a husband, girls, so temperament is paramount. Is he quick-tempered or sanguine? Is he serious or frivolous? As your parents, my brother and I shall investigate to see whether we believe you will be safe with him, and you can rely on our advice."

"Jasper says we are not to cast our eye on any of his friends," Ruby offered.

"I should think not, indeed. Those young men may think they are adults, but they are not ready to settle down, Ruby," Aunt Ginny agreed. "But it was nice of Jasper to bring his friend to our at home, was it not? That boy has a good heart."

If so, Livy had seen no sign of it, but perhaps she should reserve judgement. Seven young men in total had entered the parlor this afternoon. Jasper and his friend were off the table, which left five. If she was going to listen to Aunt Ginny, Livy must also discount the Sanderson brothers, and the remaining three were, in order of appearance unspeakably arrogant, sadly foolish, and ridiculously inept.

Truly, Mr. Bane Sanderson was the only interesting man of the lot, though Cilla seemed partial to Mr. Drake Sanderson. If the five other men were a fair sample of what the ton had to offer, thank goodness Livy had already made up her mind not to marry.

# Chapter Eight

## DRAKE

WHEN DRAKE HAD suggested a walk, he'd intended it to give him and Miss Lucilla the opportunity to talk. Given Bane's clear, if perplexing, interest in the formidable Miss Olivia, he assumed he could trust his brother to keep Miss Cilla's sister entertained. Or busy, at least.

The addition of three more girls to their excursion foiled Drake's plan, which was undoubtedly Lady Marple's intention.

Bane put it in a nutshell, saying, "Lady Marple does not think us good enough for her nieces."

"I picked that up, too," Drake agreed. "She does not get the final say, however."

"You're right. We probably need to court their father as well as our ladies."

"Our ladies?" Drake had already made up his mind to marry Cilla, if she would have him, but Bane had been counseling caution.

"They quash her, Drake," Bane replied. "You don't remember her as she was on Misrule Night—strong, triumphant, wickedly amused. That is the real Olivia. That's the woman I want as my wife. But her aunt, her father, even perhaps her sister—they all tell her how to behave. It makes her peevish. God knows, it would make anyone of spirit peevish. I want to take her from them and set her free to be herself. Whether she wants the same… why would she? But I'll make the attempt, even so. I'm better for her than dwindling away in her father's shadow, that is for certain."

From Bane, that man of few words, the spate of explanation spoke of deep feelings.

"She should be proud to be your wife, Bane," Drake insisted. "Any woman should."

Bane ignored the compliment, as he always did. Their step-mother's constant attacks had left Drake's favorite brother with a deep sense of his own unworthiness. If Miss Livy was the person who would restore Bane's confidence in himself, then Drake would bless her every day of his life.

"We're here," he commented, unnecessarily, as they arrived on the Marple doorstep. He knocked, and a few minutes later, after a brief wait in the front hall, they were on their way to the park, each brother with two maidens, one on each arm, and one walking on her own.

Unsurprisingly, it was Miss Olivia who strode along independently. Poor Bane, stuck between a couple of Marple misses. Drake at least had his preferred lady on his left arm, even if the girl on his right arm twittered like a sparrow.

She had an opinion on every gown and bonnet they passed, and was not in the least deterred by Drake's less than enthusiastic, but polite, responses. Cilla's amused smile was his reward. "Ruby, darling, I don't think Mr. Sanderson cares much about ladies' fashions," she said, after ten long minutes—the time it took them to reach the gates into the park.

"Oh," said Miss Ruby. "Am I talking too much? What would you like to talk about, Mr. Sanderson?"

That put him on the spot. What did he normally talk about? Investment opportunities? Horse racing? Prize fights? Taxes? Gas lighting? The Luddites? None of those seemed likely to appeal to

Miss Ruby Marple, though he had a suspicion that Cilla would hold her own on most of those topics.

"Horses, perhaps?" Cilla offered.

"Are you interested in horses, Miss Wintergreen, Miss Marple?"

"I had a dear little pony when I was a child," Miss Ruby said, and she was off again, describing the pony minutely and detailing several "adventures" she'd enjoyed on said pony's back.

Ahead of them, Bane and the other two Marple sisters had stopped by a woman wearing a large basket on her back and carrying a tray. Cilla's sister looked around as Drake and his two ladies approached, and grinned at her sister, who raised her eyebrows in question.

Miss Livy pointed at the ducks, who were hastening toward the vendor and her customers. *Ah!* Drake understood what had excited them. Clearly, they knew what the vendor was selling, and what happened after that. "My brother is buying bread to feed to the ducks, ladies. Would you enjoy feeding the ducks?"

"I would love to feed the ducks," Miss Ruby declared.

Bane heard, and declared, "I have purchased enough for everyone who wishes."

A cunning fellow, Drake's brother. In less time than it took to tell, Miss Ruby was tearing small chunks off a loaf of bread and dropping them as she walked toward the Serpentine, a trail of ducks processing behind her. Her sisters, with a loaf each, had hurried ahead, and were feeding those birds who had not joined the exodus.

Bane was carrying three more loaves under one arm and had offered the other to Miss Livy. They followed the Marple sisters and the ducks, but at a slower pace.

"Do you wish to feed the ducks?" Drake asked Cilla, hoping she didn't, for Bane had bought them time to actually talk, and the bread would not last forever—or even for very long, given that every waterfowl in sight had converged on the three young ladies and quite a few blackbirds and sparrows were darting under the beaks of ducks, chasing crumbs that were too small for the larger birds.

"What I would like is for us to talk, Mr. Sanderson," Cilla said. "My aunt likes you as a person, but does not approve of you as a suitor. I will make up my own mind, however. And I want to know more about you before I do." She blushed prettily. "That is, if you are courting me. Do I need to apologize for speaking so openly?"

"You do not owe me an apology," Drake told her. "Straight talking saves a lot of misunderstanding, and I'm pleased you have spoken so honestly to me. Yes, I am a suitor. Like you, I need to know more but I very much like what I have seen of you so far. Will Lady Marple's opposition cause problems? For you or for us? Or is it your father's approval that is most important?"

She tipped her head on one side and regarded him with a steady blue gaze. "My approval is most important. If you gain that, Mr. Sanderson, I shall deal with my father and my aunt."

"Then ask me questions," Drake proposed, "and I shall tell you anything you want to know. And I shall ask you questions, so I can get to know you. I promise you that you can say anything to me, Miss Wintergreen. I shall not think less of you, and shall not repeat it to others."

"A question for a question," Cilla said. "I like it. Very well, you have my promise, also. What we disclose will be held in confidence. My first question is, what do you and your brother do? For a living, I mean."

An interesting first question. How many other girls entering upper class society would ask it? "Bane and I are investors. When our sister Larkspur married, our father gave us each the same amount that he'd allocated to Larkspur for her dowry. We set out to grow it, and we are doing quite well. The interest on the original money pays enough for our rooms and our food, and the rest is in a number of different ventures."

"Such as?" Cilla asked. "No. We don't have time, for my cousins are nearly out of bread. I should like to hear more when we have the opportunity. For now, sir, please ask your question."

Drake had been thinking about it. "What do you look for in a husband?" Her answer to that should be revealing.

She was silent for a moment as she considered her answer. "In the best marriages I have seen, the husband and wife are partners and friends. I want that, Mr. Sanderson. I want a husband I can respect and who will respect me. I want to work with my husband for common goals. I want a father for my children who will take an interest in them—in the daughters as well as the son."

No mention, Drake noted, of titles or wealth. "I like that," he said. "I have not been privileged to observe that kind of marriage at close hand, but it sounds ideal. And yet, I think, achievable if both husband and wife work to the same end."

"And that is the last of it," Ruby said. "No, you horrid bird, I do not have any more. Mr. Sanderson, it is chasing me!"

Bane broke off his conversation with Livy to chase the most persistent of the ducks back into the water, and in moments, the rest of the group joined Drake and Cilla. Their interlude of private conversation was over.

# BANE

FOR BANE, IT had been an unexpectedly successful afternoon. First, he and Drake had had lunch with Lord Andrew and his investor club. They had expected a group of noble dilettantes who were dabbling in investment to amuse themselves. And some of the group were aristocrats, it was true. Lord Andrew himself, who was the fourth son of a duke, a couple of other younger sons, a baron, a viscount. But there were also two lawyers, a man who bought old houses and renovated them for resale, a bookkeeper for a brothel, a gambling den operator, and others whose background didn't come out in conversation and who were harder to place in the social strata.

What brought them together was information. They shared ideas and news that helped them to decide where to invest, either as individuals or jointly. Lord Andrew—he said to call him "Drew"—usually partnered with White, the bookkeeper, and Fullerton, a barrister. They had roomed together at Oxford, Drew told the Sanderson brothers.

He and Drake were asked to explain their successes and failures with stocks, and how their broker had contributed, which led to talking about their other investments, and then to being invited to become part of the group, which met once a week at this time.

Cautious, they had reserved their decision, but Bane thought they'd probably do it, for being part of the group committed them only to sharing information, not to any particular investment.

After the meeting, they had taken the Wintergreen and Marple cousins for the promised walk. Bane had given up hope of having Livy to himself when Lady Marple inserted her own daughters into the outing, but the Marple sisters were easily distracted with bread and ducks, and Bane and Drake were each able to cut their own quarry from the flock.

It was then that Bane faced the question most people asked, sooner or later. Usually, though, he refused to answer it, and nursed his distress at the memories for the rest of the day. Hearing the question from Livy had not upset him though. Despite his pessimism about his chances with the lady, she had a right to know the truth.

So, when she had said, "How did you become scarred, Mr. Sanderson?" he had answered her.

"My mother went mad. She became convinced that the spite and scorn of her neighbors was because of the birthmark on my cheek and my mismatched eyes, so she decided to cut them out. Fortunately, my father stopped her before she could take the eye."

She gaped at him for a moment, and he was disappointed. He had believed her strong enough to hear the hard truths of his existence. He waited for her to change the subject or even to turn away from a boy so damaged that even his own mother hated him.

At least, that was the opinion of those few who knew the truth of his scarring—that his mother hated him. He had heard both his stepmother and his father wax eloquent on the concept, and Colin had tormented him with it for years.

It was not true. She had loved him. Mostly. When she was not drunk or totally focused on Father. She had gone insane, that was all. She had truly believed them both to be in danger and had attempted her surgery out of a misguided desire to protect him from the mob.

"Mr. Sanderson, I am so sorry," said Livy. At least she was being polite. He waited for her to demand that he leave, or perhaps that he return her and the other ladies to Lady Marple's and make no further attempt to see her.

But she had something else in mind. She touched him on the hand and said, "How awful for you, and how dreadful your mother must have felt when she returned to her own mind. I must say, sir, knowing your story makes me admire you even more."

He could feel the smile spread across his face without any effort or thought on his part. Livy admired him! "Sadly, I do not know if my mother ever knew—really knew—what she had done. When I asked after her, while I was recovering, Father said he had sent her somewhere to be cared for. An asylum for the insane, I found out later. She died there a few months later, while I was still an invalid."

Again, she surprised him. "I cannot say I approve of your father having a mistress and a wife, both at the same time, and I am quite cross with him for treating you and Drake so differently to the way he treated Mr. Colin Sanderson, but he wins my respect for saving you and bringing you home with him. Yes, and giving you an education, too, for you are clearly as well-educated as your brother Drake. I am glad. Thank you for sharing your story with me. I cannot imagine you tell just anybody."

"I have never told anyone," he admitted, somewhat surprised at himself. "Except Drake, that is, when we were boys. My father knew, of course, and he told my stepmother who told Colin. Others have learned of it from them, but never from me."

"I am honored," said Livy, her voice soft and warm.

Turning the conversation in a different direction, Bane requested a dance at the debut ball. It didn't quite work out as he expected. Livy's lovely eyes sparkled with the light of mischief as she announced the request to her cousins.

"Girls, Mr. Bane Sanderson wishes to request a dance from each of us at our ball."

Bane repressed a chuckle and aimed a bow at the duck-feeding trio. "I would be delighted," he told them, and added, in an undertone that only Livy heard, "Minx."

"You are, after all, coming to a ball. I must suppose you intend to dance," said Livy.

"I like dancing," Bane conceded. "Thank you, Miss Wintergreen, for organizing partners for me. Five of them, with you and your sister. I would ask for a second dance, but I do not want your aunt to be cross with you."

"You know she has warned us not to encourage you?" Livy asked.

"I suspected."

"And yet here you are." Those silver eyes flashed as she challenged him.

"Here I am," Bane agreed, peaceably. "I'm not such a poor thing as to let a little opposition scare me away. Lady Marple does not have the power to choose your husband. Nor, for that matter, does your own father. You are of age to choose for yourself—and your nature is not the kind to bend to the pressure of others."

"You might as well give up," Livy told him. "I am not inclined to marry."

At that moment, Miss Marple yelled for help, and Bane raced to chase away a feathered bully of a duck. It was not until they approached the Marple townhouse that he had an opportunity for the final word in their conversation. He touched her arm to stop her as she was about to ascend the steps, the last in a procession of ladies. He bent closer and murmured, "I am not scared away, Miss Wintergreen. When you are ready, you can tell me your objections, and I shall do my best to counter them."

She had time for nothing more than a harrumph of displeasure before her sister called, "Do hurry up, Livy."

Bane watched her hasten inside and only then let himself smile. Yes. He was not at all displeased with the afternoon.

# Chapter Nine

## LIVY

As MORE AND more items for the girls' new wardrobe arrived, Aunt Ginny embarked on a whirl of visits and activities designed to allow her daughters and nieces the opportunity to meet other girls who were about to have their first Season.

Livy tried to cry off, since this would be her fourth year and she was years older than everyone else they would meet. Aunt Ginny refused to accept the excuse. "Your earlier seasons do not count, Olivia. Your father did his best, I suppose, but he should have called on me. These hired chaperones cannot possibly reflect credit on their charges. This time, I shall be introducing you to people who matter, dear. This year shall be different."

She must have realized that Livy was about to argue, because she played the card that always worked. "Now, dear, I know you do not wish to disappoint Cilla. She will be so much more comfortable with you there, supporting her."

And so, as the shopping wound down, the socializing ramped up. Dancing lessons with a score of girls and an equal number of reluctant brothers and cousins. Musical afternoons, where girls assessed one another's talents. Gatherings for tea and talk.

And afternoon calls. Every afternoon that Aunt Ginny was

not "At Home", she took them on a succession of calls to matrons with daughters, nieces, goddaughters, and even—in one case—a granddaughter to introduce to Society. On Mondays and Thursdays, Aunt Ginny's days for receiving calls, those matrons, their charges, and often their brothers returned those visits.

Lord Curston usually put in an appearance, as did his son. Livy did not warm to either of them on further acquaintance. They were both pleasant enough to those who were present, though they ignored the servants as if they were furniture. But at various times, Livy heard both of them tell stories about others that were meant to be funny, but that Livy found just cruel.

The Sanderson brothers were there each Monday and each Thursday, neatly dressed, beautifully behaved, and gone again after fifteen minutes. For two weeks, those brief appearances were the only times Livy saw them, for Aunt Ginny refused to allow any more outings.

Not all their time was spent on callers, calling, and other social activities. Indeed, by far the bulk of it was dedicated to the ball that would launch the five cousins into the Season. Or, as Livy was prone to point out, launch four of them, for Livy's come out was ancient history.

For several days, all five of them wrote invitations. After that, the focus shifted to the planning of the supper, the decoration of the assembly room that Aunt Ginny had hired, the selection of the music and dances, the designation and preparation of various rooms that would serve as card rooms, ladies' withdrawing rooms, the supper room, and more.

Aunt Ginny revisited every decision a dozen times before a matter could be resolved, and even then, she was prone to relitigate previous arguments several days later. Livy, who had never before been involved in planning such a huge event, was interested at first, but soon became frustrated.

As she said to Cilla, "If Aunt Ginny would just make up her mind and stick to it, this would all be a great deal easier."

"If nothing else," Cilla said, philosophically, "we are learning what not to do when it is our turn to organize a ball."

Livy did not expect to ever need to organize a ball. Nor could she imagine wanting to, though she wouldn't have minded taking over from Aunt Ginny this one time, if only to get the job finished. Aunt Ginny had still not decided, for example, whether the tulle bows on the pillars would be Saxon green or spring green. Livy wanted to say, what does it matter? What does the supplier have in stock?

And if the cook and the caterer did not both resign before the night of the ball, Livy would be amazed, for the menu changed daily, and sometimes two or more times a day.

But in some mysterious way, bit by bit, all the items on Aunt Ginny's lists were ticked. Somehow, the days passed until the day of the ball arrived. And, despite all the delays, they managed to negotiate a few last-minute changes without Livy screaming or tearing her hair out.

In the middle of the afternoon, Cilla and Livy returned to their own home to change for dinner and the ball. Pa, who was not coming to the ball, had steadfastly refused all Cilla's pleading and would not change his mind. "You do not need your old father reminding the upper sort that you are related to the likes of me," he told them.

Aunt Ginny agreed with him. "Your father is right, Lucilla. Perhaps once a gentleman's attention is caught..." She trailed off, clearly unable to think of a situation in which a gentleman suitor might want to meet Pa in a social setting.

"Since Pa is providing Cilla's dowry, which will undoubtedly be acceptable to the successful suitor, one assumes he will be willing to talk to Pa during the negotiations," Livy suggested. "Even if he has to hold his nose."

Aunt Ginny frowned, Cilla sighed, and Pa pretended Livy had not spoken.

"I should like you to dress for the evening at home, so I can see you, Lucilla," Pa said. "Olivia, too."

So, here they were, taking it in turns to sit under Barker's skilled hands to have their hair done, with Cilla thoroughly enjoying every moment and Livy trying to pretend she was not dreading the night ahead.

*This is not like previous years,* she scolded herself. *You are not without allies except for a chaperone who wishes she was with anyone else.* Balls had been a battlefield, one Livy had faced unarmed except for her sharp tongue, and without reinforcements. *Tonight will be different.* That was what she told herself, but her churning gut did not believe her.

Cilla, who was the dearest girl in the world, saw at least something of what Livy was trying to hide. "It is going to be wonderful, Livy," she said. "We shall be together, you and I, and with our cousins—and Aunt Ginny says she has organized partners for us both for several of the dances, so we need not fear sitting them all out."

"It shall be wonderful," Livy agreed, for what else could she say?

When they were ready, they went down to the study where Pa waited for them—Cilla a dream in her favorite pale shade of pink, with a white net overdress, and Livy feeling almost pretty in a color Madame Beauvillier called *damascene*, a sort of purpley-red.

"Come in, girls," Pa said, when they knocked. He stood to greet them. "Let me look at you. Turn around Lucilla. How beautiful you are. I fear some young man is going to take you away from me."

Pa took out a handkerchief and dabbed at the corner of his eyes. "Remember, Lucilla, I shall not give any man permission to marry you until I have seen our Olivia settled. Ah, Olivia, how fine you look tonight! Just lovely, turn around, my dear? Yes, lovely."

Surely Pa wasn't serious about this idea of marrying Livy off before he would let Cilla marry? For Cilla's sake, Livy decided not to say anything. Not tonight.

Papa was hunting in a drawer of his desk. "I had something…

ah, yes. Here it is. A present for each of you, girls. There, Cilla. Something for your first ball. And Livy, I realize I didn't give you a gift for your first ball, so allow me to make up for that lapse." He handed each girl a jeweler's box, tied shut with a ribbon. He must have taken advice from Aunt Ginny, for one ribbon was a pale pink and the other damascene.

"Thank you, Papa," Cilla said, and Livy hastened to add her own thanks.

They both pulled the ribbon loose and opened their boxes—a necklace each. Cilla's was a long string of pearls with a diamond clasp. Livy's was of rubies and diamonds set in gold filigree work.

"Oh, Papa," said Cilla. "How beautiful. Livy, yours is beautiful too. Let me help you put it on."

"I'll do yours, and then you do mine." She caught her father's eye. "Thank you, Pa. It is… I did not expect…"

"Just make sure you do me credit," Pa said, and Livy would have taken offense, except he was dabbing at his eyes again, and she guessed he was being gruff to defend himself against the softer emotions. She would be snarling herself, if not for Cilla.

She settled the pearls around Cilla's neck in three loops, held by the clasp, and then turned her back so Cilla could put the ruby necklace in place and fasten it.

"They suit you," Pa said. Probably to Cilla, or perhaps to them both, for he smiled at Livy, too. Cilla danced across the room and gave Pa a kiss on the cheek.

"Run along with you now. Have fun, dear," said Pa.

*I wish I could be as spontaneous.* Livy met her father's gaze, feeling awkward. Once again, she had the sense that he and she were feeling much the same. She curtseyed. "I love my necklace, Pa," she said.

"It suits you," he replied. "I know I do not need to tell you to keep an eye on your sister. She is not like you and me. She trusts people."

"She has a sweet soul," Livy said.

Pa nodded. "True. You see that. I see that. The problem is

they are not nice people, a lot of them. The upper sort. I wish she had not wanted this, Olivia. But you know how hard I find it, saying no to your sister."

"I shall watch over her, Pa."

"I know you will do your best, Livy. That's why I insisted on you coming. Your aunt—she cares too much about the silly things. Titles. Status." He shook his head and sighed. "I knew I could trust you. You have a lot of sense, Livy, and for Cilla, you will do your best. Just be careful, Olivia. Off you go, now."

Gracious. Pa was complimenting her! And her abiding irritation with being in London melted away in light of his reasons. She was here to look after Cilla. If only he had explained before, she would never have objected.

Cilla was primping in front of the hall mirror. Barker was waiting with their shawls, fans, and reticules. The butler was hovering, and as soon as Olivia descended to the hall, he said, "The carriage is ready, Miss Wintergreen, Miss Lucilla."

Livy only had time for a brief glance in the mirror, and they were on their way.

"We are going to have the best time!" Cilla proclaimed.

Livy hoped so. She certainly hoped so.

# Chapter Ten

## BANE

B ANE AND DRAKE had not been invited to dinner before the ball. They had not even known there was a dinner before the ball, until they had encountered Jasper Marple at a coffee shop that morning. They had been discussing a problem—the contract for the cutlery machine had been sent to Sheffield a fortnight ago, but they'd heard nothing back from Pentworth.

Bane was concerned. What if something had happened to their engineer or his wife? An accident, perhaps. What if he had sold the idea to someone else? Drake, as usual, was more relaxed about the possibilities.

"We can write again," he said. "Otherwise, short of going back to Sheffield, we cannot know what is going on, and I see no point in worrying about it, when everything is probably as it should be, except that our prospective partner has a bad cold, or a busy schedule, or too much to drink."

Drake might be right, but since Bane didn't have his optimistic attitude, he was going to worry whether Drake thought he should or not. And too much drink would be a problem for the project, come to think of it.

Deep in conversation, they didn't see Marple till he stood

over them. "If it isn't Sanderson and his half-brother."

"Marple," Drake acknowledged.

"Lord Marple to you, Sanderson," Marple sneered.

Bane stood and bowed extravagantly. "Lord Marple," he said.

Marple's sneer deepened. He turned his shoulder toward Bane and addressed Drake. "I see your father's bastard still hides his face around decent people," he commented.

Drake's face flushed and he half-stood, but Bane put a hand on his shoulder. "The yapping of an unweaned pup," he commented.

Marple's companion snickered, and the young viscount forgot he was ignoring Bane and attempted to loom over him. "What did you call me?"

No doubt the looming trick worked with some, but Bane was half a head taller and considerably more muscular than Marple. He raised an eyebrow. "Did you not hear it?" he lied smoothly. "From outside? It sounded like a pup."

"It did," Drake confirmed. "One that still has a great deal to learn."

"You were talking about me," Marple insisted.

"Why would you think that?" asked Bane, doing his best imitation of gently puzzled.

The friend snickered again. They had been introduced to him, Bane realized. His name was Curston and he was the son of a baron who was, unless Bane missed his guess, Lady Marple's lover, or at least a very close friend who wanted to be a lover. The younger Curston, who was a year or two older than Marple, had been at the infamous party Colin had held in Frannie's absence.

"He's got you there, Marps," Curston said. "You don't want to agree you were yapping, do you? Best leave it at that."

With a fulminating glare at his friend, Marple announced, "We had best be off. We need to dress for Mama's dinner. All the best people are invited to dinner before the girls' ball, and Mama has asked me most especially to be there, to greet the important guests."

The way he watched Bane and Drake for a reaction hinted that the exposition was for them, not for the friend. He'd have been disappointed. Drake said, "Good afternoon, Lord Marple." To the other gentleman, he inclined his head. "Mr. Curston."

"We shall see you later then," said Bane, purely to get a rise out of the arrogant young pup.

Marple grimaced, and said to his friend, "I do not know what Mama was thinking."

Bane decided he'd teased the young lord enough, and didn't need Drake's warning look to keep his mouth shut. The two brothers watched the two aristocrats leave the cafe, and Bane half expected Drake to scold him for being provocative.

Instead, his brother grinned. *"The yapping of an unweaned pup. Nicely put. Our poor ladies, with *that* for a cousin. Of course, it's his own heritage that makes him so quick to put others down. He thinks if he attacks the class from which his mother came, others will forget that she was merchant-born."

*Yes, possibly. Probably, in fact.* "You have a point. There are men in the investment club who are as high-born or higher. In Drew's case, much higher. None of them ever seem to feel the need to make me—or you, either—feel lesser."

"Yes, and there's also Wart." Lord and Lady Wharton had arrived in London last week, and Bane and Drake had called and left a card. In response, the couple had sent them an invitation to dine with them and a few other close friends. It had been a most convivial evening.

"Garry, too," Drake added. "He's never behaved as if there was any difference. Not even last time we saw him."

"A duke's grandson, and his heir, too, after his father. Blue blood on both sides, going back to the Conqueror, and further I don't doubt."

Gareth Versey, the Marquess of Thornstead, had been godson to Marple's father, and had stayed with the Marples for a couple of weeks most summers. He was the same age as Bane and Drake, and they had racketed across the countryside together whenever they could escape from their tutors, picking up their friendship each summer as if the intervening months had been a mirage.

"Last time we saw him, when he came down for Lord Marple's funeral, he had no more 'side' than when he was a boy."

Perhaps they should look Thornstead up now they were in London. Though it had been five years since they last saw him, for Lord Marple died a few months after their father. At the time, he had still been a viscount, a courtesy title as the heir's heir. And he was preparing to be married—an arranged marriage, about which he was philosophical. "Grandfather is on his last legs," he had said, "so I shall be heir to Dellborough soon enough. It's best I get on with making the next generation."

Perhaps Lady Thornstead would not be pleased to meet her husband's commoner friends. Perhaps Thornstead had grown more aware of his exalted status now his father was the duke and he, himself, had moved up to the courtesy title of marquess, rather than viscount.

Apparently, Drake had no such reservations. "We should visit him, Bane. I imagine he has children by now, do you not think so?"

"We could try," Bane said. "Don't be surprised if he no longer wishes for the connection, Drake."

As it turned out, there was no need for Bane's reservations.

Later that evening, they arrived at the assembly hall Lady Marple had hired for her ball. They made their way through the Marple receiving line, offering compliments to Lady Marple and all five of her charges—thoroughly deserved.

Miss Olivia Wintergreen took Bane's breath away in another of the rich jewel colors she'd taken to wearing—this one a sort of reddy-purple, like the pansies his mother had grown in their garden when he was a little child. The gown clung to her curves as she moved and made her eyes look even more silver than usual.

The courtesies observed, they gave their names to the butler at the ballroom door, were announced, and went in to find a place along the wall where they could observe the crowd and still watch the entrance for those in the receiving line—or, more specifically, the Wintergreen sisters—to enter the ballroom.

But they'd been there for no more than a minute when a tall blond gentleman hurried up, a pretty dark-haired lady on his arm. "It *is* you," said the man, holding out a hand to Bane. "I knew it must be. I didn't see you come in, but Jenna said you had a hood on. Jenna, my love, this is Mr. Wolfbane Sanderson, and here is Mr. Mandrake Sanderson."

"Lady Thornstead," Bane said, bowing. It had to be their old friend. The eyes were the same, though the chin was firmer and the shoulders broader.

"Lady Thornstead," said Drake. "You lucky dog, Garry."

Lady Thornstead's eyes twinkled, and Thornstead's smile at his lady was fond. "I know it, old friend. But how wonderful to see you here! Are you visiting London?"

Drake explained that they'd moved to the big city. "We were just talking about calling on you, Garry."

"We last met your husband when he came to our village for Lord Marple's funeral, Lady Thornstead," Bane explained, "before he was married."

"He has spoken to me of the friends he made when he visited Marplestead as a child. You lived nearby, I believe, Mr. Sanderson. In Marpleton, was it not? You gentlemen must call. Would you care to join us for dinner on this coming Friday? Would that suit you, Gareth?"

"That would be delightful," Thornstead said.

Drake agreed. "Tell us when to be there, and Bane and I would love to join you, Lady Thornstead."

"And what are you doing in London?" Thornstead wanted to know.

"Lady Thornstead," said a familiar voice. "Garry, Bane, Drake. Well met." It was Drew Winderfield, elegantly dressed as ever.

"Good evening, Lord Andrew." Lady Thornstead shifted in a graceful move that was not quite a curtsey.

"Drew," said Bane and Drake, and Thornstead gave a cheerful wave.

Lady Thornstead cast a quick glance at Bane and Drake, perhaps wondering how Drew came to know the two commoners, but she did not ask.

Thornstead did, with cheerful ease. "Bane and Drake are old friends of mine, Drew. How did you three come to know one another?"

"We are members of the same investment club," Drew explained. "Smart fellows, your old friends. I was sent across the ballroom by my stepmother, Bane and Drake—I've been talking about you, and she and Father would like to meet you."

"We shall come too," Thornstead decided. "My parents are talking to yours, and I'd like them to meet Bane and Drake, as well. Heaven knows they heard enough about them when I was a boy!" He offered his arm to Lady Thornstead and led the way across the ballroom.

*Heavens.* Thornstead's parents were the Duke of Dellborough and his duchess. Thornstead had married because his grandfather was dying, though he had lived for a further three or four years, until the spring of last year!

Drew's father was the Duke of Winshire, and his stepmother the Duchess of Winshire was the one the newssheets called *the double duchess*, for her former husband had been the Duke of Haverford, a title now held by her eldest son.

They were flying in high altitudes indeed!

The high-born lords and ladies were very gracious. Friendly, even, in a way that reminded Bane of village elders speaking to young men who were not yet bumptious enough to challenge the gaffers, and could always be trusted to show deference to the grannies.

The brothers were still with the group of nobles—Drake was describing the silks in a cargo of theirs that had just arrived—

when the orchestra that had been playing quietly in the background struck up a flourish and fell silent. The butler announced Lady Marple and then went on to name each of the three daughters of the house, the two Wintergreen sisters, and finally young Lord Marple.

Bane had eyes only for his Lady Misrule.

"Which lady has caught your eye?" asked the Duchess of Winshire.

He did not even think of prevaricating. "Miss Wintergreen, Your Grace. Miss Olivia Wintergreen."

"You like a challenge," the duchess surmised.

She was right. Where Cilla was a calm lake, Livy was a storm at sea. Challenging, yes, but also exciting, thrilling. A worthy opponent and an even worthier partner. "She is worth fighting for," he said. "A warrior queen. I admire her more than I can say." And why was he sharing this with a stranger when he had not even been as honest with his brother?

"Good answer," said the duchess. "I shall send you and your brother invitations to my ball, young man. The Marple and Wintergreen girls, too."

That was unexpected. Bane wrenched his attention away from Livy and turned to look at the duchess. "Thank you, ma'am. Thank you very much."

The duchess's eyes twinkled. "Miss Wintergreen has been adamant she does not wish to marry, Mr. Sanderson. So much so that she has frightened off every suitor who tried to get close for the past two seasons. I suspect most of them saw her dowry rather than the young lady herself. But not all. I shall watch your courtship with interest."

# LIVY

"WHAT IS THE Sanderson misfit doing with the Duchess of

Winshire?" grumbled Jasper. "And the duke. And the Duke and Duchess of Dellborough. How did those mushrooms finagle that?"

The Duchess of Winshire? Lady Sutton was the daughter-in-law of the Duke of Winshire, or so Livy had been told by the same person who had spoken of Lady Sutton's work with women who had been abused or seduced by men.

Livy looked in the same direction as Jasper and there was Bane, magnificent in well-crafted evening wear. He was bowing to a lady who must be one of the duchesses, while several other magnificent personages looked benignly on.

Now he stepped back so that Drake could take his place, and as he effaced himself, he turned to gaze across the ballroom. He must have been watching her earlier, for he looked first to the stairs down into the room and then to the side, where they all stood with Aunt Ginny, who was introducing each of her charges, in strict order of precedence, to the partner who would lead them out in the first dance.

He smiled when he caught her eyes, and she had to fight not to smile back. Perhaps he would introduce her to the duchess! And then what? Livy could not imagine herself asking a duchess for an introduction to her daughter-in-law.

"Jasper, pay attention," Aunt Ginny scolded in a hiss. "I shall be signaling the orchestra in a moment, and you must be ready." Jasper would take his eldest sister into the dance, of course. The other four gentlemen were sons of some of Aunt Ginny's friends. The higher-ranked men would take in the Marple twins, and the two others, Livy and Cilla. Livy would have been better pleased if she had been ignored, or if Aunt Ginny had chosen for them by height rather than by precedence.

Livy's assigned dance partner was Mr. Curston. He was almost a full head shorter than her, and would be spending the dance staring up at her or, which was worse, gazing at her chin or, worst of all, down the front of her dress. Given it was Mr. Curston, she guessed it would be the third option.

She cast another glance toward Bane. He was still watching her. He, at least, was taller than her. When their dance came about, she wouldn't feel like a rat matched with a mouse.

The orchestra played the opening chords, and Jasper and Pearl led the way onto the floor, followed by the Marple sisters and then the Wintergreen sisters in age order. They took the first five places in a long dance, but other couples crowded onto the floor.

Pearl, as the leading lady, called the first pattern, and the ball had begun. Soon enough, Jasper and Pearl handed over the lead to Ruby and her partner took the lead. So it went, with each couple taking their turn at the lead, then dancing down, the man behind the row of men and the lady behind the row of ladies, then together back up through the couples, to finish their turn by weaving back down the line again, the gentleman twirling each lady in turn, and the lady being passed from gentleman to gentleman.

Livy's partner, as she had expected, failed to meet her eyes, nor did he speak with her or show any interest in her, beyond attempting to ogle her breasts. Being ignored would have been preferable to being undressed with his eyes, but the horrid slug managed to do both. The only signs of enthusiasm he showed came when he was circling one of the other ladies, whom Livy had met as a friend of her cousins.

Apart from Bane, who was in the set with a lady Livy didn't recognize, no gentleman on the floor was as tall as Livy. The two occasions that she circled Bane were the best of the dance.

"Thank you, Miss Wintergreen," said her partner, politely. He didn't bother to escort her back to Aunt Ginny, who was, in any case, only a few paces away. He had already left her in his mind even as he half bowed, for his eyes were searching the crowd.

Livy couldn't even squash the man like the bug he undoubtedly was. Not without embarrassing her sister and her aunt. "Thank you," she replied.

Jasper was complaining to his mother when she took the few steps that brought her to Aunt Ginny.

"What is Wolfbane Sanderson doing, hobnobbing with dukes and marquesses?" he complained. "You should not have invited him, Mama. It is an insult to your guests to expect them to socialize with such a man."

Aunt Ginny frowned at him. "Jasper, please keep your voice down. Bane and Drake Sanderson have a longstanding friendship with Lord Thornstead, the son of the Dellboroughs, and they have clearly also met Lord Andrew somewhere. He, of course, is the Duke of Winshire's son. The Sandersons are personable young men."

The Duke of Winshire's son would be Lady Sutton's brother-in-law! Surely meeting the young man would be a step closer to the lady herself? Could she ask Bane to introduce to them?

"Andrew Winderfield is a mongrel, but Thornstead should know better," Jasper complained.

"Shush!" Aunt Ginny insisted. "Jasper, where the Duchesses of Winshire and Dellborough go, the rest of society will follow. If they see fit to welcome Mr. Sanderson, then you had better do likewise. We are very fortunate their graces accepted my invitation, and if you offend them, it shall be your sisters who suffer for it when the great ladies withdraw their favor."

"They cannot be such great ladies if they don't recognize a cur when they meet one," Jasper muttered.

"You are jealous of Mr. Sanderson," Livy realized, but she would have done better to stay silent, for her cousin glared at her and stalked away.

His mother sighed. "You are no doubt correct, Olivia, but it was not helpful or kind to say so."

"It seems so odd, though." Livy could not understand it. "He is wealthy and titled, and accepted everywhere. Why should he resent Mr. Bane Sanderson? It is not as if Mr. Sanderson's friendships with Lord Andrew and Lord Thornstead threaten Jasper in any way."

"My dear Olivia," said her aunt, "Bane Sanderson is an adult, and successful. Jasper is still more boy than man, and he knows it. Of course he is jealous." She sighed. "Perhaps marriage will help him to grow up."

Jasper, married? Livy could not imagine that happening any time soon, nor making any difference to his behavior when it did.

# Chapter Eleven

## CILLA

CILLA'S FIRST DANCE at her first ball was disappointing. The man Aunt Ginny had arranged to partner her seemed to think a line dance an appropriate opportunity to interrogate her about her dowry, her expectations of marriage, and how likely it was that a successful suitor would have to socialize with her father or her sister.

Given they were constantly being interrupted by the demands of the dance, his questions were delivered in snippets, but as she pieced them together, Cilla became more and more annoyed.

"For I do not suppose that Miss Olivia Sanderson is likely to marry within the *ton*," he said. "She is known to be a bit of a harpy, and if she marries in the merchant class, and you marry up, you could not expect to know her, could you? Your aunt says you are very sweet natured, and your dowry is an attraction, I have to admit."

Cilla had to admit that Livy's ability to scold would be useful at this moment. She made the attempt. "Sir," she said, "this is the first dance of my first ball of my first Season. I cannot feel that your questions are appropriate to the occasion."

They were separated again, but when they came back together, he was ready for her. "I must say, Miss Lucilla, I do not expect to be coached in proper behavior by a woman of your class."

The music came to a swirling end. The dance was over. Cilla curtseyed, and looked around for Aunt Ginny. *Ah!* There was Livy, taller than any other woman in the room. "You will return me to my aunt, sir," Cilla said, with a shallow curtsey. She did not thank him for the dance, the boring pompous ignoramus.

As she and the bore approached Aunt Ginny, Jasper stalked off in one of his pets. Livy, who was glaring after their cousin, was also seething. Aunt Ginny said something to Livy and then noticed Cilla's approach and pasted on her amiable smile for Cilla's escort. But the man stopped several paces away, gave Aunt Ginny a hasty bow, and walked away.

"Oh dear," said Aunt Ginny. "Did you offend the gentleman, Cilla? I would not have expected it of you."

"It is more likely that the gentleman offended Cilla," said Livy, loyally.

"I know that we are here in London to find husbands," Cilla replied, "but it was surely rude of that man to question me about my dowry and lecture me on my low rank and the inadvisability of me retaining a friendship with my sister."

"Oh dear," Aunt Ginny repeated. "He will not do for you, then. I wonder if Ruby…"

The three cousins arrived all together, and Aunt Ginny left the fraught question of Cilla's rude dance partner to question them about their first dances.

"If that man asks me to dance, Cilla," said Livy under the cover of the Marples' conversation, "shall I trip him up on the dance floor for you? Or threaten to gut him if he ever approaches you again?"

The offer made Cilla smile. It would not be put to the test. The man's rude remarks about Livy suggested he was unlikely to ever ask Livy to dance. But her sister's unqualified support was much appreciated.

They were interrupted by Drake and Bane Sanderson, who brought with them another man, all three of whom bowed politely to Aunt Ginny and greeted all the girls.

"Lady Marple, ladies, may I make known to you Lord Andrew Winderfield?" Drake said.

Aunt Ginny simpered at the young lord. "Delighted to make your acquaintance, Lord Andrew. May I present my daughters, Miss Marple, Miss Ruby Marple, and Miss Beryl Marple, and my nieces, Miss Wintergreen and Miss Lucilla Wintergreen."

Aunt Ginny was flustered indeed if she so far forgot herself as to present ladies to a gentleman, even one of high rank.

"We came to beg a dance with each of these lovely ladies," Drake told Aunt Ginny. "You, too, my lady, if you would be so kind."

Aunt Ginny chuckled. "I do not dance, you young scamp. Girls, I have organized partners for you for the first three dances. After that you have my permission to find room this evening for Lord Andrew, Mr. Sanderson. and Mr. Sanderson. One dance only, gentlemen."

After Aunt Ginny's warnings about the Sanderson brothers, Cilla had half expected Aunt Ginny to turn them away, but perhaps she did not wish to make a poor impression on Lord Andrew.

Drake had placed himself so he was next to Cilla—and Bane was next to Livy, Cilla noticed. "Miss Lucilla," Drake said, "you look splendid tonight. May I hope you have saved me the supper dance?"

She promised him the dance, which meant she also committed herself to sitting with him at supper. How lovely. He then spoke to Livy and after that to each of the cousins.

His brother was doing the same, having secured Livy's supper dance, and Lord Andrew was also speaking to each of the girls. Cilla promised the fourth dance of the evening to Lord Andrew, and the dance after supper to Bane.

After that, Aunt Ginny's next candidate came to be introduced and to lead her onto the floor. This dance and the next were better. If her aunt had boasted to all those assigned to Cilla about the size of Cilla's dowry and her pleasant nature, neither of the others were crass enough to mention those topics to Cilla.

The gentlemen danced well and did not attempt to converse beyond the barest social niceties. Lord Andrew took Cilla out next, and proved to be a charming and likeable gentleman, amusing her when they were waiting between patterns by his quick word-sketch descriptions of the others on the floor.

Cilla was not sure if it would be proper to ask him how he came to be acquainted with Drake, which was what she really wanted to know, so she merely enjoyed his company and his graceful dancing until the set was over.

She sat the next dance out, and was glad to do so, for two sets in a row had left her ready for a rest. Livy was on the floor with Lord Andrew, enjoying a vigorous round dance. Not one that left time for talking, but Cilla couldn't imagine that Livy had anything more to say to a duke's son than she did.

Then Aunt Ginny came and sat next to her, and spoiled her rest by quizzing her about each of her partners, especially Lord Andrew. "He is the fourth son of a duke, you know," she pontificated, as if she had not shared the same information before.

"The eldest has only daughters, and the other two are in some far-off foreign land and married, so I hear, to foreigners. I daresay the Prince Regent and the House of Lords would not object to making Lord Andrew the next duke, if it came to the point. Too high a target for you, Lucilla dear, despite his foreign mother. He might do very nicely for one of my daughters, though. Very nicely indeed. He is taking Pearl for supper. Just imagine! My Pearl, a duchess!"

Talk about building castles in the air! Cilla settled for smiling, for Aunt Ginny was not looking for any comment but had moved on to talking about other possible husbands for each of the five girls. Cilla was quite pleased when her next partner arrived.

She returned to Aunt Ginny's side after the next set to find

Drake Sanderson waiting for her. His brother was already there with Livy, and they must have been arguing, for Aunt Ginny was looking from one to the other and back again, looking both worried and confused. Cilla could have told her that Livy and Bane appeared to enjoy exchanging barbed remarks.

"Are you calling me overly large, Mr. Sanderson?" Livy was demanding as Cilla drew close enough to hear their words over the din of the ballroom.

"Not compared with me, Miss Wintergreen."

Bane was, Cilla reflected, very much up to Livy's weight, in every way.

# BANE

Miss Olivia Wintergreen was the lady for Bane. Bane still had doubts that he was the man for her, but that was a decision for her to make. And certainly, none of the popinjays he'd heard whispering about her would do for her at all.

He had been lurking in a shadowy corner, uncomfortable in the crowded and brightly lit ballroom. A group of men stopped on the other side of a potted plant to gossip about Miss Wintergreen, discussing her physical attributes as if she was a horse they were considering at Tattersalls, and not in any kind of complimentary fashion either.

One of them—cruelly, the one who planned to court her—even compared her to a plow horse! Bane had wanted to punch the man, but Olivia—Livy, as her sister called her—would not thank him for making her a scandal by standing up for her. Not that a fine Friesian or Cleveland Bay was a bad thing, and come to think of it, he was more a Shire or a Clydesdale himself, rather than a high-bred racehorse, all nerves and temperament, unfit for anything but running his heart out to win these idiots a few pounds.

Bane knew the speaker—the son of Viscount Curston—and he had meant the comparison as an insult, but Bane would pull in harness with Livy any day of the week. Unlike the men who were tearing her character to pieces with words like scold and harpy, and prescribing either exile to the country or a beating as treatment for her temperament.

The only attribute they favored was her dowry. Apparently, it was rumored to be enormous. The dastards agreed that the fortune she brought with her was worth putting up with her looks, her character, and even her low-born relatives. *Fools.*

"Not that I would allow her to see her father again," said the toffee-nosed prat who had declared his intention of marrying her. "Her sister, once she is a viscountess, but not the father."

Bane wondered why they were so certain that Cilla would be a viscountess, but his curiosity was satisfied in the next instant, when one of the gossipers asked the same question.

"Her cousin Marple is going to marry her," said Curston. "Her dowry is as big as her sister's and he has to marry. He's got three sisters to puff off, and his mother has been spending up large. She doesn't know that he's in the suds."

"I don't think Miss Lucilla Wintergreen likes him above half," one of the others said.

Marple's friend shrugged. "She spends a lot of time in his house, and he is going to get his mother to invite her to move in. If he can't seduce her, he'll compromise her. She'll marry him then, right enough. And then I'll try my luck with the shrew. She must be desperate to wed after three failed seasons, and if not, I'll take the same route to marriage as my future brother-in-law. And then I'll beat her till she learns to obey."

*Like hell.*

Bane was well aware of the disadvantages he presented as a husband, but if she chose him, he would love and cherish her every day for the rest of his life. And even if she did not choose him, he could still arm her with knowledge about her cousin's plans, and the plans of his friend.

Yes, and he'd tell his brother, too. Drake needed to know about the risk to Cilla.

The set currently on the floor was ending. Bane sidled along the wall behind the potted plants until he could emerge some distance from the pack of curs he'd been listening to, and then strode in the direction of Lady Marple.

Was the old bat part of the plot against her nieces? Marple's friend Curston had claimed that Livy's aunt did not know of the dire straits her son was in, and if that was true, Curston's father was keeping secrets from his lover. On the other hand, the young viscount was as ignorant as he was arrogant. In Bane's experience, a family's womenfolk were much more attuned to the misdemeanors of their so-called lords and masters than said menfolk wanted to believe. It was, Bane assumed, a matter of survival.

Certainly, Bane's stepmother and his half-brother's wife had known how their husbands strayed, and usually with whom—for all that they feigned ignorance to maintain the peace and their own dignity.

Livy was already with Lady Marple. "You don't have to dance with me, Mr. Sanderson," she blurted. "I will not hold you to your offer. I know your brother dragooned you into it."

Bane was amused. "Drake doesn't make my decisions for me, Miss Wintergreen," he told her.

Perhaps she thought he was laughing at her, for she lifted her chin and sniffed as if offended. "I am not interested in a pity-dance," she said, through gritted teeth.

"Good. Neither am I. I wish to dance with the only woman in this ballroom who is worth a second look."

He meant every word, but she had made up her mind to be contrary, or she thought he was spouting empty flattery for she snapped back, "Go and ask her, then."

"I was referring to *you*, Miss Wintergreen. And before you accuse me of laying it on with a paddle, I meant every word."

Was that alarm in the lady's eyes? And if it was, should he be encouraged by it or discouraged? Drake had arrived, and was raising his eyebrows at their banter. It was banter, was it not? Bane nodded at Drake but kept his attention on Livy.

"I am not sure that I wish to dance," the lady commented, crossing her arms defensively, then shooting a glance at her aunt and letting them drop to her side again. Were ladies not meant to cross arms? Bane would never understand all the silly rules these people imposed on one another.

"Perhaps you would prefer a stroll rather than a dance?" Bane suggested, as Miss Cilla joined them.

"Perhaps you are afraid I will stand on your feet," Livy retorted, which certainly sounded as if she wanted to step out on the floor with him.

Good, for he had been looking forward to this dance all evening. He grinned at her. "Deathly afraid, that a little sylph like you might damage me. Do you commonly suffer the experience of crippling your partners?"

Livy's lovely eyes were alight with the joy of verbal battle. "My previous experience is not based on dancing with elephants."

"Your previous experience is based on dancing with rabbits, if this evening is typical. An elephant is much more up to your weight."

"Are you calling me overly large, Mr. Sanderson?"

He laughed out loud at that. "Not compared with me, Miss Wintergreen." He winged his elbow at her and could have cheered with relief when she placed her hand on his arm and allowed him to lead her onto the floor.

Drake and Cilla joined them, and the dance was one where two couples formed a group of four people who stayed together through the dance, though they occasionally combined with another group to make a broader set of patterns with eight dancers.

It was a vigorous dance, too, with no time to stand out briefly and talk to one's partner unheard by the rest of the crowd on the floor.

The lady he was fast growing to love was as graceful as she was lovely. Even better, she was the right size. He didn't have to shorten his steps to match hers, or stoop to put his hands on his waist when the dance called for him to assist her in a short jump, or bend himself almost in half to go under her raised arm.

Reinforcing the point, he had to do all those things when he repeated the patterns with her sister while Livy danced them with Drake.

Bane's mind jumped to a quite different sort of dance, a private one. He was abstemious, his mother's fate fueling a disinclination to promiscuity. Even so, he was not a virgin, having been less disciplined in his youth, when his blood ran hot and his position as son—even illegitimate son—of the wealthiest man in the town won the favor of a number of daring females.

He had always had to temper his passion to the size of his lovers, fearing he might otherwise cause an injury. And if he thought any further about how Livy's height and size might change the experience, he would embarrass himself. Modern cutaway evening coats for men meant that the results of private thoughts became a matter of public display—not something he wanted to experience right here on the dance floor.

Time to think of something deflating. The missing engineer. The parlous state of the rural poor or, even worse, those who had flocked into London after last year's failed harvest, looking for work that did not exist.

For a short time, his mind ran on two tracks, one matching his movements to the demands of the dance and relishing the company of his lady, and the other adding detail to a plan he and Drake had made for funding for a dame school in the slums.

A man called Basingstoke, the vicar of an inner-city parish, was setting up a network of them, each paid for by private donors who believed that all children, boys and girls, had a better chance of escaping poverty if they could read, write and do basic arithmetic.

Calculating costs worked to subdue his animal appetites—

they'd need enough to rent a room, hire a teacher, pay for basic supplies such as slates, chalk, and coal for heating, and more. It was achievable. He hoped his courtship of Livy would likewise be merely a matter of working out the steps, calculating the costs, and putting a plan into practice. Truly, they seemed to be made for one another.

By the time the music came to an end, he was ready to give her all his attention. Now, if he and Drake could only find a table for four, so he could share what he had heard and warn his brother and the Wintergreen sisters!

He was foiled in his intentions by Lady Marple, who met them at the door of the supper room, and insisted on them taking seats at a large table where she had gathered the rest of her fledglings and their partners.

She had organized for the cur who had boasted of his intention to marry and suppress Livy to sit on the other side of his quarry from Bane, and placed her son next to Cilla, with Drake between the two sisters.

They'd have no help from Lady Marple, Bane deduced.

He managed to make it through supper without landing a fist in the cur's face, but it was a close-run thing. Both Curston and Lord Marple ignored Marple's sisters, who were their partners, to talk to Livy and Cilla, flattering and condescending by turns.

At least the next dance, in which he was to partner Cilla, was another long dance. With luck he'd be able to let her know to lock her door and be careful around Marple, and to warn Livy about the cur, the Honorable Mr. Curston. The word "Honorable" meant he could be the younger son of an earl, or the son of a viscount or baron. What he was not, was honorable in any sense of the word, except the purely technical designation of the aristocratic ranks.

## Chapter Twelve

### DRAKE

DRAKE HAD SEEN Bane in earnest conversation with Cilla during the dance after supper, but it wasn't until the brothers were walking home together after the ball that he finally had an opportunity to find out what they were talking about.

He was furious, and if Bane hadn't restrained him with a hand on his arm, he'd have turned around to hunt down Curston and Marple, and teach them a lesson.

"Think, man," said Bane. "If you attack a pair of aristocrats, who is going to end up in court charged with assault? And you'll not be able to defend yourself, either. Not without damaging the reputation of our ladies."

Blast. Bane was right. "We cannot let it sit, though, Bane," he protested. "You say you've warned Cilla and through her Livy, but Marple has the inside track, as the son of their chaperone. It is bad enough that they spend so much time in the house where he lives. But if they move in? Locking their bedchamber doors won't be enough if he's determined. Also, he'll know where they're going and who with, and will be able to tell his friend."

Drake couldn't understand how his brother was so calm. Did the man not have a heart?

"I've been thinking about it," Bane said. "I suggest a counter attack on three fronts. I've warned Cilla, and through her, Livy. That's one. Forewarned is forearmed, and they'll protect one another. The second won't work if Wintergreen is in favor of the match with Marple, but I think we must tell their father what we heard. If he objects to the plotting, he'll be able to insist that the sisters stay under his roof. The third is to tell Garry and Drew. If they enlisted the ladies of their family to look after our ladies, that would keep Livy and Cilla safe at events."

"Marrying them would keep them safest of all," Drake commented, "but would they consider it? Would Wintergreen give his permission? Is it too early to ask?"

"Look out!" Bane's warning shout gave Drake time to duck sideways, and the blow aimed at his head struck a glancing blow to his shoulder, instead. Drake twirled as he came out of his crouch, weaving to avoid his assailant's second strike, and landing a punch that not only had all his own strength behind it, but was amplified by the attacker's own forward momentum.

The man fell backward and lay still.

Bane was fighting two more men, but Drake had no sooner turned to help him than Bane managed a buffet to the side of the head of each such that he clapped their heads together, and they, too, sank to ground.

"Dead or out cold?" Bane asked, nodding toward the man Drake had dealt with.

Drake was flexing his hand. It wasn't broken, but that was an almighty punch. He checked his attacker and reported, "Out cold."

"This one isn't," said Bane, pulling one of the others up by a handful of necktie, so that the man's eyes were almost level with Bane's own and his feet dangled, just the toes of his boots scuffing the ground. "Who sent you?" Bane demanded.

The man's eyes darted from side to side, as if he searched for a way out, but Bane's grip was firm. He shook the man. "Who sent you? Answer me." Another shake.

The man squealed, "Don't know, do I? Some gent. Dressed like you. Plummy voice." He pointed the way Bane and Drake had come. "Back along there. Said to rough you up bad, and take anything you had on you. Paid us a spangle each."

Drake was investigating the pockets of the other two men. Another cosh. Several knives. Several coins, including a gold one from each villain. It was the coin known as a "spangle"—a seven-shilling piece or one-third of a guinea. Three villains, three spangles. So, someone who had seen them walking this way had paid these bully boys a guinea to assault him and Bane.

"Hand them over to the Watch?" Drake suggested.

"This man who paid you?" Bane asked the man he was still dangling. "Did he warn you that you'd need more than three of you to take us on?"

"Nah," the man said. Another of the assailants was groaning his way back into consciousness. Bane cast a glance at him then asked the first man, "The stick pin in the gent's cravat. Winged, with a blue stone? Or a bird skull?"

"Bird skull," the man confirmed. Curston, then. That had been his cravat pin of choice tonight. The winged one was Marple's.

After lowering the man so his feet were firm on the ground again, Bane let go of his necktie and stepped back. The second man was trying to sit up and the third man was stirring. "Let's not bother with the Watch. Curston will deny paying them, and they'll hang for assaulting us and probably for stealing the spangles. I don't want them to hang."

Bane's tough exterior hid a soft heart.

"At the very least," Drake said, "we should take their money. They shouldn't profit from attempting to 'rough us up bad,' as he put it." He was wasting his breath and he knew it. He sighed. "I suppose you want me to give them back their knives, too."

He sighed again and made a small pile of the items he'd abstracted from the pockets of the unconscious men.

"I think I'll have a sword stick made," he told Bane as the two of them strode away from the recovering attackers. "I can run the next man through before you have a chance to feel sorry for him."

"We should add a little chat with Curston onto our list of things to do," Bane commented.

# LIVY

Aunt Ginny's carriage drew up in front of her townhouse.

"Shall we walk to our house, or is your coachmen going to drive us?" asked Cilla.

"Come inside," Aunt Ginny said. "I daresay your father and all his household are asleep. I shall leave a message to be given to your father when he awakens to say where you are, and that you will be comfortable here with us."

"I would prefer to go home," said Cilla, remaining seated as her cousins got down from the carriage one after another.

Livy, who was about to follow them, sat down again. "Would you ask the carriage driver to take us home, please, Aunt Ginny?" she said.

She did not know why Cilla was insisting on going home, but she knew her sister. Cilla was the pleasantest and most biddable of girls. However, on the rare occasions she dug her toes in—and her tone told Livy this was one of those occasions—nothing would move her.

No doubt she had an excellent reason. Livy wondered what it could be.

"If you are going to refuse my hospitality," said Aunt Ginny, "you can walk."

Their house was on the other side of the street and a few doors down. Not a long walk, but it was very dark in between the pools of light cast by the new-fangled gas lamps, and the rain that had fallen during the evening had left the streets wet and undoubtedly muddy. Their light dancing slippers would soon soak through.

"Then we shall walk," said Cilla.

Barker, who had traveled from the ball on top of the carriage, must have clambered down, for Livy could see her hovering behind Aunt Ginny, looking anxious.

"Olivia," Aunt Ginny demanded, "talk some sense into your sister."

"We would prefer to sleep in our own beds, Aunt Ginny," Livy said, keeping her tone pleasant. Playing the peacemaker was not usually her role, but she did her best.

"Livy," said Cilla, "I want to go home to Pa." Her eyes were particularly intent. This mattered to her. Livy wondered what arguments she could marshal to gain for her sister what she wanted.

Just then, Jasper filled the doorway. "Is there a problem, Mama? Come along, cousins. You must be needing your beds."

Cilla shrank back against the cushions of the seat, and Livy narrowed her eyes at Jasper. Had he done something to frighten Cilla? If so, she would find a way to make him pay.

"Oh, Marple," Aunt Ginny complained. "Cilla is being difficult. She is insisting on returning to my brother's house."

"How foolish," said Jasper. "Selfish, too, when his house is all dark and our servants are up. Also, dear cousin, your bed upstairs has been made and is warm. Come along."

He reached for Cilla's wrist, but she shrank back in her corner, lifting her hands to her chest so that he could not reach without climbing into the carriage.

Livy opened the door on the other side of the vehicle. "Come on, Cilla," she said. "If you wish to go home, we shall go home." She turned when they were both on the road. "We shall call tomorrow, Aunt Ginny. Thank you for a lovely ball."

Cilla let out a screech, and Livy turned to see that Jasper had grasped her by the upper arms and was dragging her back toward the Marple townhouse.

"Let her go," Livy demanded, and when he ignored her as if she didn't exist, she turned on Aunt Ginny. "Tell him to get his hands off my sister, Aunt Ginny."

"He does not mean Lucilla any harm, Olivia," Aunt Ginny assured her.

Cilla screamed, startling Jasper so much that his hands must have loosened, for she spun around and punched him. Low. Just the way their father had taught them.

It worked. Jasper shrieked and dropped to the ground, hunched in on himself, his voice still shrill as he called Cilla names and threatened retribution. Aunt Ginny hurried to crouch by her son, and Livy to pull her sister into the shelter of her arm.

"You wicked, wicked girl," Aunt Ginny said to Cilla.

Jasper had no one to blame but himself, but Aunt Ginny would not listen to that tonight. The noise had woken some of the neighbors. Footmen brandishing canes had appeared on several doorsteps, and shadows in upper windows hinted at watchers.

"I shall take Cilla home and we shall talk in the morning," said Livy to her aunt, and she led Cilla away across the street to where their own front door was open, with a footman lurking on the porch and the butler, a nightcap on his head, looking out from inside.

"I assume there was a reason for that," Livy told Cilla. "We shall have some fences to mend with Aunt Ginny, I suppose."

"Jasper is planning to force me to become his wife," said Cilla. "He wants my dowry. Mr. Sanderson heard him plotting with another man. I *will* not sleep in the same house as him, Livy, and I shall not marry him even if he does compromise me. And Livy, watch out for Mr. Curston. He wants your dowry, and says he will beat you to teach you your place."

They had reached the house, and Cilla could say nothing more without the servants hearing. Livy told her, "I understand. Do not worry, dearest. We shall work out a plan." As they stepped inside, Livy looked up the stairs, where another nightshirted figure in a nightcap looked down from the landing. "Pa! I'm sorry you were disturbed."

"Virginia sent a note to say you would be sleeping at her place," her father said, frowning. "Why are you home? And what was all that fuss outside."

"Cilla does not want to sleep at Aunt Ginny's," Livy explained. "When Jasper tried to drag her inside, she punched him the way you taught us. I am certain she has a good reason, for she is not a foolish girl. But she is very tired, Pa, and so am I. Can we all sleep before we talk?"

Pa studied Cilla for a long moment. The poor dear. She was leaning her weight against Livy and the occasional shiver ran through her. Reaction to the tension of the past minutes, Livy supposed. Pa must have been able to see that Cilla was near the end of her strength, for he nodded. "We shall discuss this tomorrow. Virginia is not going to be happy, but Cilla, if Jasper behaved in a way you found offensive—and I must suppose he did, if you and Livy both say so—then you did the right thing coming home. Olivia, well done."

With that, he turned and plodded away upstairs, leaving Livy to shepherd Cilla to her room.

## CILLA

CILLA DID NOT sleep well, and Livy was heavy-eyed, too, when they came down to breakfast in the late morning. Papa was waiting for them. "Have something to eat, girls," he said, "then tell me what upset you."

But before Cilla could explain the plot against her and Livy, Aunt Ginny arrived, and went straight on the attack. "Horace, how can you be sitting there at breakfast with those wicked girls after the way they have treated me?"

Papa nodded at the footmen who stood by the sideboards and

jerked his head toward the door. Only after they left did he speak. "Well, now, Virginia, I have not yet heard what happened last night, but I am glad you are here. Come and sit down. Together, we may get to the bottom of it."

*Bother*. Cilla had guessed Aunt Ginny would be over here as soon as she was awake, but usually she did not appear until well after noon. Should Cilla disclose everything she had learned in front of her aunt? She feared that Aunt Ginny was an accomplice to Jasper's plot, and Livy—when Cilla told her the whole—agreed that their aunt would approve of their cousin's plans even if she wasn't part of them.

"What happened last night," Aunt Ginny declared, as she took the chair next to Papa, "is that, after everything I have done for them, your daughters refused to stay the night at my house, and then that little harridan—" she pointed at Cilla—"Yes, you Lucilla, looking as if butter would not melt in your mouth. Lucilla Wintergreen viciously attacked my son. He could have been crippled! Or worse!"

"Now, now, Virginia," Papa said. "Young Jasper should not have tried to manhandle one of my daughters. I daresay a tiny sprite like my Lucilla can't do much harm to a big fellow like Jasper. Now if my Olivia had hit him…!" He chuckled.

Aunt Ginny puffed up like a bantam, and if looks could kill, Papa would have been dead on the spot. "Manhandled, indeed! Jasper was only trying to help Lucilla inside. He has a great fondness for her, and he was insulted that she refused to stay under his roof."

"If Jasper is fond of Lucilla, it is the first I've heard of it," Papa commented. "Have you had your hot chocolate yet, Virginia? Olivia, pour your aunt a cup of hot chocolate."

Livy obeyed, crossing to the sideboard that held cups and hot beverages. She put the poured cup in front of Aunt Ginny then followed up with a plate of delicacies from the assortment of foods on the second sideboard.

Meanwhile, Aunt Ginny had been waxing forth about how

much Jasper admired "his little cousin", including some quite unlikely examples of complimentary things he had said about her. "Indeed," said Aunt Ginny as Livy resumed her seat, "I believe that my dear boy is quite ready to settle down and take Lucilla to wife."

"He wants Cilla's dowry," Livy observed.

"That is a terrible thing to say," Aunt Ginny declared. "Olivia, you should be ashamed of yourself, standing in the way of your sister's happiness, and poisoning her against her cousin. Lucilla, you have always been fond of Jasper, have you not?"

If ever there was a time for Cilla to speak her thoughts instead of the polite lies that made people happy, this was it. "No, Aunt Ginny. I am fond of you and of my girl cousins. Not Jasper. He has always been unkind to all of us girls, and has only ever noticed us to play mean tricks on us. I do not for a moment think that he wishes to marry and settle down."

She took a deep breath while Aunt Ginny protested, and assured Papa that Cilla had taken offense at good-natured teasing. "Boys don't understand how delicate girls are," Aunt Ginny said, "but there. Lucilla will learn to ignore their jests."

"Papa, last night, someone I know overheard my cousin's friends talking about Jasper wanting my dowry. He is prepared to force me, if necessary, to get your agreement to the wedding. Another of his friends plans to do the same to Livy. I shall not marry him, Papa."

"No, Lucilla, you will not," Papa agreed, even as Aunt Ginny protested that Cilla was mistaken, or the eavesdropper was lying.

"Horace," she said to her brother, "you cannot believe this!"

"Virginia, when I paid off your son's debts after Christmas, I told him it was for the last time. I bought your townhouse so he could no longer mortgage it to fund his excesses, and I told him to stop gambling and look after his estates. Instead, he has been back at the tables, putting you and your daughters at risk of disaster. I suppose he knows I shall not let you and the girls starve or go homeless, but if you do not want to be a poor relation continuing to live off my charity, Virginia Marple, rein in your son."

Aunt Ginny burst into tears. "How can you talk like that to me, Horace? Your daughter would be lucky to marry a Marple. A viscount, Horace! And her nothing more than the daughter of a merchant. And what was her mother? A farmer's daughter! She could be a viscountess."

"Lucilla, if you marry a wastrel like Jasper Marple, you'll not have a penny of your dowry," Papa said to her. "It would be like dropping coin into the ocean. Useless. He'd see you starve rather than miss a horse race or a card game."

"You are so unkind," Aunt Ginny complained, dabbing at her eyes with her handkerchief.

"I have said my last word on the subject, Virginia. Tell your son I shall never give my consent to a marriage between him and Lucilla, and no consent means no dowry. Remind him that, when I said I would not pay his debts again, I meant it."

He applied himself to his breakfast.

Aunt Ginny pushed back her chair and marched across the room, turning at the door to fire one last salvo. "I suppose you think I shall continue to sponsor your daughters in Society," she said.

Papa put down his knife and fork and looked his sister in the eye. "Yes, Virginia, I do think so," he said. She glared at him and he looked back, his gaze firm and unwavering. After a moment, she huffed, spun around, and marched out the door. It closed behind her.

"Oh dear," said Cilla.

"Pa is paying for our season," Livy guessed. She peered at Papa's expression, which said nothing to Cilla, but Livy must have read something, for she nodded. "And for our cousins, too."

"Don't mention that to her, Olivia," Papa commanded. "Lucilla, who told you about Jasper's plans?"

"Mr. Bane Sanderson, Papa, while we were dancing after supper. He tends to hide in the shadows. I suppose Jasper's friends didn't see him. He warned me to be careful, and to lock my bedchamber door. I thought it would be better if we didn't stay at Aunt Ginny's for the night."

"I see. And Jasper insisted."

"He came up behind me, grabbed both my arms, and tried to push me toward the house. I screamed, and when he let go, I hit him, Pa." Her voice quavered. Livy took her hand and gave it a press. Cilla squeezed back, took a deep breath, and blinked rapidly to dispel the tears Livy could see hovering. "You told us if we hit a man, to do it there," Cilla continued, her voice back under control, "because otherwise, we probably couldn't hurt him. I didn't want to hurt him, but I *did* want to stop him." She nodded firmly, and declared, "Papa, I won't marry Jasper."

"You shall not marry Jasper," Pa agreed firmly. "Furthermore, you shan't stay the night at your aunt's house, or change there, or anywhere else but here in your own home, and you will not leave this house without one of my footmen. That goes for you, too, Olivia. Who is this man who plans to force you into marriage?"

"A nasty man called Curston," Livy told him. "His father is a friend of Aunt Ginny's."

"Ah," said Papa, looking enlightened.

"What do you know of him, Pa?" Livy asked. Pa pressed his lips together. He was not going to answer, and before she could ask him again, one of the footmen knocked and then entered. "Mr. Wintergreen, two gentlemen by the name of Sanderson have called to request a moment of your time." He handed Pa two calling cards.

"Mr. Mandrake Sanderson. Mr. Wolfbane Sanderson," Papa read. He stood. "Finish your breakfast, girls. I shall speak to the gentlemen."

## Chapter Thirteen

## BANE

M R. WINTERGREEN'S DAUGHTERS had already told him about the plots against them, but he questioned Bane about the details of what was said.

"They shall not succeed," he said firmly.

"Sir, we intend to find out about Lord Marple's monetary problems, and also this fellow Curston," Bane said. "Shall we report what we find to you?"

Wintergreen smiled but shook his head. "No need. I can tell you my nephew owes money to Curston. Furthermore, Curston has his own troubles and is in no position to release Jasper from his debt or bail him out. Curston is in debt to some of the personages in the worst parts of the city. I can also tell you Jasper is a selfish and entitled brat, and my sister encourages him. However, Mr. Sanderson, that is my problem. Not yours. If that will be all?"

"Sir," said Bane, "I should like your permission to court your daughter Olivia."

"And I, your permission to court your daughter Lucilla," Drake added, anxiously.

Mr. Wintergreen tipped his head to one side as he examined

each of them in turn. "I am not willing to make such a decision at this time," he said. "My girls could marry anyone. They are attractive, intelligent, and well-educated."

"Yes, sir," Bane agreed. "They are, and they each deserve to choose the man who will make them happiest. My brother and I would like to be among the contenders."

"My sister says my daughters should not settle for a commoner, especially not a merchant's by-blow. Bane Sanderson, what makes you think you deserve to marry my Olivia?"

Bane knew the answer to that. "I do not, sir. But if she chooses me anyway, I shall love her, respect her, protect her, and support her all the days of my life."

His brother nodded. "And I feel the same about Miss Cilla, sir."

There was a long silence while Mr. Wintergreen thought about that. "I have upset my sister this morning. She will forgive me, of course, since I hold the purse-strings. But I do not wish to have yet another argument. You and your brother are not on her acceptable suitors list."

"But Lord Marple and Curston are?" Bane was aghast.

"On my sister's," said Mr. Wintergreen. "Not on mine. If my daughters have a list, they have not told me, so I assume they have not made their choices yet. I repeat, gentlemen. I am not willing to make such a decision at this time."

It was not a "no" Bane realized. He would have preferred a "yes", but it was not a "no".

"Tell me," Mr. Wintergreen said. "How would you propose to keep my daughters in the life to which they are accustomed? That is, if the time ever comes that one of my daughters indicates that one of you is a preferred suitor."

"Drake and I are happy to show you our books, sir," Bane said, "and we would encourage you to talk to our lawyer and those with whom we do business."

"Later, if the occasion arises," said the older man firmly. "Give me the highlights. What business do you do? I thought you lived on the interest of an inheritance from your father. That is what my sister told me."

"We invest, sir," Drake explained. "Some years ago, our father gave us each a sum of money and told us it was all we could expect from him, since he wanted Sanderson Medicinals to have a single master, and that would be our older brother, Colin."

"We have grown that original amount to more than double what it was five years ago," Bane said. "We have an amount invested in the Funds that is equivalent to what he gave one of us, and we live on the interest from that, but the rest is out in the world. We make use of it funding cargoes, buying shares in businesses, trading stocks."

Drake pointed out the key fact a father might be interested in. "We do not need your daughters' dowries to give them—and any children that bless our marriages—a comfortable life and a prosperous future."

"Drake is correct," Bane said. "Any money our wives bring with them can be set aside for the ladies themselves, or for dowries for our daughters and our younger sons—Drake calls the original amount our father gave us our dowry, and we intend to make sure each of our own children has funds to set themselves up in their chosen profession, and the skills to do so."

"We each received the same amount as our sister Larkspur," Drake explained. "I think it a good idea, for those who can afford it. It gives choices to the children who are not the firstborn son."

"Pull the bell rope, young man," said Mr. Wintergreen to Bane. "We shall have someone bring us coffee—or tea, if you prefer—and you shall tell me more about your investments."

# DRAKE

WHEN DRAKE AND Bane arrived home, a letter was waiting for Drake. "This is from Larkspur," he said, surprised. Apart from a brief note sent from London to thank Lark and Phillip for their hospitality, and a sweet reply from Lark to say how much the children enjoyed meeting their uncles, there'd been no further communication.

Until now.

Drake unfolded the letter and scanned the page. "Lark crosses her lines," he commented.

"Quite a bit to say, has she?" Bane asked. "Are she and the children well?"

Just a minute," Drake replied, as he studied the page, trying to untangle the lines of text across the page from those written down the page across the first set. He read it out loud as he deciphered it.

*"Dear brothers, I trust all goes well for you in London. Phillip and I are thriving, and the children are healthy and happy. Baby has a new tooth, which has been a sad trouble to him, poor little man, but the tooth is now through, so Nurse and I can look forward to better nights of sleep.*

*Phillip and I thought you should know that our brother Colin has been in Sheffield. He is seeking a new..."* Could that be supper? No, ... *"supplier for glass jars. He did not come to see me, but one of Phillip's friends knows I was a Sandman."* Oh. That must be Sanderson. *"He told Phillip that Colin is spreading dire rumors—Colin says you were thrown out of the neighborhood for licensed..."* licentious, probably... *"behavior, and that you are dishonest businessmen, making your money through fraud and lies.*

*Phillip told his friend that Colin is jealous of his younger brothers, but we thought you should know. Phillip thinks you might have a case for slander.*

*Do not forget that I am expecting you to stay with me for Christmas.*

*With much love,*
*Your affectionate sister,*
*Larkspur Hampton."*

"So, we have our explanation for why Pentworth hasn't returned the agreement." Bane commented.

"Or do we?" Drake asked. "Perhaps Colin has got to him in some way, or perhaps something else has happened. Let's write again, and then if there is no word, we had better go ourselves. Or one of us, at least."

Bane made an impatient gesture. "I'm not happy with us leaving London while our ladies are in danger. Let's try a letter."

"Mr. Wintergreen seemed open to our suit," Drake said, optimistically.

"Open, but not decided," Bane corrected. "And, in any case, it is not him but our ladies that we have to convince. He made that clear. How shall we when we cannot get alongside them?"

"It might be easier now they have moved back to their own home," Drake pointed out. "The dragon will not be monitoring them morning, afternoon, and night. Should we go to afternoon calls at Lady Marple's, do you think?"

Bane shot out of his chair. "Flowers! Drew said that men send flowers to ladies they danced with the previous night, and visit the ones in whom they are particularly interested. Where can we buy flowers, Drake?"

Drake was already across the room on his way to fetch his coat and hat. "There's a barrow just around the corner from their street. They'll have a boy to do the delivery for them, I expect. A bouquet for each of the cousins?"

"Yes, and a special one for our own particular lady," Bane decided, pulling on his gloves and donning his own coat and hat. "We'll have their flowers sent to their house, not Lady Marple's."

"And yes," Drake said, over his shoulder. "We shall make an afternoon call, and if we're refused the door, we'll know where we stand with Lady Marple, and can plan accordingly."

# LIVY

LIVY AND CILLA were changing to go to Aunt Ginny's for afternoon calls when a knock on the door proved to be the butler delivering four bouquets, two each.

"The bigger one is from Drake—Mr. Drake Sanderson, I mean," Cilla reported, reading the neatly written card. "The smaller one from his brother."

Livy craned her neck to see her own flowers. "Keep still, do, Miss," begged Barker, who was attempting to style Livy's hair.

"Read my cards, Cilla, please," Livy said, and Cilla did. A large bouquet from Bane and a smaller one from Drake. Of course, the brothers knew that Livy and Cilla had come home last night. Other dance partners might also have sent flowers, but would have assumed they were staying at Aunt Ginny's, since she was their official sponsor, and it was at her house they had been receiving visitors.

"I wonder what Papa said to them," Cilla said.

"I wonder what they said to Pa," answered Livy. If those men had cooked up a plot between the three of them to marry her off, they could think again. Not that Livy was as against marriage as she'd once thought. Not if Bane were to be her husband. Not if he still wanted to wed her when he knew what she had once done. But she would not be married without anyone seeking her consent or even her opinion.

Pa had allowed them a few minutes after his meeting to present their respects, as he put it, and had hovered the whole time. When Livy asked what they had talked about, Pa only said, "The Sanderson boys wanted to be sure you were safe. I let them know I protect my own."

Which was not very informative—as soon as she had the opportunity, she was asking Bane.

"There, Miss. You look lovely, if I do say so myself," said Barker.

Lovely might be an exaggeration, though Livy did not feel

any urge to blush for her appearance. The mid-blue she had chosen—Madame Beauvillier called it Sardinian Blue—had been made up in a round dress and trimmed around all the hems with piped lines of white and a darker blue, colors that were picked up in the embroidery on the bodice.

Cilla's gown was altogether fussier but suited her wonderfully. In another shade of her favorite pink, it was trimmed with lace and ribbon, and flounced at the hem.

Barker helped them into their walking boots and brought them their coats, bonnets, and gloves. They went downstairs to find Pa waiting in the entry hall. "I shall escort you to Virginia's house today. I want a word with young Jasper, if he is there. And I wish to make certain that Virginia does not try to bully you, or push suitors onto you."

Livy admitted, if only to herself, that she was relieved. She had been concerned about their reception after the altercation last night—or, rather, in the early hours of this morning.

As it was, Aunt Ginny must have reviewed her strategy, for she welcomed all three of them with enthusiasm. "Horace, the girls have some lovely bouquets. And even better! An invitation for all five girls to the ball that the Duchess of Winshire holds every year! My girls and the Duchess of Winshire's ball! I did tell you your girls would be a success, Horace. Girls, I spoke to Jasper, and he assures me that the conversation reported to you never took place. We must suppose that Mr. Sanderson made it up for purposes of his own."

*What rubbish.* But Aunt Ginny did not pause for any of them to comment. "I will allow Jasper to make his own explanations, Lucilla, but he assures me of his sincere regard, and of course it is ridiculous to suppose he would marry for any other reason."

"Is that so?" said Pa.

"Of course," Aunt Ginny insisted. "However, I have told him that you cannot quite like it, Horace, and that he must address himself to you. He is out at the moment for, of course, we did not expect you. Are you staying for calls, Horace?"

Pa was not staying. He excused himself, and left Aunt Ginny to usher Livy and her sister into a parlor that looked more like a flower stall, with vases on every available surface. Lord Andrew had sent flowers to all five girls. The Sanderson brothers had sent a small bouquet for each of the five girls, which was clever, since it appeared to be pure politeness, whereas the real tokens of esteem had been delivered across the road, out of Aunt Ginny's sight.

Even Jasper had sent flowers to his sisters and his cousins. Livy wondered if Aunt Ginny had ordered them on her son's behalf and paid for them, but kept the thought behind her teeth. Mr. Curston had sent flowers to Livy, but not to any of the others.

Every girl had received at least five floral offerings, which accounted for the very flowery appearance of the room. The cousins were thrilled, and they and Cilla were soon discussing the potential meaning of every blossom and every bouquet.

"Olivia," said Aunt Ginny, using the conversation as cover. "You will be nice to Mr. Curston, will you not? Lord Curston is a particular friend, you see. I would count it as a favor. And truly, my dear, he is a fine young man and would make you an excellent match."

"I shall be polite to all of your guests, Aunt Ginny," Livy assured her. Perhaps a peace offering was not too much to ask. "Cilla and I are very grateful for all you have done for us," she added.

The doorbell rang and their private moment was over. For the most part, the callers lavished their attention on the four younger ladies, while Livy knotted her reticule. This was the third she had made since coming to London. Perhaps she could give them away for Christmas presents.

Mr. Curston arrived, and paid her a few lavish compliments. Mindful of her promise to her aunt, Livy did not treat them as rudely as they deserved. In her opinion, though, it would not have been polite to let him think she was receptive to his flattery.

Better to make it clear she saw through it. Politely, of course.

"Miss Wintergreen, how radiant you are in that gown."

"Glowing, do you mean, Mr. Curston? How odd. Is my face red?"

"You are pleased to jest, Miss Wintergreen. I meant, of course, that you are the loveliest creature in the room."

Livy chuckled. "Your jest is funnier than mine, Mr. Curston. Next to Cilla? Or Ruby? I fancy most impartial jurors would find in favor of my sister or any one of my cousins."

"I am, I must admit, not impartial," Mr. Curston countered, looking a little white around the nostrils as he forced a pleasant expression onto his face. "I prefer a lady of your more mature charms."

"I see." Did the toad really think she would melt into a puddle at such verbal garbage? "What is your preferred age, sir? Or age range, should I say? Is there an upper limit to mature charms? Thirty, perhaps? Or forty?"

"You jest again," Mr. Curston's smile now looked as if it had transplanted from someone else's face and pasted on. The glint in his eye was by no means appreciative. Indeed, if Livy had not been in her aunt's parlor with her sister at hand and surrounded by cousins and other guests, she might almost have been frightened.

"It is my habit to be honest, sir," she told him. "I trust it does not offend you."

He bared his teeth in another fake smile. "I am sure nothing you did could offend me, Miss Wintergreen."

Either the man had no imagination or he had no concept of how determined Livy was to resist and deflect his charm offensive.

Fortunately, he left after the requisite fifteen minutes. Possibly, he was relieved to go. Livy would not be at all surprised. But he could not have been as relieved as Livy.

There was a constant stream of guest throughout the two hours.

Livy had not expected Lord Andrew Winderfield to appear, and he did not. Livy was a little disappointed. She had quite decided that, if he did come, she would ask for an introduction to his sister-in-law, Lady Sutton. After all, if she met the lady and announced her interest in helping women in need, what was the worst that could happen?

The Sanderson brothers were also absent. Livy did not want to admit, even to herself, that their absence—or at least Bane's absence—bothered her.

"Jasper will escort you home, girls," Aunt Ginny announced, as Livy and Cilla were putting their bonnets and coats on after the last guest had left.

"No need," said Pa, coming out of Jasper's study. Aunt Ginny flushed, looking like a child who had been caught with her fingers in the biscuit tin.

"Horace! I did not know you had come back."

"Since Jasper was not available when I was here earlier, I returned, Virginia. He and I have been having a cozy chat. I shall not trouble Jasper to escort my daughters today. Do you have an engagement with your aunt this evening, girls?"

"Yes, Pa," Livy told him. "We are invited to a musical evening at Lady Eddington's."

"Very good," said Pa. "I shall take my daughters in my carriage and meet you there, Virginia. It must be very crowded in your carriage with six ladies. I should have thought of it earlier. I shall also collect them at whatever time you tell me to be there."

"Horace, there is no need for this," said Aunt Ginny. "We are more than happy to take the girls with us."

"It is no trouble at all," Pa insisted. "We shall see you there, Virginia."

Livy wondered what he and Jasper had talked about, but what he said after they were out in the street put her cousin from her mind. "You have visitors at home, girls. The Sanderson brothers were turned away at your aunt's place, so they came across the road in the hopes that you were at home. I told them to return after an hour, when visiting hours would be over, and that they could then take you for a brief walk. Barker shall go to play propriety."

*Take that, Aunt Ginny.*

## Chapter Fourteen

### DRAKE

D RAKE AND BANE had arrived back at the Wintergreen house a little before their time. Wintergreen had welcomed them inside, gave them the newspaper, and told them to wait while he fetched his daughters. "I shall not wave a red flag in front of my sister by having you with me, gentlemen. I shall be back with Olivia and Lucilla shortly."

He was gone for no more than thirty minutes. Drake heard the front door open, and Cilla's voice greeting the butler, giving him time to stand before she entered the room, her sister and then her father behind her.

"Miss Cilla," he greeted her.

She dimpled when she smiled. "Mr. Drake."

Bane was speaking to Livy, asking her if she would care for a walk.

"I would like that," Livy commented. "We have been sitting in Aunt's parlor for two hours and I have to walk or find something to punch."

"She is quite serious," Cilla said. "She hates having to sit still. She must always be up and doing. I think that is why she loves dancing."

"I shall remember that," Bane said to Cilla.

"Mr. Wintergreen did not need to know that," Livy complained, but she was smiling.

"If you are ready," said Cilla, "we can go now."

They filed out into the hall, where the maid, Barker, was waiting, already in her coat and bonnet. The butler handed the men their outerwear and opened the front door.

"I want to know everything about you," Bane told Livy.

"I cannot imagine why," Livy grumbled.

He offered her his arm and a smile. "I think you can if you try, Miss Wintergreen."

The couple set off at a swift pace along the footpath, still arguing.

"I am beginning to believe they enjoy arguing," said Cilla as she took Drake's arm.

"I am certain they do. I imagine they will still be arguing after fifty years of marriage. We had a couple like that in our village. If he said it was a fine day, she would insist it was about to rain, and if she complained of the cold, he'd tell her he was warm enough. And yet if anyone else criticized either one of them, the other would defend them to their last breath."

"You take it for granted that Livy will have your brother," Cilla commented.

"Do you think she won't? Am I wrong to think she likes him?"

Cilla pursed her lips in a way that made Drake think about kissing—but then he thought of kissing all the time when in her company. "Livy enjoys arguing with your brother," she said. "It is a long way from that to marrying him, is it not? Livy has sworn she will never marry. She says she has never met a man she would risk giving up her freedom for."

"How do *you* feel about marriage, Miss Cilla?" Drake asked.

"I see my sister's point, Mr. Sanderson," Cilla replied. "Marriage is a gamble for both men and women, but if a woman's choice proves to be unwise, men hold most of the cards."

A fair point. "What would you need to know about a suitor to better inform your choice?" Drake asked. "We began the game of questions on our last walk, Miss Cilla. Shall we continue?"

Cilla glanced back and Drake checked behind them, too. Barker was trailing them by quite some distance—close enough to observe, but not close enough to overhear, if they were quiet.

"Very well," Cilla said. "But I should like the person asking the question to be able to ask further questions on the same topic. Is that agreed?"

"Agreed," Drake said.

"I shall go first. Do you have a mistress, Mr. Sanderson?"

"I do not," Drake was glad to be able to give that as his honest reply. To clarify, he said. "Neither Bane nor I have ever kept a mistress, and nor do we frequent brothels." That made them sound like a pair of saints, which was far from the truth, and an innocent like Cilla might not understand the difference between the various type of partner for physical intimacy. "I should add that I have had lovers, and I've also enjoyed the occasional temporary liaison."

She proved her lack of knowledge by her next question. "A brothel is a place where men buy women. Am I right?"

Rented, rather, but the more accurate term sounded disgusting. "Where men buy the right to be intimate with one of the women," he corrected. One or more, but there were surely limits to how much Cilla needed him to disclose.

"How does a mistress differ from a lover?" she wanted to know.

*How did we come to be having this discussion?* Drake could feel himself blushing. "One is obliged to pay for the time of a mistress, and probably also her housing and her servants. One understands that a lover will be receptive to gifts, but it is not so much of a contractual arrangement." Thinking of some of his early experiences, he added, "In fact, sometimes, when the lady is the wealthy one, the gentleman receives the more expensive gifts."

"Define 'temporary liaison'," the lady demanded.

*Ouch.* That was a tricky one to explain to an innocent. "Um… an agreement to be intimate with no expectations beyond the single encounter?" Or a single night or a few days. But, once again, she didn't need those details. He was feeling increasingly uncomfortable, and Wintergreen would be entitled to shoot him if the man knew what Drake was saying to Cilla.

"I see," said Cilla, without explaining what she could see.

*Drake, shut up. You are not doing yourself any favors.*

"I think this is my last question," Cilla told him. "Then it will be your turn. Do you think you shall keep a mistress or take a lover or have liaisons when you are married?"

At last! A question to which he could give an answer she would like. "No. Definitely not. I saw what my father did to his marriages—at least to the one I observed, and I assume to the others—and to his children, by being unfaithful to his wedding vows. I won't do that to my own family. I have not had any interest in other women since I met you, so perhaps I shall not even be tempted. But if I am, I shall remember my wife, my partner, my friend, my life's purpose. And so I shall turn away and come home."

"Hmm," said Cilla. "Is that true? That you have not had a lover or a liaison since you met me?"

"Yes," he said.

"It has only been a month, though," she commented. "And you have been busy."

Arguing with her would only take them back into the thorny territory of the women he had bedded. Whether or not an actual bed was involved. "My turn," he said. "For you, what does your ideal married life look like?"

"You said it," Cilla answered. "Partnership. Friendship. A husband who respects me and listens to my opinion, my ideas, my concerns. I want a man who does something with his life. I cannot understand people like Cousin Jasper and his friends, whose lives revolve around gambling, naughty deeds, silly tricks, and who has a higher status than whom."

Drake agreed. "It makes no sense to me, either. Nothing they do is of any importance. Are they not bored?"

"But not a man who works all the hours God gives," Cilla continued, ignoring his comment. "For how can I be friends with a man who is never at home? Besides, I want a husband who spends time with his children. I barely saw my father when I was a child. It was not until Mama died, which was four years ago, so I was nearly grown, that Papa began showing any interest in me."

"That must have been hard," Drake said.

"I had Mama and Livy," said Cilla, with an elegant shrug of her dainty shoulders.

Drake tried not to notice how the shrug pulled the cloth of her coat tightly across the shape of two perfectly-formed breasts, each just the size to fill one of his hands.

"I had Bane," Drake said. "My mother died when I was three, after a long illness. My father married again when I was four, but my stepmother left me to the servants, and my father was never home. Then Bane came to live with us, when I was ten. It seems to me that he was the first person to ever love me. Perhaps my mother did, though I do not remember. But I had Bane."

He hated thinking about the lonely years before Bane. Hated it. Hated the way his throat stiffened and his eyes stung. He sucked a breath into his nostrils and blinked rapidly.

Cilla had her hand in the crook of his elbow. She hugged his arm. "You will be a better father than yours or mine, Drake," she said confidently.

She had called him by his name, which cheered him immeasurably. "I shall certainly try. I know there are worse fathers than ours, Cilla, but I should like to be the kind of father who knows his children and enjoys spending time with them."

"What is going on here?" The interruption came from Jasper Marple, who had stopped his horse to glare at them from the riding path. "Lucilla? Olivia? What are you doing with those men?"

"Walking, Cousin Jasper," replied Livy. "A healthful activity. I recommend it."

"My mother has instructed you not to encourage the Sanderson brothers," Jasper said, pitching his voice to carry to all the other people who had stopped to enjoy the show.

Bane spoke up before Livy could do so. "We have Mr. Wintergreen's permission to escort his daughters and their maid, Lord Marple. Lady Marple can have no complaint."

Marple sneered. "We'll see what Mr. Wintergreen says when I tell him what I have heard from your older brother about the dissolute behavior that saw you banned from your home, and the sharp business practices and cheating that your brother has uncovered since he has been investigating."

"Drake and I shall happily submit our records and the names of our business partners to any independent and impartial investigator," Bane replied calmly. "As to dissolute behavior, you are trusting the wrong Sanderson, Marple. Surprising, given you have attended at least one of his parties. But in front of the ladies, I shall say no more on that point."

"Rubbish," said Marple. "You have been caught out, and you should slink back to the provinces where you belong."

"You are making a fool of yourself, Cousin Jasper," said Livy. "And a spectacle of us. Your mother shall be most displeased. Go away, do, and allow us to continue our walk."

Cilla was trembling. Drake placed a hand over hers. "Do not be frightened," he murmured. "We shall not allow that yapping cub to harm you."

Her face was white and her eyes wary, but she smiled up at him, the gallant lady. "He is a yapping cub, is he not?"

"Cilla!" shouted the fool viscount. "I forbid you to walk with Sanderson. Andy, take my horse. I am walking my intended home."

At that, color flooded back into the face of Drake's beloved. She yanked her hand from Drake's arm, took a step forward, and stamped her foot. "Jasper Marple, I would not marry you if you were the last man on the face of the earth. You are immature, selfish, lazy, and careless. Furthermore, you disapprove of everything about me except my dowry. My father has already told you that he will not allow you to marry me, and he will be most unhappy when he hears how you have embarrassed me and my sister today, in front of all these good people. Now go away and leave us alone."

Cilla had flushed a becoming pink. Marple turned bright scarlet. "How dare you, you impudent strumpet. You shameless hussy."

A new voice entered the fray. "Marple, I can only assume you are drunk. Andrews, take your friend home. Now." It was the Duchess of Dellborough, and with her was the Duchess of Winshire and some other ladies—grand ladies, by their dress and their company. Drake had not noticed their carriage, having been so intent on not making an even greater spectacle of the ladies by hauling Marple off his horse and punching the self-righteous smirk off his face.

A group of riders accompanied the carriage, including the husbands of the two high-ranked ladies and Drake's and Bane's friend Drew. The Duke of Winshire said, "Drew, help Andrews, will you?"

Marple let out a screech of frustration through gritted teeth, and slashed his poor horse with his whip even as he dragged its head around. He took off across the grass and poor Andrews touched his own whip to his hat in a hasty salute to the ladies before galloping after him.

"I think there is no need to bother Andrew," said the Duchess of Winshire. "Miss Sanderson, Miss Lucilla, are you well? Such an ill-bred display! One hopes your cousin will not ride out in public again while under the influence of drink."

Her voice was pitched to carry to the crowd. The Duchess of Dellborough took a more direct approach. "Move along, please. This is not a circus or a raree-show."

Muttering among themselves, the spectators obeyed, resuming their ride or their walk. But beyond a doubt, the main topic of conversation would be the confrontation between the Sanderson brothers and the Wintergreen sisters on one side, and young Viscount Marple on the other.

"If we can be of further help, let us know," said one of the duchesses, and her friends nodded. "Shall we take you home, Miss Sanderson? Miss Lucilla?" one of them suggested.

Livy replied. "We would not wish anyone to believe our cousin's calumnies against Mr. Drake Sanderson and Mr. Bane Sanderson. Abandoning them here in the park might give quite the wrong impression. But thank you, your graces, my ladies. My sister and I appreciate the suggestion and your offer of support."

Drake's own darling said nothing, but she tucked her hand back inside Drake's elbow, and he placed his hand over hers, his heart melting inside his chest.

"Then we shall leave you to the rest of your walk," the duke said, and the cavalcade moved off.

As Drake had come to expect, Livy was the first person to speak. "I apologize for my odious cousin, gentlemen. Do you suppose your brother really is telling such lies?"

"We know he is," Bane admitted. "This morning, we had a letter from our sister Lark saying he has been spreading such stories around in Sheffield. I hadn't expected him to write to Marple, but I should have. I am sorry you were subjected to such a scene. I don't suppose the duchess's claim that he was drunk will last for long. People will believe what they choose to believe. I can only hope our usual business partners won't abandon us, and that we can live this rubbish down."

It was a worry. Their entire livelihood depended on trust and honesty. Drake couldn't imagine how those they invested with might react to Colin's lies amplified by Marple's spite, but he didn't think it would be good.

"Hope is good," said Cilla. "Talking to Papa and asking his advice would be better."

"Yes." Livy nodded vigorously. "Pa has taken a liking to the pair of you. He will be as angry about this as Cilla and I are, particularly given the reason for what we did on Misrule Night."

Drake felt his eyebrows shoot up. "He knows about that?"

"Not the identity of the girl," Cilla told him. "We did try to keep it a secret from Papa, but we should have known there was no point. Someone wrote to him about the incident. Once he asked, we told him what had happened, but he agreed he did not need to know the name of the girl on whose behalf we were attempting to exact retribution."

"It could have been anyone in the three villages or the wider neighborhood," Livy commented.

Interesting, and possibly significant, that she didn't mention the ladies at the house party. Drake would keep that observation to himself.

Bane had turned back toward the park gates, and the others followed him. "I think we should go back to your father's house," he said.

"Perhaps we can walk again once this rubbish has been put to rest," Drake suggested.

"Perhaps we can walk again tomorrow," said Cilla. "Do you not agree, Livy? I shall not be dictated to by liars and bullies."

It was a brave suggestion, but Drake looked at Bane and raised his eyebrows. Bane must have read Drake's thoughts, for he said, "Shall we discuss that with your father, ladies? He may have some thoughts about ensuring your safety."

"I suppose Pa will have an opinion," Livy allowed.

Mr. Wintergreen frowned and asked a number of questions. "I shall trust you gentlemen to find a way to prove your character, and to silence your brother," he said. "I shall deal with my nephew."

Bane had a question. "Will the *musicale* tonight be safe for you and your sister, Miss Wintergreen?"

"I shall escort you," Mr. Wintergreen said.

"But Pa, you hate Society events," Livy pointed out.

"I do, and musicales most of all. But I shall be welcomed, you need have no doubt of that. Most of these people owe me money, and those who don't, use me to make them money. They will not wish to offend me, and seeing me with you will remind them they do not wish to offend my daughters."

Drake had to admit to being relieved. He had no doubt of Mr. Wintergreen's ability to deal with Marple and his mother. Curston, too, come to that.

Cilla asked about the proposed walk.

"A morning walk, I think," said Wintergreen. "While Marple and his sort are still asleep. You shall enjoy it more, daughters. Now say your farewells to your young men and go and do whatever you need to do to flossy yourselves up for dinner. I have already told your aunt that I am escorting you tonight, and shall meet her there, but I will send a note to let her know I am most displeased with my nephew for making a fool of himself and a spectacle of my daughters."

"Do you think we could get an invitation to the musicale?" Drake asked as the brothers walked home. "I would feel better if I was there myself."

Bane shook his head. "I daresay being in public with the Sanderson brothers would draw more comment than they would like."

"I do not want to go to Sheffield, that is certain," Drake commented. "Not at the moment."

But when they arrived back at their rooms, Pentworth and his wife were waiting for them.

## Chapter Fifteen

## BANE

THE FIRST ORDER of business was to call on the landlord to see if Bane could rent the currently empty rooms on the next floor down. The Pentworths needed a place to stay, for they had been more or less driven out of Sheffield. Colin had done all too successful a job of running down his brothers. So much so that, when Silas Pentworth spoke up on their behalf, he was accused of being a cheat and a liar, and his landlord asked him and his wife to leave their rented accommodation.

After some people broke into the Pentworths' workshop and wrecked the prototype, they decided that they had better get out of town. "We couldn't think of anywhere else to go," Anne Pentworth said, with the calmness of exhaustion. "Why would your own brother hate you so much that he destroys us to hurt you, Mr. Sanderson?"

Bane shook his head. "I have given up trying to understand it, Mrs. Pentworth. I am so sorry you have been caught up in our family's troubles."

He left Drake to make the Pentworths a cup of tea—much needed, Mrs. Pentworth said—and hurried downstairs to see the landlord. Accommodation arranged, he sent the boy who was usually loitering on the corner to the nearest Ordinary to buy dinner for four and returned upstairs.

Mrs. Pentworth greeted his news of a safe haven and of dinner on the way by bursting into tears, and then apologized from the haven of her husband's arms. "I am not usually prone to crying, Mr. Sanderson and Mr. Sanderson. It has been a trying time."

"Call us Drake and Bane," Drake suggested. "With two Mr. Sandersons, it becomes awkward. Do not fret, Mrs. Pentworth. You have a place to stay, and we shall find you somewhere to work. I suppose you will be able to reproduce the prototype?"

"No need," said Pentworth. "If you are still willing to fund us, we can go straight to producing the full machines. We have all the designs and calculations. Anne carried them in pockets sewn into her skirts in case we were robbed, but fortunately we had no trouble on the way here."

"Mrs. Pentworth," said Bane, "you are a marvel."

"Call me Anne," said that lady, with a watery smile. "And this is Silas."

The brothers saw the couple fed and settled into their new apartment.

"We need a council of war, Drake," Bane told his brother. "Bad enough when Colin attacks us, but when that information is used to hurt the Pentworths and our ladies? It is intolerable."

"You're right," Drake agreed. "How can we stop him?"

"Sue him for slander, like Phillip suggested. And investigate him. Heaven knows, we can probably find out plenty we can use to shut his mouth."

Drake frowned as he thought about that. "If we're going to hire an investigator, perhaps we should get him to look into Curston and Marple, too. I know Wintergreen has done so, but we might need the information to protect our own backs."

It was a good point. Bane nodded. "I wonder if Drew Winderfield knows of any investigators? Or one of the other members of the investment group? Fullerton might be able to tell us how to go about filing a suit against Colin for slander."

"Possibly libel, too, if we could get hold of his letters to Marple," Drake agreed.

"Unlikely. We can hardly ask his sisters to search his correspondence," Bane objected. *Though perhaps their cousins could ask the Marple sisters.* Bane rejected the thought. He did not want his Livy involved in what could prove to be an unpleasant business.

"We'll also have to look for a workshop where the Pentworths can build their hydraulic presses," he said. "Again, the investment group might be able to help. We'll have to ask."

"How much room do they need?" Drake asked. "I've been thinking we should buy a property of our own here in London. We're closer to the action here. We're hearing about things sooner, and more of them, so we're making more money. If we purchased our own house in an area where the prices are going up, it would take a chunk of our capital, but it would be a good investment. And it would have room for the Pentworths and perhaps outbuildings they could use for their work."

"It is a reasonable thought," Bane agreed. "Let us find out what our ladies think about it. They might have an opinion about where they would prefer to live. Meanwhile, I've taken the rooms downstairs for a month. The Pentworths can make themselves comfortable. Tomorrow, I'll get them to give me a list of what they need in a workplace."

"We cannot do much more tonight," Drake commented. "Let's make an early night of it. We have an investors' meeting tomorrow, and we'll be able to make some progress there. I hope."

*Depending on how far Colin's bile has spread.* Bane kept his concerns to himself. If Drake hadn't had the same thought, then let him wait until tomorrow to worry about it. But what were the chances that none of the investors in the group had heard the lies about him and Drake?

# CILLA

TO CILLA, IT was obvious that the scene at the park was the main topic of conversation of the evening, for people kept staring at her and Livy, and falling silent when the Wintergreens approached near enough to hear what was being said.

Livy and Papa showed no signs of discomfort. Aunt Ginny slightly redeemed herself in Cilla's eyes by a full assault on the judgmental—bustling up to those who looked most censorious to introduce, "My dear brother Wintergreen and his daughters, Miss Wintergreen and Miss Lucilla Wintergreen."

Papa had promised that no one would dare to give them the cut direct, and he was right. But no one lingered to speak with them, either, until a young lady and her husband approached to seek an introduction.

Aunt Ginny greeted them with delight. "Lord and Lady Wharton! How pleasant to see you here! May I make known to you my nieces and their father? Miss Wintergreen, Miss Lucilla Wintergreen, and my brother, Wintergreen. And you remember my daughters, of course. Miss Marple, Miss Ruby Marple, and Miss Beryl Marple. Horace, girls, Lord and Lady Wharton are neighbors of ours."

Lord Wharton bowed over their hands, and when he reached Livy, he and his wife had somehow managed to form a group with just Cilla and Livy, while Aunt Ginny and the cousins fell into conversation with another of Aunt Ginny's friends and her daughters.

Papa was a few steps away, watching benignly.

The young lord commented, "I see what my friend Bane meant about you, Miss Wintergreen. He described you as a goddess." He tossed a laughing glance at his wife, and added, "I am, of course, a worshipper at a different altar, but I understand his point."

He moved on to greet Cilla. "My friend Drake talked about you, too, Miss Lucilla."

"I imagine he did not describe me as a goddess," said Cilla.

"As a dainty maiden made of gossamer and iron," Lord Wharton replied.

*Oh my.* Gossamer and iron. Cilla was going to have to ask Drake precisely what he meant, but she liked the sound of it.

"Wharton, you are embarrassing our new friends," Lady Wharton scolded. "Miss Wintergreen, Miss Lucilla, do not listen to Wharton. Drake and Bane said only complimentary things about you, of course. Indeed, I was so eager to meet you that when I saw Lady Marple had five young ladies with her, I told Wharton that I needed an introduction, and I needed one now!"

She smiled as Lord and Lady Thornstead joined the group. "Jenna, may I present my new friends?"

"I am ahead of you, Pauline," Lady Thornstead said. "I had the pleasure of meeting Miss Wintergreen and Miss Lucilla yesterday evening. And, also, their sponsor and her daughters, of course." She looked directly at Papa and smiled. "I have not met you, sir, but I assume you are Mr. Wintergreen?"

"Lady Thornstead, this is my Papa, Mr. Wintergreen," Cilla said. "Papa, Lord and Lady Thornstead are friends of the Sanderson brothers. The good ones, I mean." She flushed as she realized that she had just said the other brother was a bad one. But it was true! She would not apologize for it.

"Gossamer and iron," Lord Wharton commented in a whisper intended just for her, but Lady Wharton rapped him on the arm with her fan.

Was that a clue to what Drake meant? That she looked delicate but was stronger than others might expect?

"You two sisters must come to my ladies' tea tomorrow," Lady Wharton said. "I call it a 'tea' so no one knows we are bluestockings. Not that anyone would dare to call us that when Jenna is a member, for she is a future duchess. We talk about books and politics and scientific discoveries and useful good works and all sorts of other interesting things, and no one is allowed to do needlework. From what the 'good' Sanderson brothers say," her eyes laughed as she used Cilla's term, "it will suit you wonderfully well."

Cilla and Livy both thanked her, and that was all they had time for. The hostess called for everyone to take their seats, for the first musician was ready to start. But when the music stopped for supper, they had time to secure an address and a start time.

What had started out to be an unpleasant evening had turned into a delightful opportunity.

# LIVY

"CILLA," LIVY SAID, as the carriage trundled through the streets of London from Pa's townhouse to Lady Wharton's, "I think we should tell the ladies we meet this afternoon about Misrule Night, and why we did it."

Her sister stared at her and then nodded. On their walk with the Sanderson brothers this morning, they had heard about the destruction of the Pentworth's machine, and what Bane and Drake planned to do to counter their brother and his allies.

"I agree, Livy. Perhaps the ladies will not approve, but we have to try." Cilla gave the decisive nod Livy knew well. Gentle and sweet as her sister was, she was immovable once she had made up her mind.

Nonetheless, Livy nearly changed her mind when she realized how exalted some of the ladies were. Jenna—the group insisted on first names—was so merry and so approachable that it was easy to forget she was married to a man who was in line to become a duke, and though Pauline was already a viscountess, she had confided she was a country girl at heart.

But almost everyone in the group was titled, and one—her name was Margaret—was a countess. Surely, they would not care about the fate of a couple of merchant's sons, one of whom was not even legitimate?

Even the ladies who lacked titles were clearly well-bred, though Livy supposed that she and Cilla presented well to those who didn't know their background. There were two Miss Worthingtons, a Miss Wharton (who must be a younger sister of Lord Wharton), and a Mrs. Paddimore, who was a widow and apparently the dearest friend of the countess.

Lady Thornstead, as hostess, called the meeting to order several minutes after Livy and Cilla arrived. "Pauline is going to read us one of her poems," she said, "then Margaret will give us a report on our donations to the clinic. We shall have afternoon tea after that, and then Eva is going to lead the discussion on our book for the month, Caroline Lamb's *Glenarvon*. After that, we shall open the floor to anyone who wishes to raise a particular issue. As always, we shall end the meeting with deciding the hostess and agenda for next week. Pauline, if you would?"

She waved a graceful hand at Lady Wharton, who stood and clasped her hand behind her back.

The poem was a sweet and rather sentimental panegyric, from the point of view of a mother cat, to the kittens who were one by one leaving her nest in the straw of the stable loft, to go to new homes. As Livy listened, she resolved that she would accept the invitation to raise an issue, and in the meantime, she would relax and enjoy herself.

It was a pleasant afternoon. Everyone praised the poet, and then Margaret, Countess Charmain, spoke briefly about how sums of money donated by the group had been spent to buy supplies for a medical clinic in the slums. Apparently, the women had also donated blankets, and these had been much appreciated.

Over tea, one of the other women whispered that Margaret was an herbalist, who worked with the doctors at the clinic and supplied them with herbal remedies from her garden. "Does her husband not object?" Livy whispered back, but the countess was that rare creature, a single woman with her own title and her own fortune! Livy was very impressed.

Livy and Cilla had read *Glenarvon* last year when it was first published and could give their opinions about the heroine and the hero. The group was split into two camps over the story of seduction and betrayal, and the sisters found themselves on opposite sides. Livy and her allies thought the heroine over-melodramatic and the hero unlikely. Cilla's side claimed that the heroine had been driven into melodrama by the hero's manipulation.

As for those denizens of the fashionable world that had been caricatured in it, the Wintergreen sisters had no personal experience to go on, but knew only what the newspapers had said.

Finally, Jenna announced that it was time to open the floor.

Livy put up a hand quickly, before she lost her nerve. "Ladies, I want to ask for your advice," she began.

"Of course," said Pauline. "How can we help?"

She laid out the whole story. How they had met someone who had been seduced with promises of marriage and then abandoned. How the man lived near Marplehurst Hall, and was therefore a fair target for a Misrule Night shaming in the village's tradition.

Pauline took over to explain the tradition of Misrule Night in Marplestead, the nearest village to the Hall. "Brentwood Court, where I live, is nearer to Fenton, the third of the three villages in the area," she explained. "I have never been to a Misrule Night, though I believe some of the Fenton villagers go. It was Colin Sanderson, wasn't it? It is not the first time he has been implicated in seducing an innocent, and the party he held last Christmas when his wife was away was notorious."

Livy nodded, and one of the other women commented, "It sounds like he deserved whatever you did to him."

"Except that we got the wrong man," Livy confessed. She told them the story of how Bane stopped the rumpus, and how Colin had tried, and was still trying, to use the tale of the shaming to blame his brothers for his own misbehavior.

"I have heard the gossip," said one of the ladies, and several others nodded their heads.

"Are you saying that one brother is a rakehell and a profligate and the other two are not?" The speaker sounded doubtful, and even slightly scornful.

"According to my husband," said Jenna, "that is correct. He has known the Sanderson brothers for many years, as Lord Marple was his godfather, and he has been visiting Marplehurst Hall since he was a child. Drake and Bane Sanderson are close to him in age, but Colin is eight years older, and was off doing young-man things when the other boys were building tree houses and chasing footballs. Even then, Garry says, there were rumors that Mrs. Sanderson chose only old maids because her husband and her oldest stepson could not be trusted to keep their hands to themselves."

"It is other bodily parts that cause the trouble," said one of the married ladies.

Livy grimaced. *And isn't that the truth!*

"You said you wanted advice. About what," Jenna asked.

"My question is, should I share the story of Misrule Night? And will it help the two younger Sanderson brothers or harm them?"

"What are the Sanderson brothers to you?" asked Margaret. "I suppose what I want to know is whether your motivation is justice or something more personal."

Cilla answered. "For me, it is both. I hope I would be concerned about anyone who was being persecuted with a farrago of lies. But also, Mr. Drake Sanderson is courting me, and I like him very much."

"And you, Livy?" said Margaret. "We know that Mr. Bane Sanderson is courting you. Do you feel about him as your sister does about his brother?"

"How can one know?" It was a cry from Livy's heart. "When we marry, we put our lives into the hands of our husbands, and if one makes a mistake… 'A man may smile and smile and be a villain.' Didn't Shakespeare say that? It certainly applies to Mr. Curston, who has also announced his intention of marrying me. He tries to flatter me, but with compliments that mean nothing, for he does not notice me at all. And the things I hear about him confirm that he is horrid—for one, he was at Colin Sanderson's party. He is friends with my cousin Lord Marple, who is a bully and a spoilt boy. Marriage is too big a risk, or so I have always thought."

"But Bane Sanderson is giving you second thoughts." Jenna made it a statement, not a question, but Livy answered it. "Yes. No. I don't know." The last three words were almost a wail.

Bane confused her. She responded to his kindness, his respect, even his teasing—for she had known from the first that the arguments they had every time they met were intended as entertainment, by them both.

She admired him, too. "My mother did it," he had said about his face. Just the facts. No bitterness or anger, even against the father who neglected him and the stepmother who despised him.

On the other hand, he was a man. How was she to know whether he was just after her dowry? Or whether he would turn into a bully and a tyrant behind closed doors?

"I like him," she admitted. "But I am… cautious."

"Afraid," accused Mrs. Paddimore—Regina, rather. "And who can blame you? When we marry, we give ourselves, our property, our future children—if we are blessed with children—our happiness, all into the hands of a man. He has all the legal power in the marriage, and we have only what we are permitted."

"We marry so we can have children," said another of the women, "and children make it worthwhile."

"Or we refuse to marry so we do not have children," said another. "Children might be one's reward for marriage and childbirth, but I can enjoy my nieces and nephews without risking either."

Jenna spoke from the perspective of the happily married. "If we are fortunate, we marry a kind man who respects us. A man who will be our partner and our friend, as well as our lover."

"But how is a person to know?" Livy asked.

"It is harder when we have more to offer than ourselves," Margaret said. "That is why I am still single, in fact. Perhaps some of my suitors have wanted more than my fortune and my title, but most of them were single-mindedly in pursuit of what I would bring to them, with never a thought of what they would bring to me."

"We have our intelligence," said Pauline. "Margaret, you have used it to assess your suitors and have found them wanting. And Livy, you have already rejected Mr. Curston, and I applaud your good sense. Cilla, the same applies to Lord Marple. Neither of those gentlemen evidence any interest in settling down and being good husbands."

"That is true," said Jenna. "And we have our feelings. Are our doubts based on our personal fears, or on something that the suitor has said or done? Let us trust our own instincts, particularly if a suitor seems intellectually a good match but we just cannot warm to them. At the same time, let us not allow our feelings to override our good sense."

"Lastly," said one of the other married ladies, "we have advisors. Our parents, perhaps, or our friends. People who can give their opinions about our suitors, and perhaps even investigate finances or behavior. If I had taken advice, my first marriage would never have happened. Though, to give Fairburn credit, at least he had the courtesy to catch an ague in one of his low dives, and die of it."

"Christiana," said Pauline, "we all love you, but you are giving Livy and Cilla a misguided opinion of you."

Livy smirked. She had a feeling that she and Christiana had a very similar outlook on the world. As to the advice? It was practical and reassuring. She would have to give the whole Bane thing further thought. But perhaps—just perhaps—he might be worth taking the risk.

# Chapter Sixteen

## BANE

DRAKE AND BANE arrived at the investor group meeting to discover that Colin's poison had done its work on the minds of some of the members. "Lord Andrew," said one man, before they could even take their seats, "you proposed the Sanderson brothers as members, and we were guided by you. However, in the light of the scandalous—and may I say illegal— conduct that has come to light, I propose that they be ejected."

Two of the others said, "Hear, hear."

Drew raised an eyebrow. "I quite agree that we should hear. We should hear the rumors themselves, and the Sandersons' defense before we sit in judgement. Bane? Drake? Please be seated. Bagshaw, you mention scandalous and possibly illegal conduct. Please be specific."

"Well," said Bagshaw, "what is most relevant to this group is that they have been accused of fraud and cheating. In business, I mean."

"By whom?" Bane asked calmly.

"By your older brother, for one," retorted Bagshaw. "He says you kept the books for your father, and he has spent years cleaning up the mess. I have it from my cousin, Curston, and he is

150

a friend of Colin Sanderson's. Your brother also says that you have cheated investment partners, which is how you have made so much money."

The barrister leaned his elbows on the table and folded his hands in front of his chin. "In law, we call that *hearsay*," he said. "Do you have any evidence for these contentions?"

"This is not a court of law, Fullerton," Bagshaw said.

"Indeed," Fullerton agreed. "And these are accusations that should be heard in a court of law. Has Colin Sanderson laid information with a magistrate?"

Bagshaw shook his head. "I have no idea. Not that I have heard."

"If he did," said Fullerton, turning his attention to Drake and Bane, "How would you answer the charges?"

"I kept Sanderson Medicinals' books up to the time of my father's death," Bane said. "My father reviewed the accounts monthly and was satisfied with my work. The last time I worked on the books was the day before he died suddenly of an apoplexy. He had all of his wits about him until that day. Colin had me ejected from the house immediately after the funeral. If the books have been tampered with, it was after I had access to them. If Colin is cleaning up a mess, it is of his own making."

"As to the accusation of cheating, we have detailed business records of all of our transactions," Drake said. "They will show there is no substance to the charges, and those with whom we have invested will stand witness to the same."

"Which is why Colin and his friends are using rumor and gossip to discredit us, instead of going to the law," Bane added.

"Before we extended the invitation to the group, we made the usual enquiries," said Mr. White. "Mr. Bane Sanderson and Mr. Drake Sanderson are highly respected in the investment community, and Mr. Bane Sanderson is remembered in the business community as a trusted servant to his father, who was also highly respected. Unfortunately for the legacy of Sanderson Medicinals, Mr. Colin Sanderson, the current owner, is developing a reputation for slap-dash work, cost-cutting on materials, and sharp business practices. I can share that evidence with any of our members who may be interested."

"My cousin has a great deal of respect for Colin Sanderson," Bagshaw insisted.

"You are certainly welcome to look into the evidence," Drew said. "And to share the results with your cousin, by all means."

"Then there is the question of their moral probity," Bagshaw insisted. "Do we want to be associated with men who were driven out of their district for debauchery?"

"My dear Bagshaw," said White. "We are here to discuss investment opportunities. Not to exchange gossip in tones of moral outrage. What a man does in private, as long as it is not illegal and does not involve coercion, is his own business."

"Though the group may wish to know that the gossip is incorrect," Drake pointed out. "The person responsible for the debauchery and his friends was not, in fact, driven out of the district."

Bagshaw leapt to his feet and leaned over the table, resting his weight on his hands. "Do you deny that you were the subject of a shaming on New Year's Eve by the women of the village of Marplestead?"

"Half a shaming," Drake corrected. "I was not the Sanderson who should have received the letter that lured me into their trap, but the messenger made a mistake. Once Bane turned up and showed them it was me, and not Colin, the ladies set me free."

Bagshaw sneered. "I heard you were drunk, naked, and driven through town with an ass's head attached to your shoulders. And that the ceremony ended in a dunking."

"I was drugged, not drunk," said Drake. "Bane, you remember more than I do?"

"Drake was stripped to his breeches and tied backward on an ass, with a carnival mask of a goat's head over his head. I got there in time to stop them from dunking him. I convinced them that he wasn't our older brother, and they let him go."

"I don't know whether they intended to punish a specific sin of Colin's or whether it was a pattern of behavior, but I cannot say I was surprised," said Drake. "His wife was away for the Christmas holiday, and he and his friends brought in a carriage load of soiled doves to entertain them while she was absent. In his own house, in front of his wife's servants. My father was not an abstemious man, but he would never have insulted his wife in such a situation."

"Hearsay!" Bagshaw used Fullerton's term in Colin's defense.

"Ask your cousin Curston," Bane suggested. "He was at the party. You might also ask him whether his enthusiasm for this attack stems from our rivalry over the right to court a lady whose name I will not bring into disrepute by mentioning it."

"Olivia Wintergreen," Bagshaw sneered. "As if she would choose the bastard son of a merchant over a viscount."

"Gentlemen," said Drew, "I trust I do not need to remind you that anything we discuss during our meetings is strictly confidential. Anything. Including the name just mentioned by our colleague Mr. Bagshaw. We have addressed the question, raised by our colleague, of whether we should eject Mr. Bane Sanderson and Mr. Drake Sanderson from our group, given the questions that have been raised in recent gossip about their honesty. The other questions—of who is or is not of good moral character, and of the possible motivations of Bagshaw's cousin, Mr. Curston— are beyond the scope of this group and of no interest to us. Fullerton? How do you propose we proceed?"

"A vote," said Fullerton. "Three options. Yes, we eject the Sandersons. No, we do not eject the Sandersons. No decision, we take time to further investigate." He raised his eyebrows in question and looked around the table. The members, even Bagshaw, nodded.

"Sorry Bane, Drake," said White, with a grin. "You do not get a vote, I'm afraid."

On a show of hands, the decision was overwhelmingly "no", with Bagshaw a "yes", and two others voting for "no decision".

"The Sandersons stay," said Drew. "Gentlemen, on the table before us today are the proposed ship extension to the Newcastle canal, Mr. Linton's proposal for an improved gas lamp for household use, and a report from our Madras agent on a new source of textiles that may prove lucrative. Does anyone have anything else to add?"

"I hesitate to raise our problem," Bane said, "given the time already given during this meeting to the attack on our reputation, but could I please have a few minutes to seek help finding new premises for a project in which we have invested? I can explain when my turn on the agenda arrives."

Drew looked around the table, ascertained the agreement of the others, and nodded. "Very well," he said. "White? You were looking into the canal extension."

Bane and Drake left the meeting an hour and a half later with the satisfaction of knowing most of the group believed them, and with a possible new home for the Pentworths that would include sufficient space to build the hydraulic presses that were already on order. If those who had made the orders would honor them.

Stopping Colin—and Curston, whose motive for destroying Bane's reputation was obvious—was a priority. Fullerton had given them the name of an attorney, and also of an investigator whom Drew also recommended. "Wakefield is something of a connection," said the young lord. "He was a protege of my father's duchess, as is his wife, who is also his business partner."

He added, "If you don't mind, I'll also have a talk with my stepmother about how to handle the gossip at a social level. Aunt Eleanor is an expert in that arena. She says it is almost impossible to prove innocence in the court of public opinion. Some people will always believe the worst. But it is good enough to persuade the majority to assume innocence."

"We would appreciate it," Drake said.

All in all, a good meeting, though the day was marred by another attack by footpads as they made their way home. This time, the men came at them with knives, but gave up quickly and ran off when Bane and Drake fought back.

## Chapter Seventeen

### LIVY

Cousin Jasper had left town, and taken Mr. Curston with him. Apparently, they had gone to a house party just out of Brighton, a place which saw a much faster set than Bath, since it was popular with the Prince Regent and his hangers-on.

Livy was delighted to see them go. Aunt Ginny was inclined to grumble. "Horace, you did not need to drive my boy away," she said to Pa.

"I did not drive him away, Virginia," Pa told her. "I did tell him that he needed to stop seeing marriage to Cilla as a solution to his financial problems, for he would never get his hands on her dowry, even if she agreed to marry him, which she would not."

"It would be a good match," Aunt Ginny insisted, "with benefits on both sides."

"Virginia, your son is a spoilt boy who would make my Cilla miserable," Pa said. "He spends money he does not have, chases after anything in skirts, cannot resist a horse race, a prize fight, or a wager, ignores his responsibilities, and has no sense of purpose. I ask you, where is the benefit to Cilla?"

She did not counter any of Pa's criticisms, but only made the same old claim. "He is a viscount, Horace. She would be a viscountess." True but irrelevant. Cilla didn't care about titles.

"If he does not mend his ways, my lass, he will have nothing left except the title, and where will that leave you and the girls?"

Aunt Ginny burst into tears, and it was left to Cilla to comfort her, since Livy shared Pa's opinion that it was all, or mostly, an act.

With Jasper and Curston out of town, Pa relaxed, and once again Livy and Cilla were left to travel to and from events with Aunt Ginny, though Pa had solved the crowding problem by purchasing a coach that had enough room to fit all five girls, plus Aunt Ginny, with Barker and one of the Marple maids relegated to the roof.

On several occasions, Livy saw Pa giving Aunt Ginny a purse, or asking her to explain items in the accounts that arrived from the dressmaker, the candlemaker, the cobbler and dozens of others. "I had not realized until now," she said to Cilla, "that Pa is paying *all* the costs of Marple's household as well as his own."

It made her even less inclined than before to indulge her aunt's whims about what to wear, where to go, and who to be seen with. She and Cilla might owe their aunt thanks for being their sponsor, and Livy was grateful. But Aunt Ginny and the cousins owed Pa for the food they ate, the roof over their head, and the clothes on *their* backs.

She and Cilla continued to sleep at home, under their father's roof. After all, as Cilla said, who knew when Jasper might return from his house party?

But also—Cilla didn't say this, but Livy certainly appreciated the advantage—they could walk with the Sanderson brothers in the mornings, without having to endure Aunt Ginny's opinion on the matter.

Aunt Ginny usually had plans for them in the afternoon and evening. She was inclined to be indignant that her nieces chose to attend the weekly meeting for Jenna's ladies—mostly because she was not invited. Cilla soothed her ruffled feathers by explaining that the group met to discuss books and current affairs, which

Aunt Ginny thought was a complete waste of a marriageable lady's time.

"I cannot see the point, Lucilla. You do not need to know such things in order to make an eligible marriage."

However, given the families represented among the ladies, and the titles, she conceded that the connections her nieces were making might have some value, and only grumbled when the meeting times conflicted with her own plans for the girls.

Livy and Cilla were making not just connections but friendships.

Cilla was taking lessons from Margaret in the cultivation of herbs and their medical use. Livy, pursuing her own interest in help for the less fortunate—particularly unfortunate women who had been victims of selfish men—found that Regina taught reading once a week to girls at a local "house of refuge"—a place where those who were unmarried and with child could go to be given a roof over their head and food to eat in return for their labor.

"No, Livy, I cannot take an unmarried woman into Magdalen House," Regina said bluntly. "Just entering such a place will destroy your reputation and will do the women no good at all. You can help, though, if you wish. Talk to your friends and relatives. We need baby clothes. We need jobs, particularly jobs in the country, particularly jobs where a 'widow' might be permitted to have a baby with her. It is safest for the women to pretend they are widows. Donations of most kinds are appreciated—food, clothing, money."

How irritating that Livy's chastity would be called into question for as simple an act as walking into a building that contained "fallen" women. And how annoying that at least some of the men who had copulated with those women populated the ballrooms of London without censure. Even if their part in fathering children outside of wedlock was known, they would be criticized only for failing to provide for the child, and not for the acts that had led to the child's existence.

How hypocritical. Particularly since, in most cases, the men participated in such activities fully aware of the potential outcomes, but not caring. And why would they? Any consequences would fall almost entirely on the women.

Whereas, and Livy could speak from experience, many women had no idea that a little flattery and a kiss might make a man feel entitled to take more. Still other women—like the poor girl at the house party—trusted promises and avowals of love that were lies.

However, at least she could be useful in some small way. She abandoned her netting projects for knitting and persuaded her father to let her send the kitchen's leftover food to Magdalen House. Her father, after some searching questions, harumphed gruffly, then agreed. Livy was somewhat stunned to realize he seemed proud of her new interest.

The Duchess of Winshire's ball was three weeks after Livy's and Cilla's debut ball, and put the less prestigious event entirely in the shade. Aunt Ginny was in altitudes every time the ball was mentioned, and as the date approached, she planned every detail of the girls' garments, jewelry, and coiffure, then changed her mind and planned again.

Livy was delighted to learn, during one of their morning walks, that Bane and Drake had also received an invitation. She and Cilla agreed to keep that morsel to themselves. Let Aunt Ginny find out on the night.

Indeed, Bane and Drake were being invited everywhere, thanks to their own connections and—Livy believed—the ladies of Jenna's group. Aunt Ginny was torn between being annoyed at their success and delighted that her nieces and daughters were benefiting.

And the rumors that painted their reputations in the darkest of colors had disappeared as if they had never happened.

Jasper remained in Brighton. Aunt Ginny complained to the girls about his absence, but Livy could not see that any of them were disadvantaged. Certainly not his sisters, who had barely seen him since the day after their debut ball. He had put himself out to attend that event and to induce his friends to dance with them, and he had turned up at their first afternoon at home.

Apart from that, he had only seen them when they happened to be present during the farce that was his courtship of Cilla.

Aunt Ginny might have worried about what he was up to while out from under her eye, but at least she did not know. And since she had no influence over him whatsoever, not knowing what he was doing must be less disturbing to her peace of mind. Or, at least, that was Livy's opinion.

Cilla was thrilled to have him absent. "The way he looks at me makes me want to go and scrub myself all over, with soap and hot water," she told Livy. Since Livy felt the same way about Curston, she absolutely understood.

# BANE

BANE AND DRAKE were visiting the Pentworths' new workshop, which had been set up in a building owned by Drew's father. Drew's younger brother, Lord Barnabas, who was himself an engineer, had his own workshop in the same building.

They had been introduced to Lord Barnabas when Pentworth gave them a tour. The two engineering workshops each included copious storage and even a room with a desk for paperwork and a bed for nights when they worked too late to go home. In addition, the building housed a blacksmith's forge.

"The blacksmith works for the duchy," Pentworth told them, "but we have the use of the forge by arrangement with him, and he will also take commissions to do the more crucial pieces that require a higher level of precision."

"It could not be more perfect." Mrs. Pentworth was close to gushing, which was far from her usual practice. "And the new rooms you found for us, Mr. Sanderson, are just a two-minute walk away."

The couple were now living in a mews behind some large houses that had been split up into apartments. Many of what had once been stables and carriage houses for the former owners had also been converted into pleasant, if small, dwellings for rent.

"My sister in Sheffield writes that the men who were sharing the lies about you and us have been exposed, and are facing charges," Mrs. Pentworth added. "Silas and I must thank you for that, too."

Drake said the right thing before Bane had managed to think of an answer. "The attacks on you were because of us, Mrs. Pentworth—because you and your husband allowed us to become your investors. It was only right that we did what we could to restore your reputation along with our own."

The investigators had done their job, finding who was spreading the rumors and tracing them back to Colin. Bane's half-brother had not replied to the lawyer's letter, which warned him that evidence had been filed and a suit for slander laid. But he had withdrawn to Marpleton and—the investigator must have suborned the postmaster—stopped sending letters to his crony in Sheffield and to his friend Curston.

As for Curston and Marple, they also received letters, and withdrew from London entirely. The surge of gossip when the accusations were first made had died down to nothing in their absence. Thanks, in large part, to Livy's ladies—Bane knew, for Jenna Thornstead had told him, that Livy had rallied her and her friends to Bane's and Drake's cause, and with them, their powerful mothers.

Livy. She consumed Bane's thoughts. A lady of fire and steel, and yet with deep veins of vulnerability that she barely showed him and never showed the world. She feared marriage. He had gathered that. She feared the loss of control that marriage implied, and Bane was both unsure that he could convince her to trust him and certain that all his happiness for the rest of his life depended on him finding a way to do so.

"Do you agree, Mr. Sanderson and Mr. Sanderson?" Mrs. Pentworth said, bringing Bane out of his thoughts. He had no idea what he had just been asked, but Drake was nodding and smiling.

Bane was about to admit that he had not been paying attention when they were interrupted. "I believe the gentlemen you seek are through here," said Drew's voice, and it was Drew who looked around the door. "Bane and Drake? There is a messenger here for you. He says it is urgent."

Lord Barnabas threw a sheet over the pile of iron on the floor, and Mrs. Pentworth folded up the engineering diagrams and put them into a drawer.

"Bring the messenger in, Lord Andrew," Pentworth said.

Drake recognized the visitor before Bane did. "Caleb! What are you doing here?" It was a footman from Bancroft House, their old home, and he was wearing a black armband.

"Frannie? The children?" Bane asked.

"It is Mr. Colin, sir. Dead. Mrs. Sanderson sent me. There's a letter." He fumbled in the satchel he wore around his neck and handed a thrice-folded and wax-sealed piece of paper to Bane. "She needs you, sir, and you, too, Mr. Drake, sir."

Bane opened the letter, and Drake came to stand by his elbow and read it with him.

*To my esteemed brothers-in-law.*

*My husband, your brother, has been shot. It may give you comfort to know that he died quickly. I found his last will and testament, and if I could bring him back to life, I would, just so that I could kill him again.*

*He has appointed two of his horrible friends as guardians of our children and trustees for our eldest son, who inherits everything. I need you both, and especially you, Bane, for you know the business. Colin has been bad enough for it. What Marple and Curston will do to it I dread to think.*

*Please come.*

*In frantic need, your devoted sister-in-law,*
*Frances Sanderson.*

"We have to go," Drake said to the Pentworths. "Our brother has died, and his wife has sent for us."

"Caleb, when did you last eat? Or sleep?" Bane asked the footman. The poor man looked exhausted.

Caleb shook his head, frowning. "I rode through last night, Mr. Bane. Had a pie in…" he gave the matter some thought. "Baldock. I think."

The last stage before London. "Right. We'll take you back to our rooms. You can eat again while we pack. I suggest we hire a coach, Drake. Caleb can sleep on the way."

"I am sorry for your loss, Bane and Drake," Drew said. "Please, let us loan you a carriage. I know Father would wish to help you reach your sister and her children as quickly as possible."

Lord Barnabas and the Pentworths echoed the condolences. "I'll ask for a carriage to be prepared," Lord Barnabas told his brother. "Bane and Drake, I'll only be a few minutes."

He was as good as his word, and the carriage was far more comfortable than anything they could have hired. The Winshire stables also provided the horses for the first stage—not the prized Turkmen horses, but superb specimens of horseflesh, nonetheless. And with the carriage came two coachmen, so one could spell the other and they could drive through the night. They had barely pulled away from their own front door before Caleb was asleep.

"Cilla and Livy will be safe while we are gone," Drake said, as if he was trying to convince himself. It was thanks to Cilla and Livy that Caleb had found them at the Pentworth's workshop. Their landlady had sent the footman to the Wintergreens, and the sisters had known their plans for the day.

In his note to Livy, sent with Drake's to Cilla, Bane had thanked her, told her he would miss her, and begged her to be careful. "Mr. Wintergreen knows the danger," he told Drake.

"And the ladies themselves are aware, and have a lot of good sense."

There was no point in regrets. They had to go to support Frannie. Bane wondered how Colin had died. No doubt Frannie would tell them.

# BANE

COLIN HAD BEEN shot by an angry husband who had found their brother in his bed with his wife. Frannie was furious. "I daresay some part of me will grieve for the worm at some point," she said to Bane. "He was, after all, the father of my three children, and I loved him once. When we were first married. Before he disappointed me. At the moment, though, I am so angry with him I have no room for any other emotions. How could he leave me without any way to support the other children? How could he leave us all at the mercy of those two degenerates?"

"Frannie, we will challenge the will," Bane assured her. "Surely no court will give the control of young children—not to mention the business—into the hands of men who are so deeply in debt?"

There was a lot to do. Bane picked up the various threads of the business and Drake spoke to the coroner to find out when the body would be released and then to the vicar and arranged the funeral.

They both spent some time with their nephews and their niece. Only Lewis, the eldest, really understood that his father had gone for good. He did not seem particularly bothered. Apparently, he had not seen his father more than a couple of times a month, and even then, according to Frannie, Colin showed no interest in the lad.

Bane had assumed that Frannie had been largely running the business, and that was confirmed during the next few days.

Colin's contribution had been to cancel her orders, interfere with her decisions, take money from the safe for his own spending, and otherwise hinder her efforts. If Lewis's guardians and trustees left Sanderson Medicinals in Frannie's hands, he would have a healthy company to inherit when he reached twenty-one.

"It is over to us to make certain that happens," Bane said to Drake.

Reluctantly, they made certain that a message was sent to Brighton, to Curston, and Marple. Since they were so prominently named in the will, they should be at its reading, which would take place immediately after the funeral.

By return mail, Frannie received two elegant expressions of condolence, formal phrases with little substance.

Bane also wrote to the lawyer Fullerton had recommended, outlining the problem and asking him what could be done to protect Frannie, the children, and Lewis's inheritance. The brothers braced themselves to confront and oppose the two men when they arrived. But when the day of the funeral came around, they had still not appeared, and the reading of the will went ahead without them.

It was as Frannie had said. Colin had made no provisions for his wife or his two younger children. He had not even left the customary legacies to long-standing servants. Instead, the will left "Everything of which I die possessed to the eldest son of my marriage, Lewis Sanderson." It went on to make provision, in the event that Colin died before Lewis reached his majority, for "my dearest and most esteemed friends, Jasper Viscount Marple and Arthur Curston, to act as guardians of my son Lewis, and trustees of the properties, estates, businesses, and personal possession that I leave to my son Lewis."

The solicitor was a little annoyed that Marple and Curston were not there for the reading, and demanded to know why Frannie had not contacted them.

"The gentlemen were both notified," Bane informed him. "You will stop hectoring the widow."

The solicitor sniffed. "Since Mr. Sanderson did not appoint a guardian for the younger children," he said, "the Court of Chancery will do so. Probably the gentlemen that Mr. Sanderson appointed for Master Lewis Marple, since that would be convenient."

"Those gentlemen are not fit to be guardians for any child, let alone a daughter," Frannie protested.

"We shall challenge their suitability in court," Bane told her. "And Frannie? Since Colin did not leave you anything in his will, you are entitled to the one-third dower portion that is yours by common law."

Or so the London lawyer said in the letter Bane had in his pocket.

"Well," said the solicitor, reluctantly, "that is probably true. Unless there is a reason for the appointed guardians to challenge that amount."

When the sour little man packed his papers back into his briefcase, Frannie gave a sigh of relief. "I know this isn't over," she said to the brothers, "but at least I did not have to deal with Lord Marple and Mr. Curston today."

But why? That was what was bothering Bane. Why had Colin's "dearest and most esteemed friends" missed his funeral? Because they did not care for Colin the way he cared for them? Or was there a more sinister reason?

"Frannie, we have to go back to London."

Frannie's face fell. "Of course, Bane. I have taken you away from your work."

Bane shook his head. "There's nothing we cannot handle from here. At least for a short time. But Frannie, there are two ladies we care about. Marple and Curston have been threatening to force them into marriage. I'm worried…" He trailed off, his concerns too formless to articulate.

"Hell!" Drake cut the expostulation off and shot a shame-faced glance at Frannie. "Sorry, Frannie. Bane, do you really think…? But we cannot take the risk. Frannie, if all is well, we shall come back straight away. We will not leave you to deal with those two horrid men on your own."

Frannie's frown had deepened as they spoke. "You must go. Marple is a stupid boy whose mother has spoiled him, but Curston is vicious. Save your ladies, and write to tell me what I must do next."

She was pulling the servants' bell as she spoke, and when a maid hurried into the room, she gave instructions for "my brothers' carriage to be prepared. They need to hurry back to London."

# Chapter Eighteen

## CILLA

PAPA HAD NO hesitation in permitting Cilla and Livy to join Aunt Ginny and her daughters for a garden party two-hours' drive outside of London. He insisted on sending his own coach driver and a couple of footmen, but none of them expected trouble.

After all, the troublemakers were safely in Brighton.

The garden party was just outside of Watford. The house belonged to a friend of Aunt Ginny's, and the garden was beautifully landscaped into dozens of different spaces, some enclosed with shrubberies, others sunk into the ground, still others with hedges or stone walls. Indeed, though more than one hundred people must have been at the party, Cilla and Livy found themselves following Beryl along a path with no one else in sight except one of Papa's footmen, who had attached himself to the party.

"Are you certain Aunt Ginny said to meet her along here?" Livy asked Beryl.

"She did," Beryl insisted. She seemed sincere, and Beryl had always been an open book, so the sisters descended a flight of stairs and followed a path around a fountain and down another flight from which they could look across a picturesque stand of trees to the spreading waters of a lake.

"I wonder what she wants us for?" Livy commented.

"Surely, it is not much further," Cilla said. They had been walking for a good five minutes, and she could no longer hear the sound of the band that was playing on the terrace outside of the house.

"It cannot be," Beryl agreed. "Mama said through the rose garden, along the yew walk, down two flights of stairs, and across the park to the trees. She is going to meet you there. She did not tell me why. Come on. This is the park and those must be the trees. We are nearly there."

It was still several minutes' walk. Livy was frowning as they strode out across the grass. "After all," whispered Cilla, "what can happen? We are in a private garden, and we have Henry with us."

Livy's frown deepened, but she kept walking, following Beryl.

Then she stopped. "Cilla, this is stupid. If it happened in a horrid romance, we'd be shouting at the heroine, 'Do not go into the woods!' Let us go back to the party. If Aunt Ginny needs us for something, she can find us and tell us."

She was right. Cilla nodded her agreement.

"Mama will be so angry," Beryl whimpered. "She told me it was important. She said she was depending on me."

"We shall tell her not to blame you," Livy assured her. Cilla imagined that Aunt Ginny would be cross with Beryl anyway, but what Livy said about horrid romances had set alarm bells pealing in Cilla's mind. No, not that, exactly. Rather, Cilla had been suppressing her instincts that something was wrong, telling herself that she was being silly. But after all, how much did she trust Aunt Ginny?

*Not very much.*

When they turned back, Henry looked relieved, but they had only taken a few steps before rapidly approaching hoofbeats had them turning. Four men on horses had burst out of the woods and were galloping toward them.

Everything happened so fast! Henry flung out his arms, as if he thought he could stop four horsemen. Three of them swerved and one charged straight at him, swerving to brush past him at the last minute.

Cilla was occupied with the others, but from the corner of her eye she saw the rider raise some kind of a club and strike Henry down.

Beryl had started to scream. The riders were all wearing handkerchiefs over the lower part of their faces, but one of them swore at Beryl in Jasper's voice. "Shut up or I'll lock you in the cellar with the spiders. In the dark."

Beryl subsided into sobs and whimpers.

"Jasper. I might have known," said Livy. She eyed another of the riders. "Curston, I shall not marry you."

"You shall," said Curston, as he dismounted. "Once you are ruined, you will have no choice. Jasper, we are going to have to take your sister, too."

"Idiot girl," Jasper complained. "Why couldn't you leave them to find their own way like you were told? You were not meant to be here."

Jasper was now on the ground and so were the other men. One of them was left to hold the horses while Curston produced rope and he and Jasper proceeded to tie Cilla's hands behind her back. "Don't attempt to run away," Jasper told Cilla, "or I shall tie your legs and throw you over the horse. Livy, stay put."

"I am checking to see whether your accomplice has killed Henry," Livy replied, calmly, and kept walking the few steps to where Henry lay on the grass.

"He's not dead," said the man who had hit him. He sounded nervous. Cilla could not place the voice, but it was not quite an upper class one. He tried, but some of his vowels hinted at an origin in Birmingham or some other Midlands city.

None of the men interfered when Livy bent over and placed her hand on Henry's neck to take his pulse. He shifted at her touch, and Curston growled, "Enough. He is alive. Come here and be tied up."

"No," Livy replied, and without warning, began to scream at the top of her voice.

In half a dozen strides, Curston was on her, and he felled her to the ground with a single blow. After that, though she struggled and it took all three of them, they gagged her and tied her, hands, and feet, and slung her over one of the horses.

"I do not have to tie you, Miss Beryl, do I? You will walk along with us without trouble?" The tone of Curston's question made it a threat, and Beryl shook her head and then nodded it, her eyes wide in her pale face.

There were too many of them and they were too strong, so Cilla walked when she was told to walk. Beryl kept babbling, "I didn't know. Cilla and Livy, I didn't know," until Jasper threatened to gag her if she didn't shut up.

"Don't make out it is a tragedy, you stupid girl," he said. "Curston and I are going to marry the sisters, and we're better matches than girls like them could expect. We are doing them a favor. You'll see."

Cilla would not marry Jasper. No matter if he compromised her. No matter if he gagged her and dragged her before a bribed priest—for such matches were illegal and invalid, and she would escape him at the first opportunity and sue for an annulment.

There Livy's fascination with the crimes of men against women was proving useful, for if she had not read out loud about such a case, Cilla would not have known that, if he forced marriage on her against her will, he would not be able to keep her *or* her dowry. Yes, the woman mentioned in the newspaper lost her reputation—which was so unfair, because it wasn't her fault. Better that, though, than a lifetime with Jasper.

They had entered the woods and passed through them. On the other side was a bridle path where another man waited with a carriage.

This was it then. No last-minute rescue. They were being abducted.

# BANE

ONCE MORE, THE brothers finished the distance from Marpleton to London in an astoundingly short time, stopping only to change horses and to swap drivers, and arriving in the mid-afternoon. The carriage dropped them at the front door of their lodging house, but before Bane could put the key in the door, he was interrupted.

"Is one of you gentlemen Mr. Sanderson?" The inquiry came from a small non-descript man who had been sitting on the steps, looking so inoffensive that both brothers had ignored him. Jumpy as they were, the act, if it had been one, was impressive.

"My brother and I are both Sandersons," said Drake. "I'm Drake, and this is Bane."

"Then my message is for you both, sirs," said the man. "David Wakefield sent me."

Wakefield. The investigator—or *inquiry agent*, as he called himself.

"Wakefield sent two of us to Brighton to keep an eye on Mr. Curston and Lord Marple, sir. I am sorry to say, sirs, that they evaded us yesterday evening. It took us a while to pick up their trail. They came back to London, and visited Lord Curston, Mr. Curston's father. Lady Marple was also at Lord Curston's house. Fortunately, Wakefield had an agent watching Lord Curston's house, and he was able to report their arrival. It appears, sirs, that Lady Marple had spent the night and was preparing to leave for home when her son and Lord Curston's son arrived."

Bane raised an eyebrow. Someone—he forgot who—had suggested that Lord Curston and Lady Marple were more than friends. Apparently, it was true. "Are Marple and Curston still in London?" he asked.

"No, sir. That is why I am here. They rode out in the direction of Watford. As did Lady Marple, a few hours later, with Miss

Wintergreen and Miss Lucilla Wintergreen."

Bane turned away from the door, energy surging into his muscles as his every instinct ordered him to speed to wherever Livy might be.

"Mr. Wakefield has gone to report to Mr. Wintergreen," the agent was saying. "He suggests we meet you there."

They ran, stopping only when they were hailed by Wart, who offered them a lift in his curricle—"To wherever you need to be in such a hurry."

They explained as he drove, keeping the horses at a trot and weaving expertly around any obstructing traffic. When he dropped them at Wintergreen's door, he said, "I'll be back shortly with horses for you."

"Thank you," Bane said, fervently, while Drake hammered on the Wintergreen door.

# DRAKE

MR. WINTERGREEN INSISTED on coming in his traveling carriage, but Drake and Bane soon outstripped him on the borrowed horses. Wart had come, too, and Garry, who had joined the expedition when he had arrived at Wart's to pick up his wife from a visit to Jenna. At a mile-swallowing canter, they rode the distance to Watford in under an hour and a half.

Drake ignored the fear coursing through him, telling himself over and over that they would arrive to find that the girls were safely in Lady Marple's care and that Curston and Marple had not been unable to reach them.

No such luck. They arrived to find Lord Curston handing Lady Marple into her traveling carriage. At a glance, Drake could see that Ruby Marple had been crying, and Pearl looked anguished. Of their sister Beryl, and of Cilla and Livy, there was no sign.

Bane wasted no time on courtesy. Dismounting, he demanded, "Where are the two Miss Wintergreens?"

"Gone," Pearl answered on a wail. "Beryl, too. Mama will not say…"

"Be silent, you foolish girl," said Lady Marple. "This man has no right to demand answers from us."

"Nonetheless." Bane took a couple of steps closer, until he loomed over Lady Marple. He pushed his hood back and glared down at the woman. "Where are they?"

"She would not let us look for them," Ruby told him, choking back a sob. "She said they were being looked after."

"Mr. Sanderson and Mr. Sanderson!" Drake recognized the speaker as one of Wintergreen's footmen. He was being half supported by another of them, with a third man hovering behind. The carriage driver called out, "There you be! You near got left be'ind!"

"Henry, isn't it?" Drake remembered.

"Yes, sir. They came out of the woods, sir. Four of them, on horseback. One of them coshed me, and I don't know what happened after that."

"Did you recognize any of them?" Bane asked.

"Yes, sir," said Henry. "Lord Marple and Mr. Curston, sir. Also Mr. Curston's valet. He was the one what coshed me."

"Where did they take the ladies?" Bane demanded of Lady Marple, who shrank away from his harsh tones and burst into tears. Or perhaps it was his face that frightened her, for he was pale, and his knot of scars stood out red against his white skin. His mouth was set in a snarl, and his mis-matched eyes blazed.

Bane turned on Lord Curston. "Where?"

"See here, young man," Curston blustered. "I do not appreciate your tone."

"And I do not appreciate you conniving at the kidnapping of my betrothed," Bane snapped back.

"I say." The speaker was another of those present—there were perhaps twenty or more finely-dressed ladies and gentlemen on the carriageway, or on the steps leading down from the house, all gawking at the spectacle of Bane confronting Lady Marple and Lord Curston.

The portly gentleman who spoke was not wearing boots or a traveling coat, so in all likelihood was the host. "I say," he repeated. "What is going on?"

"This peasant has attacked and maligned me, Lord Finch," said Curston, his chest swelling.

"Three young ladies who arrived here with Lady Marple are missing," Drake said. "Miss Wintergreen, Miss Lucilla Wintergreen, and Miss Beryl Marple. The Wintergreen's footman, Henry, was with them, and was knocked out by four assailants on horseback."

"Nonsense," said Lady Marple, who seemed to have remembered her backbone. "My nieces have accepted a ride with my son and Lord Curston's son, and my daughter has gone to chaperone them. Nothing wrong with that. No doubt these louts have paid this servant to malign our dear boys, just because the Miss Wintergreens prefer suitors with breeding." She stuck her nose in the air and sniffed with contempt.

"'Enry 'ere were knocked out right enough," said the man with the two footmen. "Me an' George found 'im 'obblin' in from the park, all woozy, like."

"The guests at the garden party did not go down into the park," said the lady who had come to tuck her hand into the host's arm. Lady Finch, Drake presumed.

"Livy and Cilla did," Ruby said. "Beryl took them there. She said Mama wanted to meet them in the park. She went with them to show them where."

The last sentence was shouted over Lady Marple's demands that she shut her mouth, and from behind Bane, where she had taken refuge from her mother's attempts to strike her.

"Who are you?" Lord Finch demanded of Bane, who was occupied in trying to protect Ruby without taking hold of or otherwise assaulting Lady Marple. Drake envied his control. He wanted to tear the sister's aunt limb from limb until she disclosed the whereabouts of the girls.

He forced himself to an assumption of calm. "I am Mr. Drake Sanderson." Drake took a leaf from Bane's book and claimed a status that would give him the right to pursue the kidnappers. "I am Miss Lucille's betrothed, and my brother, Mr. Bane Sanderson, is betrothed to Miss Wintergreen. Our companions are Lord Thornstead and Lord Wharton."

The introduction set the onlookers twittering.

"The Duke of Dellborough's boy?" said Finch.

"The same, sir," said Garry, with a bow. "May I have your permission to check the place where the footman was assaulted, to see if we can find any trace of the stolen ladies?"

"Carry on," said Lord Finch, with a wave of his hand. "Are you up to showing them the way, lad?" he asked Henry. Drake's opinion of the man went up a notch for his kindness.

"I'll take you up behind me, Henry," said Garry, and they set off, with the other footman jogging alongside.

Lady Marple was still denying everything, but Lord Finch had clearly decided there was at least a case to answer. Lord Curston, on the other hand, was sidling toward another carriage.

"Lord Finch," said Drake, "are you the local magistrate, sir?"

"I have that honor, Mr. Sanderson."

"Then can you please insist, sir, that Lady Marple and Lord Curston remain here until Mr. Wintergreen arrives? He is the father of two of the missing ladies, and follows us here by carriage."

Lady Marple heard that and stopped in mid-sentence. "Horace is coming?" she demanded, and then bolted for the carriage, shouting up at the coachman, "Drive on. Quickly."

Lord Finch raised his eyebrows and gave the coachman a look. "No problem, me lord," the man said. "Me an' the 'orses'll just stay right 'ere till yer lordship sez the word."

Two of Finch's footman, at a gesture from their master, were ushering Lord Curston back into the house.

"Can you let Mr. Wintergreen know that we and Lord Thornstead will search until we find the ladies?" Bane said to Lord Finch. "Come on, Drake, Wart."

"Sir," Drake said, "could you spare us fresh horses? And a couple of grooms to ride back and forth with messages? That way, you can let us know if Lady Marple or Lord Curzon disclose anything that would help. And we can keep Mr. Wintergreen informed."

"Good idea," said Lord Finch. "Albinus, my boy? Erasmus?" A pair of young men who looked like an amalgam of Lord and Lady Finch stepped forward. "Go with these gentlemen, my lads. My sons, Mr. Sanderson."

"We'll fetch enough horses for us all and follow you, sir," said one of the men.

*Good enough*. Bane was waiting impatiently. The brothers left their mounts to the care of Lord Finch's stables and strode together in the direction that Garry had gone.

Chapter Nineteen

## LIVY

L IVY HAD EXPECTED they would throw the three of them into
the carriage and continue on horseback. That way, she and
Cilla could persuade Beryl to untie them.

No such luck. Jasper and Curston crowded into the carriage,
and Curston sat between her and Beryl, while Jasper took the
back facing seat alongside Cilla. Livy hoped they were not
traveling some distance, or over a rough road. Cilla had never
been able to manage for long in a backward facing seat, and she
was gagged, so if she became sick…

Frightened for her sister, Livy tried to speak, to warn the
men, but Curston laughed at the noises she made.

"I cannot understand you, Olivia," he said. "Stop trying, or I'll
give you something to make a noise about. Jasper, I might keep
her gagged until she learns to obey me. What do you think? No
one needs a wife who is a scold."

"She's trying to tell you…" Beryl began, but Jasper hissed,
"Shut your mouth, Beryl, or I'll gag you, too."

Curston put his arm around Livy and pulled her against his
body, and then pawed at her breasts. "They're as big as they
look," he said to Jasper, sounding delighted. Fear, disgust, and

anger made a nauseating mix. Livy's gut might prove to be as treacherous as her sister's. Though it would serve this cur right if she choked on her own vomit right in his lap, she forced herself to swallow the reaction. She would live to see him suffer for this, dammit.

"Here, Curston, let her go," Jasper ordered. "You cannot paw her like that in front of my sister."

"But we agreed that the sooner—" Curston began.

Jasper interrupted. "Not in front of my sister, I said. We'll have to wait until we get to the cottage. We have plenty of time. Even if they find the footman, Mama and your father will stop people from following us. And even if someone does come after us, they won't know where to go."

Jasper had a thread of decency left. Was there hope in that? Not enough to rely on. *But Henry was conscious. He winked at me. With luck, he will get help and pursuit will not be far behind.* Livy was holding to that thought with all her might.

"That's true," Curston acknowledged. "Very well. Stop the carriage. If I can't have my way with your cousin, I'm going to ride."

"Good idea. Let's tie Beryl up so she can't untie the others, and I'll come too."

Jasper banged on the hatch between the carriage interior and the coachman, and ordered the carriage stopped, then Curston descended, leaving the carriage door open.

"Cilla gets sick in carriages," Beryl whimpered to Jasper. "Please take her gag off, Jasper." *Thank goodness Beryl spoke up.* Livy had been terrified for her sister.

"You're making that up. I've traveled with her before."

"Short distances, and when she is facing the way carriage is going," Beryl insisted. "Please, Jasper. You can't marry her if she chokes to death."

*Good girl, Beryl.*

Cilla, her eyes wide above the gag, nodded vigorously.

Curston climbed back aboard with a coil of rope. Jasper reported, "We need to put Cilla in the forward-facing seat and take the gag off. Beryl says she gets sick in carriages."

"We'll tie Beryl up first." They did so, Curston binding her hands behind her back and Jasper tying her ankles together. Then Jasper untied Cilla's gag, lifted her, and put her on the other carriage seat.

"Me, too," Livy did her best to say, but could only make noises. Nonetheless, Jasper understood and went to undo her gag, but Curston stopped him. "Not Olivia. Let her remain gagged. I don't trust her not to be plotting against us."

He was quite right, too, the dastard. But if he thought Cilla would not be plotting against them, he didn't know her at all.

Moments later, they were gone, and the carriage was underway again. The three girls looked at one another. "Beryl," Cilla said. "I mean no offense to you, but I am not going to agree to marry your brother under any circumstances. And Livy will not agree to marry Curston, will you Livy?"

Livy nodded, which was the best she could do. And if he went through some form of ceremony anyway, she would run at her first opportunity, and Pa would help her to have the marriage annulled.

"It won't be a legal marriage, Beryl," Cilla explained, "if we do not consent, or if our consent is forced from us."

"I can see why you do not want to marry Jasper," Beryl admitted. "I would love to have you as a sister, but I would not want to be married to someone like Jasper. As for Curston…!" She shuddered, and Livy agreed wholeheartedly.

"Then we can count on your help?" Cilla insisted. "If there is a chance to escape, you will help us to take it?"

"Mama wants this marriage," Beryl said, doubtfully. "She says we would be out in the streets if it were not for Uncle Horace. She says she does not want to be going cap in hand to your father all the time. We need your dowry, Cilla, for Jasper cannot seem to mend his ways, and he is very expensive."

She turned to Livy. "And she wants your dowry for Lord

Curston, Livy, for he and his son are very expensive, too. I think they gamble a lot. Mama, too. Uncle Horace told her he will pay for her servants and her clothes, but not for her card parties."

Tears filled Beryl's eyes. "She says they are debts of honor, and she has had to borrow to pay them. If she does not pay the loan people, we will be out on the streets. I don't want to be out on the streets, Livy, Cilla. Where would we sleep? Where would we keep our gowns?"

Beryl had no idea, obviously. If Livy could have spoken, she would have told her that she and her sisters, without Pa's help, would be working for a living—as governesses, perhaps. Of very young children, for none of the three had much of an education. Working in a respectable position, and fighting of the advances of an employer or an employer's son. Or worse. Working in a non-respectable position, where accepting advances was part of the job.

Gentle Cilla was instead explaining that, even if Pa withdrew his support from Aunt Ginny, as he had from Jasper, he would continue to keep his nieces fed, clothed, and housed. "It is foolish, what your brother is doing," she pointed out. "He won't get his hands on my dowry by forcing me to the altar. I am not of age, so the marriage is invalid even if I consented, and I do not. Anyway, without Papa's consent, he is under no obligation to pay the dowry to my husband or to Livy's, for that matter."

Beryl shook her head. "Mama said he will have to pay the dowry, once people know that you and Jasper have been alone together. For days!"

*And nights.* Livy shuddered.

"He will not do it," said Cilla, firmly. "Not to mention that, if for some reason I am unsuccessful in getting the marriage annulled, I shall very likely finish up smothering my unwanted husband with a pillow. I know he is your brother, Beryl, but I really do not like him."

Perhaps not so gentle Cilla, then. Livy heartily approved of the sentiment.

"Oh dear," said Beryl.

"Can we count on your help, Beryl?" Cilla insisted, "Or must we fight you as well as those two villains?"

"Oh dear," Beryl said again. "Oh, very well then. Yes, Cilla. You and Livy can count on me."

*Not*, Livy thought, *without our eyes wide open*. Beryl had always been the most suggestible of their cousins, and she was frightened of her mother and brother both.

"You and Livy can count on me" lasted until the carriage stopped outside a little cottage surrounded by trees. Jasper untied Beryl so she could walk. The coachman, another servant who appeared to be Curston's valet, and the fifth man, who was obviously a groom, were sent off to rooms above the stables. Jasper and Curston carried the sisters inside.

"Beryl, you can have the cook's room," Jasper said. "It is off the kitchen. There are only two other bedchambers."

"Can I not share one of them with Livy and Cilla, while you and Lord Curston share the other?" Beryl asked.

Jasper rolled his eyes. "I am sharing with Cilla, and Curston is sharing with Livy, you silly girl."

"Cilla says she will not marry you, and that her father will not give you her dowry even if she does," Beryl reported. "She said if she cannot get an annulment, she will smother you with your pillow."

If looks could set one on fire, Cilla would have gone up in smoke from the glare that Jasper shot at her. "You *shall* marry me, Lucilla Wintergreen. If you do not, you will be ruined. You will have to retreat from Society, and everyone will shun you. You'll never find a decent husband. As for your father, Mama says he will not wish to see you living in poverty. He will have to give me your dowry, or you will suffer."

Cilla snorted. "Do you think I care what a lot of spoilt aristocrats think?" she said. "As for a decent husband, Jasper, do you think you will be one? For I do not. You are a spoilt brat with no talents or self-control, who only wants his own way."

"Why, you…!" Jasper took an angry step toward the couch on which he had deposited Cilla, but hitting a bound woman was apparently a step too far, even for him.

"Lock your sister in her room and let's get to it," Curston said. "The sooner they have no choice, the better."

"You can bed me," Cilla commented. "You are stronger than I am and you can force me. But you cannot force me to consent to marriage with you. Perhaps I shall suffer, Jasper, as you say. But you are facing hurt that you have never conceived. And this applies to you, Curston, too. Force us, and my father shall destroy you. The Sanderson brothers, too, shall not cease until they have taken everything from you, and you are forced to dress in rags and beg in the streets."

"Gag her again," Curston advised. "I certainly do not plan to take Olivia's gag off. Indeed, I daresay she would like to unman me with her knees, so I shall tie her to the bed. In fact, if you want to help me tie Olivia, I'll help you tie Lucilla."

A spark of unholy excitement lit his eyes as he made the proposal. He clearly liked the idea of making Livy immobile, unable to resist, unable even to participate.

"That is horrible," said Beryl. "Jasper, you mustn't. It is wicked."

"Shut up, Beryl," Jasper told her. "You should not even be here."

"I need to use the chamber pot," Cilla announced. "Livy? Do you need to use the chamber pot?"

Livy nodded. Delay. That was the best bet. Give any pursuers time to catch up. *If they are coming. If they have not lost our trail.*

*No.* She must not let herself despair. Hold on to anger. Delay as much as she could. Besides, she really *did* need to use the chamber pot.

There followed an unpleasant interlude. Curston refused to allow their arms to be untied or for any of the women to leave the room. Jasper baulked at either man attending the ladies in such an intimate task. So Jasper had Beryl untie Cilla's legs, and hold the chamber pot for her, while arranging her gown to protect her from the men's view—Beryl told the men that they must turn their backs, and Jasper did, but Curston leered until Jasper noticed and punched his arm.

Once Cilla had finished, Beryl, who was crying in embarrassment or shame or a combination of the two, performed the same office for Livy. Livy kept herself from such emotions by focusing on her anger. Jasper and Curston would pay. Especially Curston. Livy would make sure of it.

# BANE

BY THE TIME the two sons of Lord Finch joined the hunt, Garry had found a trail through the woods, and carriage tracks leading away. The young men had had the forethought to bring a groom with them to lead Garry's bay and Wart's chestnut back to the stables.

"They have a thirty-minute head start on us," Bane said. Thirty minutes was more than enough for a ravishment, especially if they did not wait until their destination, wherever it was.

"I don't think they'll rape our ladies in the carriage," Drake pointed out. "Not with Jasper's sister present."

That was true, and something of a comfort. Not that it changed Bane's determination to offer Livy the security of his name, but at the idea of his Livy suffering an intimate assault, he wanted to howl. He wanted to tear Curston limb from limb.

"We are here far sooner than they could have expected," Garry said. "Even checking every offshoot of the path, we shall make up much of the time, especially if they have any distance to travel."

They took off from standing to a full-out gallop, watching both sides for any indication of a side path, slowing to a walk from time to time to make certain they were still following the carriage and horse tracks. The trail soon turned to run between dense hedgerows with few gates, and with the late spring growth lush and tall around many of those, so that a carriage and escort of horses, such as they followed, could not have left the road without leaving obvious signs of passage.

At the few side lanes or forks in the road, they paused to confer about which way their quarry had taken. "Garry must have eyes like a hawk," Drake muttered at one of their stops. Bane was glad of it. Garry had dismounted to check some tracks that Bane and Drake had not even noted.

"They stopped here," he said. "Two people—probably men from their weight—left the carriage and mounted horses."

Without further words, he wheeled the mount Finch had supplied and rode off at a slower pace toward another crossroads.

"He must be a good hunter," one of the Finches commented.

"Very," said the other. "Was the bay with the white blaze his? Came from London in under two hours, and looked ready to keep going."

"It is part Turkmen," Bane told them, "from the Earl of Sutton's stud." The Earl of Sutton, the Duke of Winshire's heir, was crossing his stallions and mares with the best that England had to offer. "If you have a lot of money, you might be able to buy one," he said.

Garry had chosen a road to follow, and the other five riders turned in that direction.

The young man's eyes lit up. "Did you hear that, Ras?"

"Doubt your allowance'll run to it, Albie," said his brother.

At that moment, they reached another long stretch where they could give their horses their heads, and there was no more talking.

Ten minutes later, Garry stopped again. "They turned off here," he reported, pointing to flattened grass and fresh wheel ruts and hoof marks barely visible in a patch of dry earth where a gate into an overgrown lane had been pushed back until it was half open, leaving a space barely wide enough for a carriage to edge through.

He dismounted and began walking cautiously along the edge of the lane, keeping low, scanning the terrain as he walked.

A turn in the lane brought them within view of a barn, with a glimpse of a cottage beyond. "Let's tie the horses and go on foot," Wart suggested.

They were skirting the barn when they heard voices from an open window above their heads. Men—at least three of them, by the different voices—arguing about whether or not they needed to set a guard.

Garry pointed upward and jerked his head toward the side door to the barn. Would the kidnappers have taken the women to the barn loft? Surely not, and Bane's heart yearned toward the cottage. Every second they spent here might be one more second of suffering for Livy and Cilla.

But they had to check the barn. There were too few of them to risk splitting their forces. He exchanged glances with Drake, who had also been gazing in the direction of the cottage. Bane pointed to Garry, Wart, and the Finch brothers and up toward the barn loft, then to himself and Drake, and to the cottage.

Garry nodded, and led the way into the barn through a side door.

Bane and Drake continued on around the barn. From above, the voices continued arguing until they were suddenly cut off. One man had time to yell, but as Bane and Drake approached the cottage, the bulk of the barn muffled the noise from the open window on its far side.

It was a small cottage—the kind that had bedchambers in the roof and a simple downstairs plan of several rooms. From within came the sound of a woman, shouting.

"You can't, Jasper. It is wicked. Don't do it. Don't let Curston do it." The voice was somewhat familiar. Not Livy, nor Cilla. Beryl, then. Drake was at Bane's shoulder as he hurried toward the door.

"Get out of my way, you silly bitch." That was Curston.

"Don't shove my sister!" Jasper shouted.

"Do you want to swive your Cilla, or not?" Curston demanded. "Shut your stupid sister in the cook's room and let's get to it."

*We are not too late.* Fury flooded Bane's mind to the exclusion of all except that single bright thought. He was about to put his shoulder to the door when Garry ran up, reached past him and opened it. The three of them crowded inside, to see Curston standing over Beryl, who was standing with her arms outspread in front of Livy and Cilla, both of them bound, and Livy also gagged. Jasper was beside Curston, grimacing in discomfort.

For a moment, the two men were too focused on the women in front of them to hear the commotion behind them, and by the time they turned, it was too late. Bane's fist met Curston's chin, and for a brief time, he was focused on pounding the fiend into flinders.

It was Livy's voice that brought him back to himself. "Bane, he is unconscious. Stop now, please." His mind struggled to surface from his killing rage, but her next words acted like a bucket of cold water, washing away the heat of battle. Or not the words so much as the fact that his dear Amazon's voice shook when she said, "I need you."

He dropped Curston, leaving him to Garry who was standing ready to bind the villain as Wart was already doing with Jasper. Someone must have untied the sisters while he was dealing with Curston, for his beloved was standing, rubbing her wrists. He opened his arms and Livy walked into them. She rested her head on his chest and sighed, small quivers that were not quite sobs running through the body that he cradled in his arms.

"What took you so long?" she asked.

"Livy!" Cilla objected from her own haven in Drake's arms, but Bane laughed. That was his warrior queen, making jokes even now.

"I apologize for my tardiness, Livy," he said, and she looked up.

"I am so glad to see you, Bane." Her smile was all the reward he needed.

# Chapter Twenty

## DRAKE

T HE FINCH BROTHERS had been left to truss the henchmen—
three of them—and had done a good job of it. They put the
five miscreants into their own carriage, trussed up like poultry for
the oven.

Just to be sure, Wart found a hammer and nails in the barn,
and nailed both doors shut. If anyone escaped their bounds, they
were going no farther, though Drake rather wished Jasper would
succeed. The man had gone down at the first blow. Deprived of
the fight his rage needed, Drake would welcome an excuse to
punch Jasper again.

Wart announced that he had driven a carriage before, and
proceeded to demonstrate, and Albinus Finch went on ahead to
give news of the rescue to their father and Mr. Wintergreen, who
should have arrived at Lord and Lady Finch's by now.

Garry apologized to the three ladies. "We don't have sidesad-
dles for the horses, ladies."

"I do not need a sidesaddle," Beryl declared. "I can ride astride
if someone helps me to mount, but Cilla and Livy do not ride.
They will have to go up behind someone."

Drake turned to Cilla and she nodded before he had asked.

Good, for he was not letting her beyond the reach of his arm.

Bane was already unbuckling the girth of his horse's saddle. With the help of the other men, the two of them rigged a pad out of a colorful blanket behind the saddle, anchoring it firmly under the saddle.

Drake mounted, and Bane lifted Cilla up behind him, to sit sideways behind the saddle with her knees together on one side and her arms around his waist. At the touch of her, his emotions began to settle. Garry, meanwhile, lifted Beryl up and then mounted his own horse.

Bane indicated a mounting block, half-hidden in weeds. He escorted Livy up onto the block while leading his horse, then mounted and rode his horse to where Livy could simply take the hand he offered her to help her balance, and sit down.

Typical Bane. No showy moves. Just planning, resolve, and efficient action.

"Are you comfortable, Cilla?" Drake asked.

"I am," Cilla said.

His heart settled a little more.

"We shall walk," declared Bane. "Both for the ladies' sake, and for the horses, who have already traveled eight miles here, and must cover the same distance back."

"Did that fiend hurt you in any way?" Drake asked quietly, once they were out in the road, part of a long line of horses following the carriage.

"Jasper? My cousin is too much of an idiot to be a fiend. I'm not saying he might not have gone along with Mr. Curston if Beryl hadn't been there. But he felt compelled to be at least a little bit of a gentleman in front of his sister."

"I'm grateful for it," Drake said. Although it didn't make him feel better about Jasper. The wretch had threatened Drake's lady. He must never be able to do so again.

"I am, too," Cilla said. "Beryl did her best, Drake. She is afraid of her mother and her brother, but she helped as much as she could."

What was Beryl's role in the kidnapping? Why were the three ladies out on the park where they could be captured? Drake had his suspicions. He changed the subject.

"I told Lord Finch and Lady Marple that we are betrothed," he admitted. "She was trying to stop his lordship from sending out help—though we would have come anyway, so she was doomed to fail. But it was better to have the magistrate on our side."

"Betrothed?" Cilla repeated.

"The thing is," Drake continued, "most of the guests hadn't left the party, and a lot of them were listening. Do you mind very much?"

"Mind what?" Cilla suddenly sounded very much like her sister. "Mind being kidnapped? Mind almost being assaulted? Mind being rescued? Mind being informed—informed, mind you, not asked—that I am suddenly betrothed?"

"Um—" Drake sensed the need for caution. "Three out of four? I do not suppose you mind being rescued." It suddenly occurred to him what she was saying. "All were without your consent. That was wrong. I understand that. I spoke without asking you first. I am sorry for that, but it seemed essential at the time. To protect your good name, and perhaps—if the worst had happened—give you grounds for an annulment."

"They are sound reasons, I suppose," Cilla admitted.

"You forgive me, then? For saying that you and I are betrothed?"

"Yes? But you don't have to… We can change our minds when the fuss dies down."

"I will not change my mind, though you can, if that is what you truly wish. I have been courting you for months—or weeks, anyway. Lucilla Wintergreen, would you do me the very great honor of marrying me? I am not the richest of your admirers, or the most talented. I am certainly not the best looking. I have no title and my blood is not blue. But not another man in the world esteems you as I do. And not another man needs you as I do. As my wife, my partner, my friend, my lover. When I arrived at the Finches' and found you gone, I glimpsed the void my life would be without you in it." A deep dark hole with no light and no hope. "Rescue me, Cilla, my love. Marry me."

Cilla had been holding lightly onto his coat with one hand while sitting upright on the pad of blanket. She leaned against him now, reaching her hands around him as far as she could, and resting her head against his back. "Yes," she said. "Oh, my darling. Yes, I will marry you, and be all those things you just said."

He freed one of his hands from the reins to press it over hers, where they clasped together in front of his chest. "My wife, my partner, my friend, my lover. For all of our lives together."

# BANE

LIVY WAS SITTING stiffly, quietly, behind Bane, her only contact with him one hand gripping his coat.

He endured the silence for as long as he could, understanding her need to retreat into herself after such an experience. When he could stand it no longer, the words that tormented him burst out. "Did he hurt you?"

Had he been too late, he meant, but she took the words at their face value. "Some abrasions from the rope on my wrists and ankles. Some bruising from being tossed around like a sack of grain. A horrid taste in my mouth from the rag they stuffed into it. Considerable injury to my dignity."

*Is that all* would be the wrong thing to say. If she had been violated, she was not prepared to talk about it, and he would not further damage her dignity by being more specific in his questions.

He would settle for doing something about the taste in her mouth. He reached around inside his coat with one hand without taking his eyes off the road. There it was. His inside pocket, and within it, his flask, which he handed over his shoulder.

"Here. Have a sip of this. It is brandy, and will help with the taste."

Her fingers touched his as she took the flask. A moment later, she said, "It bites. I am not sure that I like it."

"Give it a minute, and you will get the flavors," Bane said. "A couple more sips would not hurt, either."

"Sort of sour and bitter, but fruity." She was silent again for a moment. "A sweetness, too. How odd. It helps, Bane. Thank you."

"Keep the flask," he offered. "Sip when you wish, but be cautious. It is very strong. If you are not accustomed to strong drink, it might affect you more quickly than you expect."

"Not necessarily a bad thing," she mused.

That she was arguing was a good sign, surely? "It will be if you fall off the back of the horse," he retorted, and was rewarded with a hiccup of a laugh.

"If I fall off, I shall blame you," she retorted.

He should tell her that they were betrothed. No, that he had claimed they were betrothed, and she would need to agree to save her reputation. She was not going to be pleased, and he didn't want to upset her. Wasn't it better for her to have the peace of the journey before she had to deal with the turmoil that was sure to be waiting for them?

But no. She deserved to be warned, but he could wait until they were nearly at the Finches'. They rode on in a companiable silence.

The distance they had traveled at such speed a short time before was farther than he'd realized. It must have been nearly an hour before he could see the towers of Finch Court ahead of him. "Livy, there is something I need to tell you. At Finch Court, when we confronted your aunt and Lord Curston, Drake and I told them and Lord Finch that we were betrothed to you and Cilla. A lot of other people were listening."

Livy stiffened. "Oh," was all she said.

Bane felt the need to explain. "Lady Marple and Lord Curston were claiming that you had gone willingly with their sons, that you had consented to marry them. Saying you were already betrothed to us gained us Lord Finch's support to pursue you, and gave you some protection from the gossips. I am sorry if you do not like it."

"I do not plan to marry," said his future wife, firmly. "You know that. The whole world knows it. Cilla, I think, favors your brother. She can wed him, and I shall retire to Liverpool and ignore the Polite World."

"Is it that…?" He had left it too late. They had turned in at the gates to the mansion. The Finch brothers and a dozen other people crowded as close as they dared to the horses carrying the rescued maidens, their words consoling and encouraging, and their eyes avid with the glee of a good scandal.

With no further time for private conversation, Bane had to leave it, and hope that she would at least understand the sense of using the cover of the fake betrothal today, and until the fickle ton had turned their attention elsewhere.

# Livy

PA WAS WAITING for them, striding impatiently back and forth across the forecourt of Finch Hall, his balled-up hands clenched at his side. Lord Finch and several of his guests stood on or by the steps to the front door, and started forward as the riders approached, with the carriage containing the villains behind them.

Ignoring everyone else, Pa made straight for the horse bearing Cilla, and was there to lift her down and fold her in his arms as soon as Drake halted the horse.

Bane waited until Drake had dismounted and the horse had been led away to bring their horse up beside Pa, but he had all his attention on Cilla and didn't notice. It was Drake who helped

Livy to reach the ground, and Bane who said, "Mr. Wintergreen, here is Livy."

Keeping one arm around Cilla, Pa reached out the other. "Olivia, my dear girl. Olivia, I have been so worried. I should have abandoned that rapscallion to the debt collectors months ago! I should never have listened to Virginia when she told me he was reforming."

"She was part of this, Pa," Livy told him. "She and Lord Curston."

"Why have you tied up my son?" The bellow came from Lord Curston, who had emerged from the house and was glaring at the carriage, where Garry was supervising as some of Lord Finch's men passed out the bound forms of the kidnappers.

"Your son," Pa bellowed back, "abducted my daughters."

"*If*—and I say 'if'—my son offended your daughters, the remedy is easy." Curston was no longer shouting, but his voice was still pitched to carry to the furthest corner of the courtyard. "He will give Olivia the protection of his name, and in due time, the title of viscount. What do you say to that, eh?" His smile spread wide, he clasped his hands behind his back, and bounced up and down on his heels, as if he had just accomplished something praiseworthy.

"Your son will not be permitted to benefit from his perfidy, you scoundrel," Pa declared. He, too, managed a volume worthy of the finest of actors. "Fortunately, both of my daughters are already betrothed."

His arm tightened around Livy for a moment. "To two fine upstanding young men who are already on their way to becoming men of real worth—both financially and in character."

Livy opened her mouth, and Pa whispered, "Let it be, Livy. For Cilla's sake." Livy looked around at the curious crowd, avidly waiting for some piece of scandal they could use in a letter. For Cilla's sake then, and for the moment. She would clear the error up after this was all over.

Meanwhile, Bane had moved up beside Livy, and on Pa's

other side, Drake stood protectively beside Cilla.

"Lord Finch, perhaps we could continue this without an audience," Bane said to their host.

"Good thinking, good thinking," said Lord Finch. "Bring the prisoners inside, Lord Thornstead." He turned to speak to his butler, who had appeared at his side, though Livy had not seen Lord Finch summon him.

"The servants into the cells," he said in a low voice that Livy only heard because she was just a few feet away. "Lord Marple and Mr. Curston can bide there, too, until I have questioned the witnesses." The butler led away the parade of footmen and bound men, with Lord Thornstead striding alongside and Lord Curston scurrying behind.

"Miss Wintergreen, Miss Lucilla, and Miss Beryl, do you feel up to answering questions?"

Livy nodded. Might as well get it over.

"May I request tea and refreshments for the ladies?" Bane said to Lady Finch. "And, forgive me, but the opportunity to—er— freshen up? They have been through quite an ordeal, and have been given nothing to eat or drink since they were taken from here several hours ago."

"I shall have tea served to Lord Finch's study," said Lady Finch.

"I must be there if my daughter is to be questioned," Aunt Ginny insisted. She might have been there for a while, standing with the other onlookers, but Livy hadn't noticed her until now.

"I will speak to the three young ladies alone, with Lady Finch as their chaperone," Lord Finch insisted.

Pa glared at his sister. "I suggest you go to your room, Virginia, and contemplate your future. You and your son are dead to me from this day."

Aunt Ginny stomped her foot, burst into tears, and rushed back into the house. Livy wondered what would become of her. Pa would look after his nieces, of course. But he was not one to easily change his mind, and Aunt Ginny and Jasper had directly and repeatedly flouted his direct wishes.

Bane was offering her his arm. "May I escort you to Lord Finch's study? And afterward, we should talk."

"Yes," she said. Yes, they needed to talk. Livy was suddenly and overwhelmingly weary. Would this day ever end?

It did, of course, after many questions from Lord Finch. Then more—intrusive and not to the point—from the guests, who should have gone home by now, but who were hanging on for fear of missing something. The grueling inquisition was cut off by Bane, who firmly announced that the Miss Wintergreens and Miss Marples were tired, and that their carriage was waiting.

Sure enough, Pa had apparently gone to bespeak his carriages as soon as Lord Finch finished with the three of them.

"What will happen now?" Cilla asked.

"Mr. Wintergreen is taking you all back to his place," Bane answered. "Lady Marple and Lord Curston have been asked to remain here to 'help Lord Finch with his inquiries'. What will happen to any of them remains to be seen." He sighed. "People of their class seldom pay for their crimes."

Drake was escorting Cilla to the carriage, the two of them with their heads together for all the world as if their betrothal had already been announced. The three Marple sisters were already waiting by the carriage. Beryl had been crying and she and Ruby had their arms around one another. Pearl was pale and serious. Whatever happened, this was going to be a tragedy for them.

"This Season in London, their first, has been the most important thing in their lives for years, Bane. I hope we can save some of it for them."

"Their brother deserves punishment," Bane commented. "Their mother, too."

"But public condemnation for those two would mean ruination for these three," Livy pointed out.

"Perhaps. Or they could make their curtsy in the merchant world, as the nieces of a prominent man," Bane argued.

It was a fair point. Why had Livy and Cilla been so focused on an upper-class debut? *Because it was all Aunt Ginny talked about,* Livy realized. "That could work," she acknowledged.

Bane stopped before they were in earshot of the others.

"*We* could work," he said. "Can we at least talk about it, Livy?"

"Come as usual tomorrow morning," she said. "Take me for a walk."

He nodded. "I'll be there." He proceeded to hand her into the carriage and say farewell to them all. He and Drake were staying until Lord Finch was ready to talk to them, and would then ride back to London.

It would be wonderful to be married to Bane, Livy thought. But she was certain. He wouldn't want her once she told him her history.

## Chapter Twenty-One

### BANE

B ANE BARELY SLEPT. He had no idea whether Livy was just humoring him by giving him a hearing or whether she had something to say. She didn't want to marry. He knew that, so what could he tell her that might change her mind?

He spent the whole night imagining conversations. Any one of them could go horribly wrong, depending how Livy reacted, but he had decided a starting point by the time dawn slipped sullenly through his window, hampered by clouds and an incessant, light rain.

The weather did not improve. "Bane, the weather isn't going to change because you want it to," Drake reminded him. "You have risen to look out of the window nine times in the last hour."

"I promised to go for a walk with Livy," Bane explained.

"Or we could sit in comfort in their parlor for a quiet conversation, and stay dry," Drake said comfortably.

It was all very well for Drake. His lady had agreed to marry him. He had confessed his love and Cilla had returned the sentiment.

Bane wanted the privacy of a walk in the park for his and Livy's talk, but when the brothers left their rooms to walk to the

Wintergreens' townhouse, the steady drizzle continued—light enough to deceive a fool into thinking he could hurry through it without an umbrella, persistent enough to soak anyone so deceived to the skin.

The Sanderson brothers were not deceived. They took a large umbrella each, walking together under one so they could converse, and carrying the other in its furled state, so it was dry at the other end, while the wet one could drip in the Wintergreen's umbrella stand.

When they were shown into the parlor, it was clear that the sisters had had a very similar conversation, for Cilla was comfortably ensconced behind the tea tray, and Livy was just donning her coat, gloves, and bonnet. "Pa sends his complements, Bane, and asks us to be back by noon. He is at Aunt Ginny's going through her study with the magistrate to see if they can find any letters that have passed between her and her son. And no, I do not know what he plans to do. Are you ready?"

Bane held the door to the parlor for her. "Do you need to wait for a maid to chaperone?" he asked.

Livy blushed. "Pa says there is no need. The maid will sit in the parlor with Drake and Cilla." Even as she spoke, the maid, Barker, slipped past them and entered the parlor, closing the door behind her.

Bane opened the front door and put up his spare umbrella under the portico before offering Livy his arm. They stepped out into the rain, two of the few pedestrians out on the path.

"I have a question," Bane said. "Two, rather. What is your objection to marriage? What must I agree in order to satisfy your concerns?"

"Straight to the point," Livy noted. "Bane, can I answer once we are in the park? What I must tell you… we need to be private."

That sent Bane's mind teeming with further questions, but beyond trying to see her expression—and failing, for she had her head down, and her face was hidden beneath her bonnet—he saw no other reaction. She had, at least, agreed to answer his questions, though she sounded as nervous as he felt.

They walked in a silence that was not uncomfortable, passing between the gates of the park, and turning onto one of the pedestrian paths. The rain pattered gently on the oiled fabric of the umbrella, and seemed to enclose them in their own world. He waited for her to speak, but he did not expect what she said.

"Bane, I am unchaste."

Curston. That unspeakable cur. The fury that surged through Bane flooded all of his senses, so that for a moment he was blind, and deaf to all but the roar of anger in his blood. "I'll kill him," he declared, through a stiff jaw.

"He has been dead for years," Livy told him.

Bane blinked, his rage-soaked brain slow to understand. *Not Curston, then. We were in time.* The relief was almost as disabling as the wrath. He had to focus on suddenly weak knees in order to keep walking.

"For years," he repeated.

"And I consented," she added. "I would not want you to think… That is, he did not force me, Bane. Though if I had not thought he meant marriage… I am telling this out of order."

*For years.* The pieces were falling into place. A youthful mistake, a disappointment with a man that she widened to all men. His relief that she had not been violated by Curston was growing to include a new understanding. She was telling him this story expecting him to reject her, but still trusting he would keep her secret. His mind settled with that knowledge, and his heart swelled.

"Tell me in order, then," he suggested.

"It was during my first season. Mama was already ill, though she hid it from me. But it made her, perhaps, less careful, and Aunt Ginny was sure that Gray—my most persistent admirer— intended marriage, and so did not complain if we slipped outside for a few minutes. He said he loved me, that he couldn't wait to make me his, that he would die if he could not sip the sweet nectar of my lips, and other rubbish like that."

"The words of a seducer. He promised marriage?"

"He did not mention marriage at all, and after—you know. Did I say he was a soldier? He was, and he said that he was going off to risk his life for king and country, and so I let him…" She threw her head back to let out a growl of self-contempt. "After *that*, I asked if we would marry before he rejoined his regiment. And then he reminded me he had never mentioned marriage, and he would say nothing about what had happened as long as I said nothing."

"You were eighteen, and the two ladies responsible for your protection left you to the wiles of a practiced seducer," Bane said. "Did he die in battle? I hope he got camp fever and died a horrible death in a pool of his own wastes."

"Bane!" She looked up at him, her eyes reflecting mingled shock and humor, then the bonnet brim dipped again, and she continued talking as she walked. "No, he fell off his horse while on parade and hit his head. According to the story I was told— one of my cousins knew his sister—he was drunk at the time. He never regained consciousness."

"Too good a death for him," said Bane, disappointed. But there was nothing to be done about it. Gray—whatever the rest of his name was—was gone beyond Bane's retribution. Bane's lady was right there on his arm.

"Were there… consequences?" Bane asked.

"I did not have a baby, if that is what you mean. I told Mama what had happened, though, and she explained to Pa and Aunt Ginny that she was too ill to stay in London, and that I did not want to remain without her. Both of which were true, as it happened. She never told Pa, for the man was the son of a man of high estate, and what could Pa do? Ruin me in the eyes of the world for no purpose."

Bane nodded. Women seldom received justice. *Ah! That is why Livy is so ardent in her desire to help those who have been cheated out of their virtue!* Well. And good for her. In her name, and as a counterbalance to Gray Scum-sucker, Curston, and all their ilk, he would help her in that cause.

First, though to address the idea that he guessed she had eating away inside her.

"Livy, it was not your fault," he said. "You were the victim of an older and more experienced man. But even if you had had a wanton affair, why should that stand in our way? I have already told you that I am not a virgin. What a hypocrite I would be to expect you to be one."

She stopped in her tracks, looked up at him, and examined his eyes. What she saw there must have reassured her, for she began walking again. "Most men are hypocrites, then," she said.

"Many men of wealth or position, I suspect," Bane allowed. "I am not. And neither is Drake. *Is* that your objection to marriage, Livy? That a scoundrel once lied and charmed his way under your innocent skirts, and so you think I will reject you?"

"Are you saying you will not?"

Every conversation with Livy seemed to become a tennis match. "I want you as my wife, Livy. Nothing you have said dissuades me."

"Why?" his darling demanded. "Why me? I am old, contentious, not particularly pretty, and used goods."

That sparked his anger, partly at her for believing such nonsense, but mostly at those who had eroded her confidence in herself. He wished he had Drake's silver tongue, but he would have to rely on the plain unvarnished truth, since that was all he could command.

"Why? Because I found myself face to face with you on Misrule Night, and you were magnificent. Powerful. Confident. Lovely as the night. An armful of a woman who was physically a match for an overgrown gowk like me, but also a woman of character I could spend my life striving to deserve. Since then, I have come to know you, and found that all of those things are true. You say *old*, I say *just the right age for me*. You say *contentious*, I say *challenging and interesting*. I know you will require me to be the best version of myself, and will support me as I try."

He was reaching her. A smile was dawning, and her silver eyes were intent on his.

"You say *not particularly pretty*, my darling, and there, I must take issue with you. To me, you are indescribably lovely. I love how you look. I could spend hours worshipping every inch of your body, and I hope one day soon to have the right to do so. As for 'used goods', I beg you never refer to yourself that way again. What happened to you long before I knew you only matters to me because it hurt you. On the other hand, it meant you remained single, and I can only see that as a gift to my heart, for here we are at last. Together. Are we together, my love?"

"Am I?" she demanded. "You have said you love how I look, but do you love me?"

"*Gowk!*" Bane called himself, thumping his own thigh. "I have not said, have I? Not in those precise and precious words. I love you, Olivia Wintergreen. Thoughts of you consume my mind and haunt my dreams. My heart belongs to you. Everything I am and everything I have is at your feet. Will you pick it up, my love?"

She said nothing and his heart sank. "You don't have to answer now," he assured her. "If you do not love me, and think you can never love me, allow our betrothal to stand until the gossipmongers find something else to care about, and then you can go your way, and I will at least have been of service to you. Or, if you care a little, let me use our fake betrothal to court you. Give me, give us a chance."

"No need," said Livy, and he thought she meant to dismiss him immediately, and wanted to howl, but in the next moment she elevated him from hell to heaven in a few words. "I think I began to fall in love with you that night, when you came alone to face us all, for the sake of your brother. And then we met at the inn, and when I scolded you, you turned it back on me with a quip on your lips and a smile in your eyes. Let us not bother with a long betrothal, Bane. Let us marry and begin our lives together.

I am yours if you are mine."

Bane lowered the cup of the umbrella so that their heads would be hidden from anyone who was out in the rain at this unfashionable hour, and bent, but only slightly, to present his lips. After a moment's hesitation, his brave lady stood on tiptoe and pressed her mouth against his.

Either she had not been kissed enough to master the skill, or she had been kissed by idiots with no idea of how to treat a woman. Bane lost himself in the glory of her mouth, relishing her wordless sounds of pleasure. If not for the need to hold the umbrella and the hinderance of their coats, he might—he would—have taken things much further than his lady was ready for. Thank goodness for the rain.

Even so, he walked her back to her home with his mind in a whirl, and she, to his secret joy, seemed even more dazed than he. He was going to be wed! And he could not have been happier.

# CILLA

CILLA AND LIVY insisted that Jasper and Curston needed to face justice. Papa pointed out that they couldn't have a trial without the whole matter becoming public, especially since Lord Marple would need to be tried by the House of Lords. And then Cilla and Livy would be found guilty and condemned by the court of public opinion. Also, Pearl, Beryl, and Ruby would not come out of such an ordeal unscathed.

"We cannot just let them go," Livy declared. Cilla nodded. She quite agreed.

"We cannot see you punished along with them," Drake pointed out.

"We will not," said Bane. "Would you accept permanent exile as an appropriate punishment? For all four of them? The Curstons and your aunt and cousin?"

"Aunt Ginny would never willingly leave England," Cilla said. "And what of her daughters? Even Beryl did not want to obey her mother, and Pearl and Ruby have done nothing wrong."

"My sister will not be given a choice," Papa said, sternly. "And my nieces will be remaining with me."

"How?" Livy asked. "How can you be certain they will go and stay away, without first taking them to trial?"

Papa explained that he and the Sanderson brothers had been buying up all the debts owed by the four miscreants. "Bane's investigator even prepared us a list of loan sharks and gambling dens to approach. And the two dukes whose sons he and Drake know have been collecting chits for private bets, too."

"The duchesses have done the same with your aunt's chits," said Drake. "Between us, we can ruin the Marples and the Curstons. Financially and socially. We can take everything that is not entailed, and leave them to slowly starve, without two pennies to rub together."

"Not that there is much," said Bane. "Both viscounts have neglected their estates and sold off unentailed land and even paintings and other such items. Or your aunt has, during your cousin's minority."

Papa steepled his fingers in front of his mouth, a sign that he was nearly ready to make a deal. "We can provide them with tickets on a ship to the Americas or the other end of Africa. Virginia can sell her jewelry to help them to start a life there. It won't be what they are used to, but it will be better than the alternative."

"We shall promise them that, if they ever return to England, we will call in their debts in full," said Bane.

Livy was nodding thoughtfully. "It will do," she decided. "It seems unfair on wherever they decide to live, but I shall console myself with the thought that, if they break the law there, they will not be protected by their titles and social status."

Cilla could see another benefit. Two, in fact. "Make sure that Jasper and Curston also sign a document refusing the appointment as guardian to your nephew," she advised. Drake had told her about Colin's will. "Also, Papa, you need to bring our cousins to live with you. You will need company to keep you amused now Livy and I are getting married."

# DRAKE

SINCE WINTERGREEN OWNED a shipping line, the arrangements to deport the Marples and the Curstons were easy enough. Drake and his brother had little to do with it.

Wintergreen arranged for his sister and nephew to sign the agreements to leave the country permanently in return for a small annual allowance—enough not to starve, but not enough for luxury—and to put the Marple estate into Wintergreen's hands as administrator until such time as they were able to pay off all of their debts—with a provision for the next generation if that unlikely instance never came to pass. He also arranged Marple's repudiation of Lewis Sanderson's guardianship.

The Duke of Dellborough and the Duke of Winshire, prompted by their sons, both offered their services to negotiate with the Curstons. They ended up doing it together, two formidable dukes who outranked Viscount Curston by several rungs in the peerage. They came out with the same agreements, Dellborough adding the Curston estates to those he already managed on behalf of one of his dependents.

Within a week, the four of them were being escorted onto a ship that was sailing around the Cape of Good Hope to India, where Lord Curston seemed to think they would all be able to make their fortunes. "Not with barely enough to live on and no idea how to work," Drake said to Bane. Success in that far-off country depended on more than a proud attitude and a title.

Next on Drake's and Bane's list was a house each to bring their brides home, but at this time of year, with Parliament in session and the season in full swing, housing was in alarmingly short supply. They could not find one suitable place, let alone two.

Wintergreen came up with a plan. "If I move into the Marple townhouse with my nieces, you two and my daughters can occupy the house I have leased for the season," he suggested. Cilla and Livy agreed it was a good solution. "We do not mind sharing a house," Cilla assured Drake. "It is what we are used to. It will give us time to find something permanent when there is more available on the market."

The Winshire Ball was a week before the wedding. The ball was, Cilla said—and Jenna Thornstead agreed—the event of the social season. It would apparently set the seal on Livy's and Cilla's—and Bane's and Drake's—acceptance in society. Cilla was having a new gown made, and another for the wedding. Drake was not allowed to see either, though he escorted Cilla to Madame Beauvillier's for fittings, while Bane escorted Livy, and Barker came along to make sure that nothing naughty happened.

More's the pity.

Drake had managed to steal a few kisses despite Barker's vigilance. They only made him all the more impatient for the wedding to be over and done.

The brothers decided to sell some bonds or redeem some investments in order to pay for a few things to make life more comfortable and pleasant for their brides. Some new furniture, a carriage and pair, a wedding present for their brides, and other items of importance to those just embarking on life's marital adventure.

It proved unnecessary. Fortunately, a cargo of tea came in— all of it of very high quality and most of it pre-ordered. The influx of cash was welcome.

It was in their new carriage that they called for Livy and Cilla on the night of the ball. Mr. Wintergreen was taking his nieces in his carriage, and had consented for Drake and Bane to take their brides. "After all, you will be married by this time next week," he said.

He waited with them in the entry hall, while a maid went upstairs to let the ladies know the carriages were at the door. The Marple sisters came first, pretty girls in pastel colors, like sweet spring flowers. To see them chatting and laughing, no one would believe that their mother and brother had committed crimes and been exiled. Drake supposed they had been largely raised by servants, like the children in most noble houses. He and Cilla had already agreed they would not follow that practice.

Then Cilla came down the stairs. Drake's brain noted Livy was directly behind her, but most of his attention was riveted on his betrothed. He could not have described her gown in fashion terms. He didn't know any of the fancy names for the shade of blue she had chosen. He only knew it was almost a perfect match for her eyes.

Nor could he have spoken about the type of ruffle or lace, or named the sleeve or the scoop of the neckline. Indeed, until he began taking Cilla to her dressmaker's appointments, he had not known particular types of sleeves and necklines had their own names. But he did recognize that this neckline perfectly framed her throat, and the line of the gown, from neckline to hem, skimmed her dainty figure so perfectly that his mouth dried as she smiled down upon him.

"You take my breath away, beloved," he said, holding out his hand to her.

Beside him, Bane said, "My thoughts exactly. Livy, you are magnificent tonight."

## Chapter Twenty-Two

### LIVY

REFLECTED IN BANE'S admiring eyes, Livy saw a powerful, capable, beautiful version of herself. She liked it. He and Drake gave her and Cilla the forward-facing seats and sat opposite them, and for the next thirty minutes, they discussed the changes to the townhouse, where both couples would live after their wedding.

Pa had purchased it from the landlord and given it to his daughters as a wedding present.

"We are all moving to the Marple townhouse in two days, so the servants can give our townhouse a thorough clean, and set up our suites," Cilla explained, and blushed.

Was she imagining sharing a bed with Drake in the bedchamber that would be theirs? Being with Bane was certainly on Livy's mind. One of the reasons for vacating the townhouse was they were going to make over Pa's suite of two rooms into a bedchamber and sitting room for Livy and Bane, and the sisters' adjoining bedrooms into a bedchamber and sitting room for Cilla and Drake.

And downstairs on the next floor, the family drawing room and the guest parlor would be assigned one to each couple, so they could see guests of their own separately, or open the doors between them for joint entertainments.

The discussion was practical. The way that Bane was gazing at her was far more primitive. By the time the carriage pulled up at the foot of the Winshire House steps, she had enjoyed half an hour of admiring looks from her soon-to-be husband, and was feeling hot and prickly. The kisses they had managed to steal had hinted that her long ago experience with Grayson Fletcher was not the measure of what to expect in her marriage. One more week. She could hardly wait!

The Duchess of Winshire's ball was the highlight of the social calendar, and also the first one she had held as Winshire's duchess. Livy knew about this contradiction because Aunt Ginny had spoken of little else since the invitations arrived.

Apparently, as the Duchess of Haverford, her grace was frequently asked to sponsor children for baptism. When the first group of those goddaughters reached the age to be presented to the ton, her grace held a ball for them. For the last quarter of a century, the ball had been a yearly event, although last year she had been the dowager duchess, and she and her daughter-in-law were joint hostesses of the event.

Now she had remarried, she was a duchess again, standing in the receiving line with the still handsome duke, who had apparently set the Polite World on its ear when his return from many years of exile revived an old feud with the Duke of Haverford.

Lord Andrew was one of Winshire's sons by a Central Asian princess, and he and other sons and daughters were also in the receiving line. At long last, Livy was presented to Lady Sutton, wife to Winshire's heir.

"Drew tells me you wish to know more about the work my aunt-in-law started at our estate in Essex," she said to Livy, referring to the village where women could go to escape abusive husbands. "Come and visit me when you return to society after your wedding, Miss Wintergreen. Our group can always use new members."

It was a wonderful evening, culminating in the moment just before supper when the Duke of Winshire honored Livy, Cilla, Bane, and Drake by announcing the forthcoming weddings.

Drew, whose table they joined for supper, explained, "Our step-mama, Aunt Eleanor, suggested it. She said that seeing you are accepted at the highest level would put that nasty gossip fully to rest. Father said the wealthy of the merchant class are the future of Britain, and what awaits those of his class who will not diversify their holdings to work with people like Bane and Drake, is financial annihilation."

He raised his wineglass. "To the imminent merger between Wintergreen Shipping and Sanderson Investments, and an ongoing partnership with the Winshire duchy and the Winderfield family."

Garry, who was also at the table, added, "And the Dellborough duchy and the Versey family. We have no intention of being tomorrow's amusing antiques."

Livy exchanged a smile with Garry's wife Jenna, and with Pauline Wharton. She could not have imagined this four months ago. Aristocrats who were friends? A marriage within her own class that came with a welcome into some of the highest houses in the realm? A bright future with the friend and lover who had given her his heart and who held her own? Who would have thought a crown in a Christmas pudding and a misdelivered letter could have led to such a result?

# BANE

"WE SHALL SEE you at home," his lady told her father and cousins, and allowed Bane to escort her out to the carriage, where Drake was already handing Cilla up the carriage steps.

Cilla took the forward-facing seat, leaving room beside her.

Livy sat on the other seat. Drake was ahead of Bane, but surely he would have the sense to do the sensible thing. *Drake, take the seat beside Cilla.* Drake did just that, leaving Bane to sit beside the lady he loved, trying to fit his large frame into half the space on the seat.

"Do you have your fan, Livy?" he asked.

"Why?" asked Livy, lifting the fan up from her skirts and flicking it open. "Do I need to rap you for impertinence?"

"On the contrary," he replied, keeping his mouth solemn, though he was certain that his eyes must be laughing. "The fan is to assist me to be impertinent."

He pulled down the blind on the carriage window on his side, and Drake, sitting opposite Livy, did the same on theirs.

"If you open your fan," Bane said, "and hold it up as a screen, it will work nearly as well as an umbrella."

Her eyes lit up, and she held the fan as commanded. "Do not mess my hair," she scolded, "or muss my gown. Pa will notice."

"No, ma'am," he replied obediently, then touched his lips to hers and forgot the rest of the world entirely.

It was a busy night on the London streets, and the carriage frequently stopped and started. Bane neither noticed nor cared. He had suggested to Drake that the trip might allow time for dalliance. He had instructed the driver to knock on the intervening panel when they were a street away from the Wintergreen townhouse, and the footman not to open the door until he was told. All his thinking had been done, and now all that mattered was feeling.

It was only a kiss—or kisses, rather. Kisses that flowed into one another, as he explored her lips and her mouth, and she did the same for him. From the sounds that penetrated his concentration, Drake and Cilla were similarly occupied.

Clearly Livy realized that, too, for the fan had been abandoned some time ago, so she could use both hands. His cravat was now a disaster, though he and Drake could easily set one another to rights. Hopefully, Livy and Cilla could do likewise, for he had, he was certain, mussed her hair.

After a long time, the carriage stopped. The knock came. After a moment, the carriage started up again. Bane lifted his head, feeling as if he was surfacing from deep under water. Livy, too, looked dazed.

"We have perhaps a minute and a half, or a little more," Drake said, perhaps in answer to something Cilla had said, for she ordered, "Change places with Livy, Drake darling, so that Bane can fix your cravat and I can tidy Livy's hair."

"And I yours," Livy retorted. "Do you have spare hair pins, dearest, or do we need to scrabble around and find them?"

Cilla produced a handful of pins from her reticule. They hadn't done too much damage. A couple of curls needed to be re-pinned, and the aforementioned cravats retied. Hopefully Mr. Wintergreen would not notice the slight puffiness of Livy's lips. Cilla's, too.

Now the knock came again. They were here.

*And that*, Bane thought, *will have to suffice until we are married.* Only another week. It seemed a lifetime.

# DRAKE

THE DOUBLE WEDDING at St. George's church attracted a much larger crowd than the small invitation list predicted.

In the front pews, the Marple sisters were there for the brides and Lark, Phillip, and Frannie for the grooms. Both the investment club and Jenna's ladies' group were out in force, with their spouses, and the Dukes and Duchesses of Winshire and Dellborough set the seal of approval on the match by their attendance.

Behind them sat reporters for the gossip sheets, a caricaturist sketching furiously, and a number of fashionably-dressed people that Drake recognized by sight from the various entertainments he had attended over the past couple of months, but otherwise didn't know.

Beyond them were those who had apparently come along on the coat-tails of those with a whisper of an excuse to be there, and the crowd who had seen people gather and had therefore joined the throng in the hopes of some excitement.

Drake could not have cared less, as he stood at the front of the nave, watching Cilla walking toward him. Beside him, Bane stared at Livy, who walked at her sister's side. He'd left off the hood, so the besotted smile on his face was clear for all to see. No doubt the smile on Drake's face was just as beguiled.

It was time at last. They would say their vows and with those vows, make official in the eyes of God and the assembled congregation what had been true for months. They were made for one another—Drake and Cilla, Bane and Livy.

Drake and Bane had been brothers by blood since before they were born. Then, when their Father brought Bane home, Drake had sneaked into the sickroom and they had become brothers by love. In a few minutes, they would become brothers again, this time by marriage.

Four people who shared their lives, their work, their love. Each to all the others, a gift to the heart.

# Epilogue

## CILLA

*Marplestead, 1826*

MARPLEHURST HALL HAD come alive in the last week, with every guest chamber allocated and the nursery and schoolroom full. Papa had lived here for several months every summer when the Marple sisters were still under his care, but since the last of them married years ago, the house had been empty, except for caretaker servants.

The steward of the estate, the man Papa had appointed to care for it in its owner's absence, had his own cottage nearby. He had overseen the attic-to-cellars cleaning of the house in the past month, and had appointed a full staff of servants to serve the current house party.

It was a great opportunity to see one another all at once. Marriage had scattered the three Marple sisters—one to Devon, one to Yorkshire, and one to Shropshire. As for Cilla and Livy, they lived partly in London and partly in the Middlesex country-side, an easy two hours from their London townhouses.

Thanks in part to the success of the Pentworth engine, and successive designs by Anne Pentworth, they had been able to purchase the townhouse next door to the one they received as a wedding present. They had introduced connecting doors between the buildings. The fourth floors had become one large complex of nursery rooms, schoolrooms, and bedchambers for their children. Other doors allowed free movement from one building to the other on every floor, and made it possible to open the reception rooms up into a single space if they wanted to host a ball.

They'd done the same with their country home, Cowcroft Court. Bane and Livy had their realm in the west wing, Drake and Cilla in the east, and the children—as in Town—shared one of the upper floors of the main house.

All five cousins, their husbands and children, and Papa had arrived at Marplestead several days ago. Lark and Phillip, too, but they were staying with Frannie at Barlow Hall, and the path between the two neighboring estates had seen much traffic in the past few days.

Today, though, Lark, Phillip, Frannie, and their respective children had stayed at home.

"We are not relatives," Frannie had said. "His sisters and cousins should welcome him and his wife home. We neighbors will wait our turn."

"Pa! Pa!" That was Livy's Gareth, shouting at the top of his voice as he and Cilla's own son Alfie burst into the drawing room where the adults were gathered. "The carriage is coming, Pa. We saw them turn in through the gates. I think it is them!"

"Gareth," said Bane, "this is a drawing room, not a barnyard. No shouting."

"Sorry, Pa. Sorry, Ma and aunties. But they're here. They're really here."

The other children came racketing down from the nursery, the whole tribe of them—even the babies in their nursemaids' arms. They must have heard the shouting, for they were doing a bit of it themselves. "Auntie Mary's here! Uncle Jasper's here!"

Several years ago, to her utter surprise, Cilla had received a letter from Jasper Marple, in which he acknowledged his villainy and made what sounded like a sincere apology. Livy was inclined to think it was some sort of trick, but Drake, Bane, and Papa, who had been keeping track of her cousin—the only surviving member of what Bane called "that cabal of villains"—said that he seemed to have settled down, was earning a respectable living as the factor of a merchant, and had recently married.

Jasper appeared to have learned from his mistakes and grown up.

Unlike Curston and his father, who had been shot attempting to steal an East India Company pay chest, and Aunt Ginny, who had shortly after disappeared from view—some said into the seraglio of a sultan.

Cilla wrote back—just a couple of pages of news about his sisters, their husbands, and their babies. She had not expected her brief note to initiate a correspondence. Letters went back and forth. Jasper's wife Mary became something of a friend to all five cousins due to those letters, and eventually most of them, even Livy and Papa, were convinced that Jasper's change of heart was real.

It was not only letters that went back and forth, but presents. Western toys and treats from England for three little Marples. Wonders from India for his nieces and nephews, and his cousins' children. Now Jasper and his family were coming home, and the assembled children were beyond excited to finally meet the source of such amazing gifts.

Everyone but Papa crowded out onto the steps to see two carriages, both heavily laden, make the final turn into the courtyard. Cilla found herself nearly as excited as the children.

Drake had their little Olivia on his shoulders, with Gareth beside him. Horatio, who was inclined to shyness, clung to Cilla's skirts. As the carriage drew up, Drake came up beside Cilla and put his free arm around her shoulders. While he had agreed with the majority decision to invite Jasper to return, he was still wary.

Jasper was the first out of the carriage, flashing a grin at the crowd on the steps before turning to assist out two little girls, barely more than toddlers and then a diminutive lady who looked nearly as round as she was tall.

She faced the welcoming party with wide and anxious eyes the same brown as those of her twin daughters. The last of the party followed her from the carriage, taking his father's hand to support a jump to the ground.

Pearl took the initiative, coming down the steps with her hand out. "You must be my sister Mary," she said. "Come inside, dear. Such a long journey, and in your condition! The others will help my brother and the children."

She linked arms with Jasper's very pregnant wife and led her inside.

# DRAKE

PEARL'S ACTION BROKE the ice. Beryl and Ruby hurried after their sister and Marple's wife, and the older children approached Marple and his children with eager smiles. "Cousin Jasper?" asked Gareth, who was as much the leader of the children as Bane was of the adults.

Marple put out his hand. "You would be Gareth Sanderson," he said. "Yes, I am your Cousin Jasper, and here are my son Peregrine and my daughters Bethia and Mercy. This tall fellow must be Alfie. Won't you introduce me and my family to my other nieces and nephews, and my cousins?"

Nicely said, and the man seemed sincere. Drake stayed back with Cilla as the children were all introduced, Marple's brothers-in-law stepped forward to introduce themselves, and Bane and Livy took their turn at speaking to the scoundrel. Or possibly the ex-scoundrel. Drake had to acknowledge that the man had changed in more than appearance.

He not only acted more mature and responsible, he seemed at ease in his skin in a way totally foreign to the status-driven pack-follower of yesterday. And the way his children stayed close to his legs, as if confident of their father's protection and support, suggested he was a good father, too.

The second carriage had disgorged a cluster of servants, including a woman with black hair and eyes, a costume composed of a colorful wrap of fabric, and a queenly carriage. While the other servants began to offload the luggage, she came to Marple's side and held out her arms toward the children.

Marple spoke briefly, and then picked up the two girls, seating one on each arm. The woman bowed and stepped back.

Once the babble of introductions and welcomes died down, those on the carriageway began to make their way up the stairs, Marple still carrying his daughters, and the nurse—if that is what she was—leading little Peregrine. Marple stopped a step below Cilla, so their eyes were level. She said nothing. Drake tightened his grip, hugging her closer. Marple looked up at him and inclined his head in acknowledgement. "I have changed," he said. "But I understand your caution."

He continued up the stairs, surrounded by a sea of adults and children.

"Perhaps he has," said Cilla.

"People can change," Drake commented. But he would reserve judgement until he saw the evidence for himself.

The man put on a good show the rest of the day. Pearl, as Marple's eldest sister, had been acting hostess since they arrived. She had planned daytime meals that the children could join. "Mary will not want to be separated from her little ones in a strange house, and if all our children are around, the adults will be on their best behavior," she had declared at dinner last night.

So perhaps that was it. Perhaps Marple could keep up the show for the rest of the day. What about after the younger children had been sent off to bed and the older ones back up to the schoolroom?

The time came. The nursemaids appeared, the Marple's nurse with them, and the little ones went off to their nursery tea. The governesses, too, arrived to conduct the older children to their tea, though Alfie suggested that, at nine years of age, he and

Gareth should really be counted as adults. "Daddy," he said to Drake, "I am, after all, your little man."

"A good try," Drake told him. "Give it another six years, my boy."

"With family, and only if you behave," Cilla added.

"Daddy," Alfie complained. "Cousin Jasper said he would tell us about hunting tigers from elephant back."

"If your father permits, Alfie, I'll come up to your room after the adults have had dinner to give you and Gareth that story," said the scoundrel, which put Drake in a difficult position, for he would be the villain if he said no.

"Please, Daddy," Alfie pleaded.

"If your Cousin Jasper doesn't mind," said Drake.

Which was why, a little over an hour and a half later, Drake was standing in the room that Alfie shared with Gareth, listening to Marple tell a thrilling story about a hunt for a man-eating tiger. Having said his good nights, he would normally be downstairs himself, drinking port with the other men. Or perhaps in his bedchamber, with Cilla, who had gone upstairs to bed. She was with child again, and these early months always left her exhausted.

But if Marple was spending time with his son and nephew, Drake wanted to keep the man under his eye.

After the story was done and the boys were left to blow out their candles and whisper in the dark, Drake and Marple left the boys' room.

Marple put a hand on Drake's arm. "Will you spare me a moment, Mr. Sanderson? Come this way. There's a room by the stairs where we might talk without disturbing the children."

Drake followed him, wondering what the man was up to. "What are you about, Marple?" he asked, keeping his voice down in deference to the young potential audience.

Marple stopped to light a candle at the hall table on the landing, and then led the way into the little parlor. Drake closed the door behind them. "Well?" His single word contained all his frustration.

"Words are cheap," Marple said with no delay. "I can tell you I have changed, but why should you believe it? What I attempted to do to my cousins—it was wrong. I knew it at the time, but I ignored my conscience. It has bothered me, though."

*Play the violins. Poor, poor Marple.* The sulky boy had not changed his ways at all. Just got better at hiding them.

Perhaps Marple read Drake's thoughts in his face for he made an impatient cutting gesture with one hand. "It is not about me. I know that. For you, it is about Cilla. For me, Mary. I don't want to see her hurt, in any way. She has been so excited about meeting you all."

"Does she know what you did?" Drake demanded.

Marple hung his head. "Yes. I told her." He shuddered as if reliving the occasion and a flush crept up his cheeks. "Up until then, I really had not considered what it must have been like for my cousins. Mary was good enough to explain it to me." The shake of Marple's head expressed a wistful awe. "My wife can be… formidable."

*Good.* Marple deserved to suffer.

"It was six months before my wife forgave me enough to let me back in her bed. She is a saint, my wife. I don't deserve, nor do I ask, for your forgiveness, Sanderson, nor Cilla's. All I do ask is that you do not spoil this homecoming for my wife. Please, I beg you, try not to glower at me whenever you must be in my company. I shall avoid you and your wife as much as I can, consistent with hospitality."

Had he done that on purpose? Brought in the fact that Drake was staying under Marple's roof? As if it mattered. Marple Hall would have been sold long ago if Papa Wintergreen had not saved it.

That said, Drake would enjoy watching Mary Marple keep her husband in line. "I shall try not to glower," he said.

With a nod, Marple left him to go downstairs. As for Drake, he had a different destination in mind. His wife was in their bedchamber, and Drake could do with a hug.

# BANE

"MY NEPHEW SEEMS to have grown up," Pa Wintergreen commented to Drake, Bane, and his daughters a few days later.

Since Marple was currently involved in riding an old tin tray down a grassy slope with one of his nephews between his knees, the remark seemed out of place, but Bane knew what his father-in-law meant.

The Viscount Marple of yesteryear would not have been seen dead joining in with the play of children, let alone behaving like a great overgrown boy for their entertainment.

Drake made a disbelieving grunt. He was going to take quite a bit more convincing, and Bane sympathized. Marple had threatened, kidnapped, and manhandled Cilla. Bane didn't think he would ever forget the horror of those moments when he feared they would be too late to save Livy. Cilla gave his arm a sympathetic squeeze.

"Can a leopard change his spots?" Drake asked.

"He will make a good viscount," Wintergreen commented. "He needs to learn more about English farming, but he understands bookkeeping and how to manage servants." Wintergreen had spent hours over the past days closeted with Marple in the book room, or riding out with Marple and the steward over the estate.

"I do not trust him," Drake growled.

"He does seem to have changed," Cilla said. "Mary loves him, and she is no fool, that woman. I like her."

"He was a weak boy who did a terrible thing, and would have done worse if you had not stopped him," Wintergreen commented. "In the past decade, Drake, he has paid for those sins. Not as the Curstons did. As you know, they gambled with and lost the money the four of them had on the ship that took them to India. When they could not live off their names and rank, they gambled again, this time with theft and robbery. Their deaths wiped that slate clean."

"Not clean, no." Bane did not agree. "If there is justice after death, they are both in hell."

Drake nodded.

"Be that as it may," Livy said, "They are gone, and by their own misdeeds, furthermore. They are out of our lives forever."

"As for Aunt Ginny," said Cilla, "we shall not see her again. Mary says that she became a sword wife of the Maharajah Amarsinha, and is not permitted out of the seraglio. Sword wife is a lesser form of marriage, Mary says. In India, those who are wealthy and titled might have several principal wives and any number of lesser wives, as well as concubines. It is very interesting."

Bane had become used to his sister-in-law's fascination with other times and cultures. He exchanged a smile with his best beloved. Livy's approach to life was far more practical, just as he preferred it.

Cilla hadn't finished. "Once Jasper married, Mary—as Aunt Ginny's daughter-in-law—was allowed to visit her. That was several years after she entered the seraglio, of course. Apparently, at the time Lord Curston died, she was advising one of the principal wives on European fashion and customs. The queen asked her husband to marry Aunt Ginny, to protect her and give her a home."

"Was it the maharajah who found Jasper a position?" Bane wondered.

"Wintergreen shook his head. "He had the position before the Curstons died. He says he had cut ties with them, and was slowly working his way up in the office of an American shipping company. As you know, he had become their chief agent in Bombay before his return to England."

"And Marple did not think to bring his mother home with him?" Livy enquired, with a touch of disdain. She hated injustice to women, even a woman like her aunt.

"Even if the maharajah would have permitted it," said Mary, who had approached with none of them noticing, "what is there for her here in England? Would an English woman who left under a cloud of scandal and became the divorced lesser wife of an Indian Maharajah be welcomed back into English Society?"

She raised her eyebrows in question, and Livy was quick to shake her head. "I see your point."

"It was your aunt's point," Mary explained. "When we decided to leave India, Jasper sent me to see if she wanted him to petition the Maharajah for her release from the seraglio so that she could come home with us, and she refused. It is a cage, the seraglio—luxurious and gilded, but still a cage. But Mother Marple likes better to be one of the lesser lights around whom the place turns, than to be a mere dowager viscount, and one with a stain on her character."

"It is justice," Livy decided. "She is in a prison, of sorts. And in her own way, when her own interests were not affected, she was kind to us."

"You have been kind to Jasper," Mary blurted. "I know his offenses against you. Especially you, Livy and Cilla. But you have welcomed him home and given him back his patrimony. I want you to know I am grateful, and I shall make sure that he is worthy of the trust you have placed in him." She then blushed scarlet and hurried away across the lawn to join the whooping laughing crowd at the bottom of the slope.

Alfie and Gareth broke free of the group to race toward their parents and grandfather. "Pa," Gareth screeched. "Did you see me coming down the hill on the tray? Grandpa, I was the fastest."

"Not as fast as me." Alfie gave him a friendly shove, which Gareth returned, saying, amiably, "You were faster. Grandpa, Alfie and I were fastest."

Bane ruffled his son's hair. He'd do his best to make sure the boy never got into bad company, but if he failed, he hoped someone would give Gareth a second chance. Perhaps, after all, Marple had changed.

# LIVY

LIVY WAS GLAD to be back in London, after a week at Marplehurst and another few days at Barlow Hall. Gareth put it best, when he leapt out of the carriage that carried the older children, not waiting for the steps to be lowered.

"Home!" he yelled, with his usual exuberance.

Bane turned back from the front door to smile at his son. "I thought you enjoyed spending time with all of your cousins, my son."

"I did, Papa. I really did. But this is my own place, and all the most important people in my world live here. And at Cowcroft Court, of course. All our things are here, mine and Alfie's. And our cats, our dog, our other pets. I wonder if the rats have had babies while we were away. Come on Alfie, let's go and see! Hello, Wilson." With a wave to the butler, he was off up the steps and in through the front door, Alfie keeping pace behind him.

Livy shuddered. She had still not quite reconciled herself to the pet rats her son and Alfie shared, though she had to admit that they were clean and tame, and that the babies, once their pelts were grown, were quite sweet.

"How did you and I have such a loud and boisterous son?" Bane asked Livy. "Do you think he and Alfie got swapped at birth?" It was a constant joke between the four of them, that Bane's outgoing eldest son had somehow become confused in the nursery with Drake's much quieter, more reserved child, who had been born four weeks later.

Never mind that it was impossible, since they had been easily distinguishable from birth, each taking after his father in size and coloring, even Gareth's eyes—by the time he was six months old—showing one brown and one green, while Drake's and Alfie's were blue.

None of the other births had been quite as close. Cilla had

another son eighteen months after Alfie, and Livy produced a daughter a year after that, and there was also a year's gap between Cilla's daughter and Livy's younger son, who was still an infant.

"Are you going to stand on the steps trying to pass your son off as my own?" Drake teased them. "Or are you going inside? I need to take my wife to our rooms for a rest."

"A rest, you say?" Bane asked. He grinned at Livy. "Darling, do you need a rest after that long, tiring carriage ride?"

"I should see the children settled," Livy said. But when she looked back at the carriages, the last of the nursemaids was just disappearing through the front door to the other townhouse, leading her smallest son.

"Wife," Bane said, "the children are pleased to be home and can safely be left to settle in. Come and lie down with me. I am so tired."

"Me, too," Drake claimed, gifting his wife with a leer that left no doubt what kind of a rest he had in mind. Cilla giggled, and—since Livy and Bane still stood on the top step—led her husband by the hand down the steps and along the pavement to their own entry.

"If you are tired," Livy said, "what use will you be to me, Bane?"

"Come along, wife," Bane told her, "and I shall show you."

She followed beside him. "I was thinking," she started.

"Uh oh," he answered, giving her a sideways grin. "You know what they say about a lady who thinks."

She gave him a glare. As he expected. "Of how this all started. When I was the Lady of Misrule."

"Oh?" Her husband's grin grew into a smile.

"I should like to relive that role. The one where I am in charge of the proceedings." She gave him as coy a look as she could manage.

Her husband blinked and grabbed her hand. "You know, my lady, that I will do whatever it takes to please you." He sped up his steps as they walked, and because she was tall, she easily kept up with him. "I bought some cotton rope," he confided. "It is softer than the jute we used last time. Shall we use the mask?" Livy grinned. "Wait and see," she advised. Which was part of the game, of course. In truth, whatever they did, they would decide it together. Whoever played the one in charge, it was always about them both. Both in bed and out of it, she was his and he was hers. And to think it all began with a thrice-blessed mistake.

AUTHOR'S NOTES

## Tatterhood

This story was inspired by Tatterhood, a Scandinavian folk tale, in which a woman wishes for children. She is advised to put two seeds under her bed. When they grow, she is told, she must ignore the ugly one, and eat the beautiful one. But the beautiful one is so delicious, she eats the ugly one as well, and in due course, gives birth to twins. One is lovely; the other so ugly she is actually born wearing a hood!

Fast forward to when they grow up. The two sisters are devoted to one another. When the castle is attacked by magic wielders, the beautiful sister has her head stolen and replaced by an ass's head. So Tatterhood, as the ugly sister is called, sets off with her sister to track the head down and swap back.

That done, they arrive at a kingdom where the king falls in love with the beautiful sister and asks to marry her. (Just as well she had her proper head back.) The sister will only agree if the crown prince marries Tatterhood. He does, reluctantly, but of course, marriage transforms her into a bride even more lovely than her sister and they all live happily ever after.

## Invention of the hydraulic press

The hydraulic press is a highly versatile piece of equipment used in all sorts of manufacturing. It works on the principle that pressure in a closed system is constant, so that a small amount of mechanical force in a small area will allow a large amount of mechanical force to be applied in a large area. It was invented by a man called Joseph Brahms and was patented in 1795.

And hydraulic presses for cutlery making were developed in the 1810s, but my inventors the Pentworths are entirely fictional.

## Umbrellas

Umbrellas were used in China as early as 3,500 BC, and water-proofed with a combination of wax and lacquer by 3,000 BC. They came to Europe through ancient trade routes, but were considered appropriate only for women. In England, they were still considered a female accessory as late as 1790, but a man called Jonas Hanway ignored popular ideas of suitability, and used an umbrella for decades. By the early 19th century, men and women in England both used umbrellas. The folding umbrella, though, would not appear until the 1850s. To this day, a neatly furled umbrella is a gentleman's fashion accessory, and one of the songs of my young adulthood was all about a romance under an umbrella. (Bus Stop, by the Hollies.)

## Crossing lines in letters

When paper was expensive and postage went by weight, thrifty people used to fill their paper with closely written lines, then turn the page one turn, and write more. This was called "crossing the lines".

## Little boys love rats

Rats as domestic pets might have been familiar in Europe as early as the seventeenth century, and this was certainly the case in Japan. We have excellent documentation for domesticated rats in England in the early nineteenth century. In fact, the ancestor of many of today's pets might have been raised by Jimmy Shaw or Jack Black. (This might not have been his legal name, but it is the name under which he was interviewed by Henry Mayhew. The interview with the two men was published in a book titled *London Labour and the London Poor*.)

Jack and Jimmy were ratcatchers. Jack was ratcatcher to the king (among other things) from 1825, and supplied live rats to the rat pits, a popular blood sport that didn't end until 1912. Another lucrative income source for him was breeding from rats that had different colored coats. He told Mayhew: "I have 'em fawn and white, black and white, black white and red. People come from all parts of London to see them rats. They got very tame, and you could do anythink with them." He sold them as pets or curiosities, mainly to young ladies. Jimmy Shaw was even more interested in the odd rats. If today's pets are not descended from those kept by one of these two men, they no doubt originated in a similar way.

Laboratory rats appear to have been used in research from at least 1828, and probably were also saved from the rat pits or bred from such animals. The albino rat often used in laboratories or as pets is also known to have been around for a while. There was apparently a wild colony of albino rats in Bath in 1828.

Have you ever wanted something so much you were afraid to even try? That was Jude ten years ago.

For as long as she can remember, she's wanted to be a novelist. She even started dozens of stories, over the years.

But life kept getting in the way. A seriously ill child who required years of therapy; a rising mortgage that led to a full-time job; six children, her own chronic illness… the writing took a back seat.

As the years passed, the fear grew. If she didn't put her stories out there in the market, she wouldn't risk making a fool of herself. She could keep the dream alive if she never put it to the test.

Then her mother died. That great lady had waited her whole life to read a novel of Jude's, and now it would never happen.

So Jude faced her fear and changed it—told everyone she knew she was writing a novel. Now she'd make a fool of herself for certain if she didn't finish.

Her first book came out to excellent reviews in December 2014, and the rest is history. Many books, lots of positive reviews, and a few awards later, she feels foolish for not starting earlier.

Jude write historical fiction with a large helping of romance, a splash of Regency, and a twist of suspense. She then tries to figure out how to slot the story into a genre category. She's mad keen on history, enjoys what happens to people in the crucible of a passionate relationship, and loves to use a good mystery and some real danger as mechanisms to torture her characters.

Dip your toe into her world with one of her lunch-time reads collections or a novella, or dive into a novel. And let her know what you think.

Website and blog:
judeknightauthor.com

Subscribe to newsletter:
judeknightauthor.com/newsletter

Bookshop:
judeknight.selz.com

Facebook:
facebook.com/JudeKnightAuthor

Twitter:
twitter.com/JudeKnightBooks

Pinterest:
nz.pinterest.com/jknight1033

Bookbub:
bookbub.com/profile/jude-knight

Books + Main Bites:
bookandmainbites.com/JudeKnightAuthor

Amazon author page:
amazon.com/Jude-Knight/e/B00RG3SG7I

Goodreads:
goodreads.com/author/show/8603586.Jude_Knight

LinkedIn:
linkedin.com/in/jude-knight-465557166